PEANUT, BUTTER, & CRACKERS

PAIGE BRADDOCK

Coloring by Kat Efird

VIKING

To Buddy Barker, Otis, and Charlie—P. B.

VIKING
An imprint of Penguin Random House LLC, New York

First published in the United States of America by Viking,
an imprint of Penguin Random House LLC, 2020
First paperback edition published 2021

Viking & colophon is a registered trademark of Penguin Random House LLC.

Penguin Books & colophon are registered trademarks of Penguin Books Limited.

Visit us online at penguinrandomhouse.com.

Manufactured in China

LIBRARY OF CONGRESS CATALOGING-IN-PUBLICATION DATA IS AVAILABLE
ISBN 9780593524213

1 3 5 7 9 10 8 6 4 2

RRD

Book design by Paige Braddock, Jim Hoover, and Lucia Baez

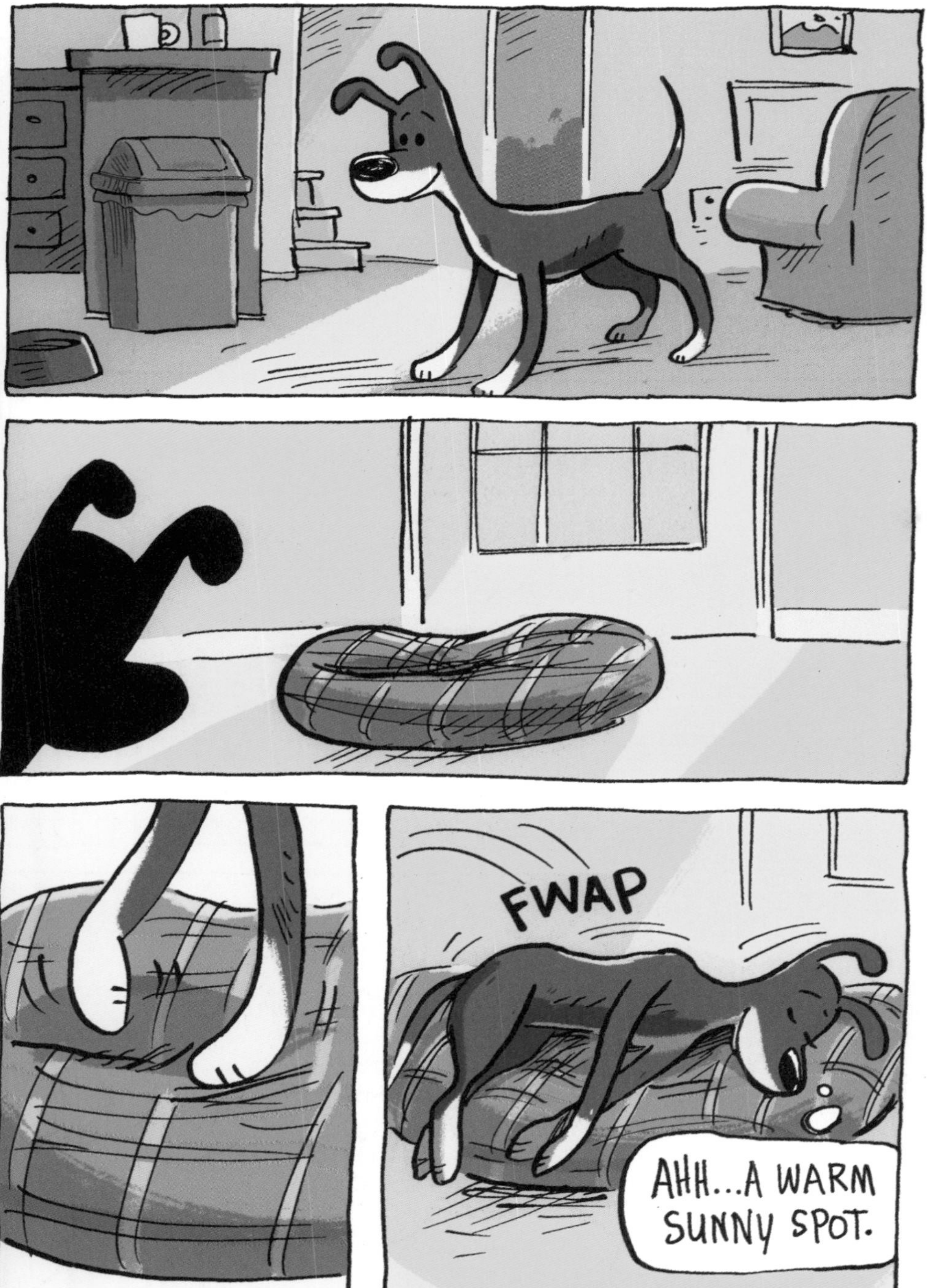
FWAP
AHH...A WARM SUNNY SPOT.

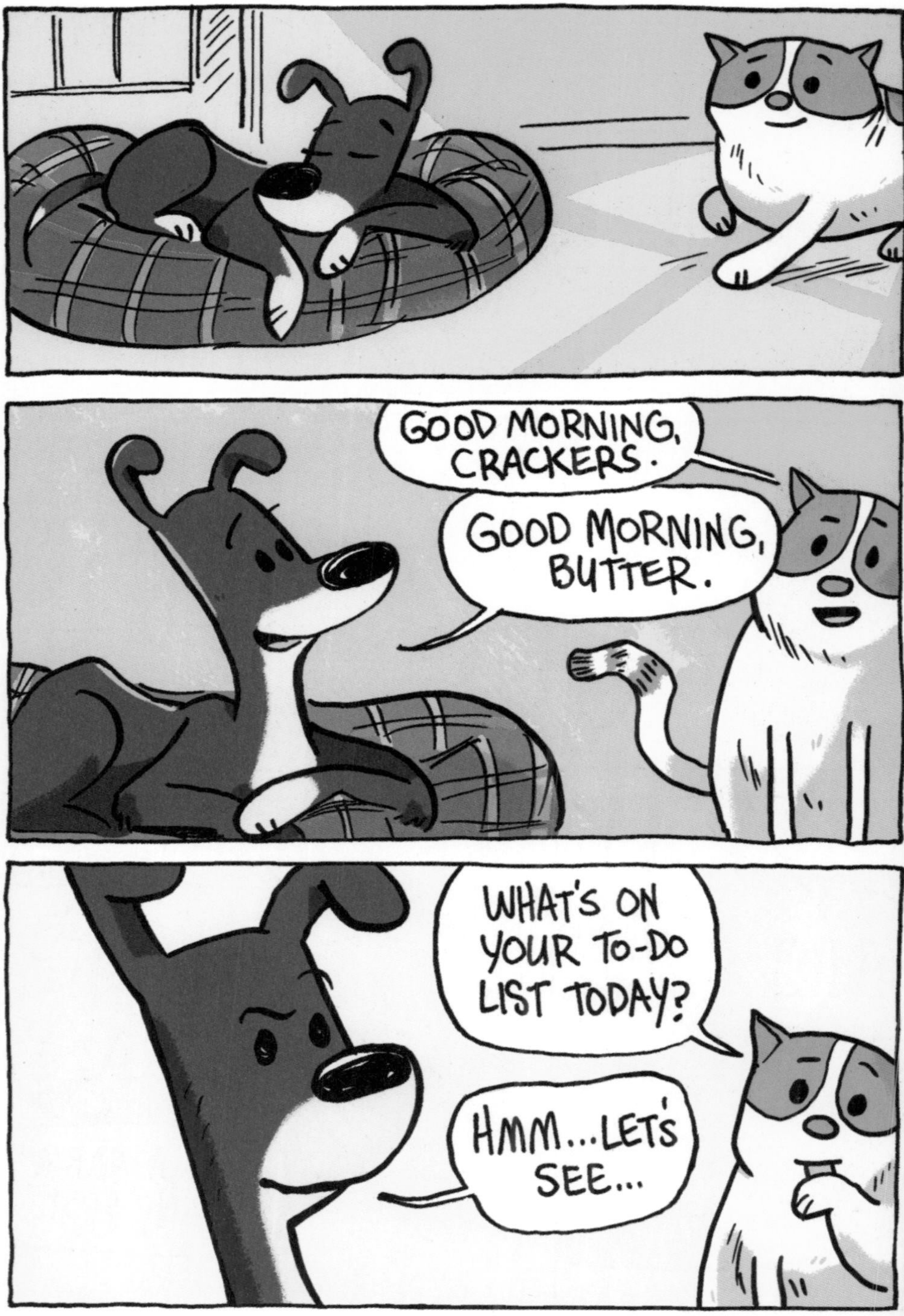
GOOD MORNING, CRACKERS.
GOOD MORNING, BUTTER.
WHAT'S ON YOUR TO-DO LIST TODAY?
HMM...LET'S SEE...

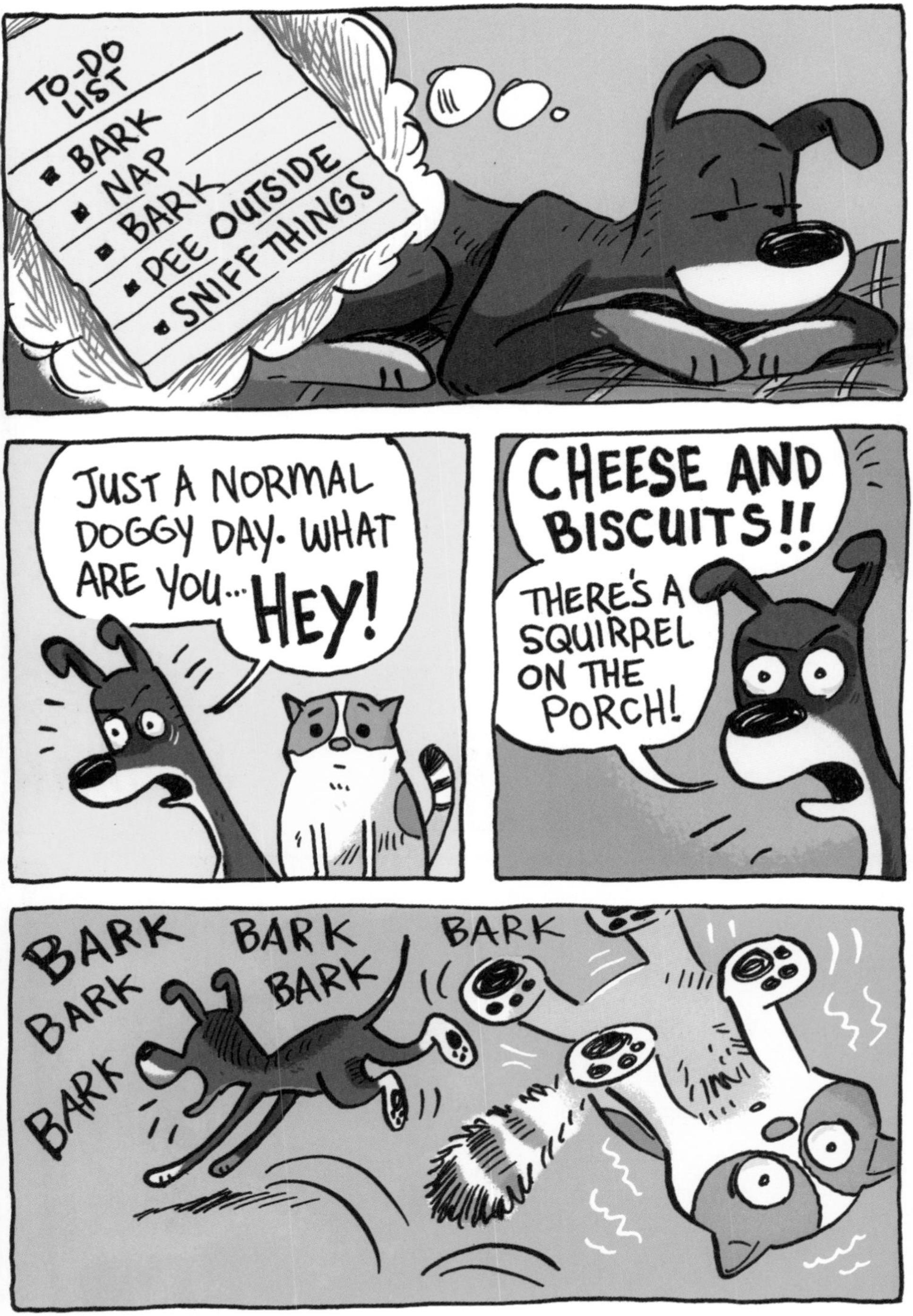
TO-DO LIST
BARK
NAP
BARK
PEE OUTSIDE
SNIFF THINGS
JUST A NORMAL DOGGY DAY. WHAT ARE YOU... HEY!
CHEESE AND BISCUITS!!
THERE'S A SQUIRREL ON THE PORCH!
BARK BARK BARK
BARK BARK
BARK
BARK

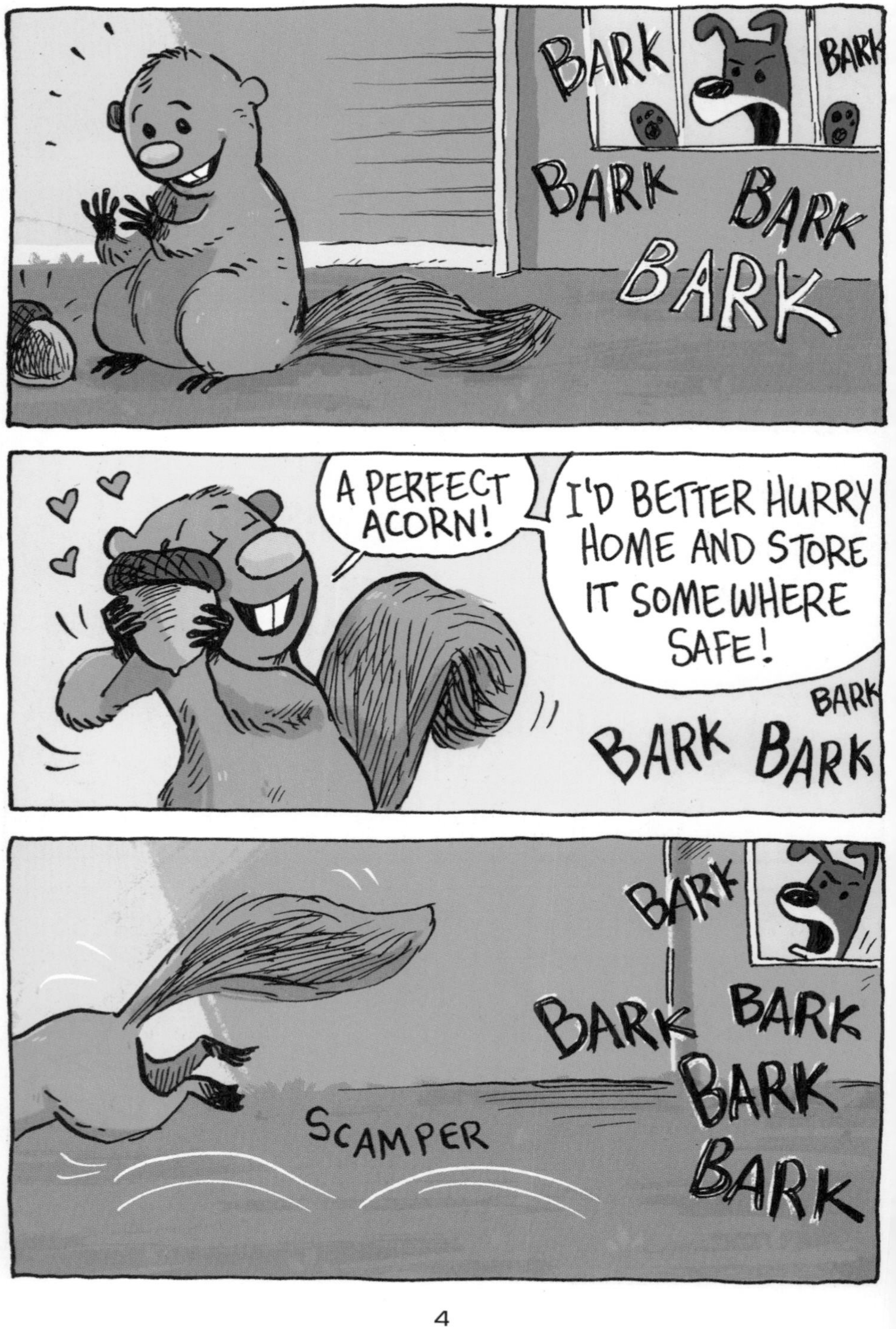
BARK
BARK
BARK
BARK
BARK
A PERFECT ACORN!
I'D BETTER HURRY HOME AND STORE IT SOMEWHERE SAFE!
BARK
BARK
BARK
BARK
BARK
BARK
BARK
SCAMPER
BARK

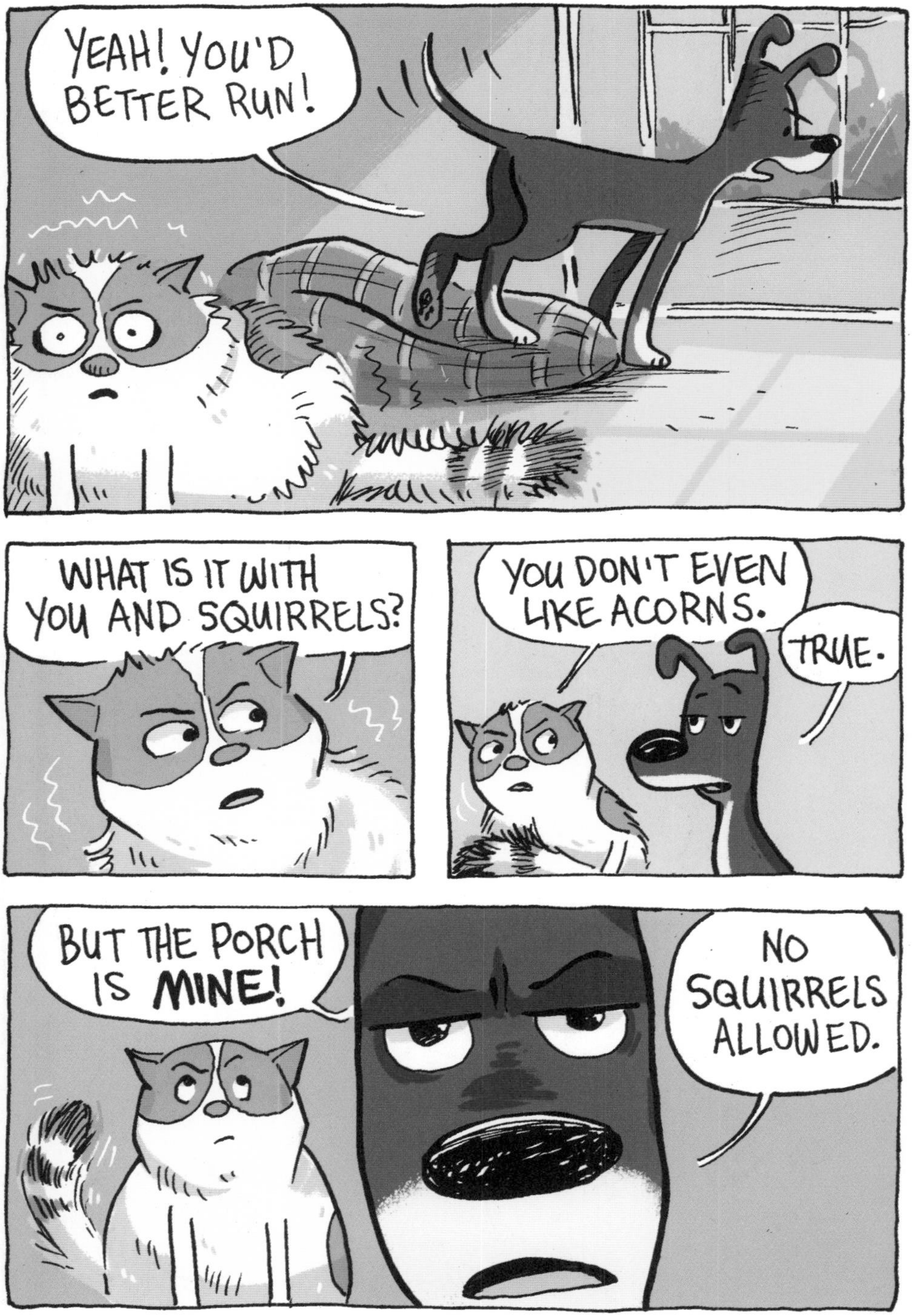
YEAH! YOU'D BETTER RUN!
WHAT IS IT WITH YOU AND SQUIRRELS?
YOU DON'T EVEN LIKE ACORNS.
TRUE.
BUT THE PORCH IS **MINE**!
NO SQUIRRELS ALLOWED.

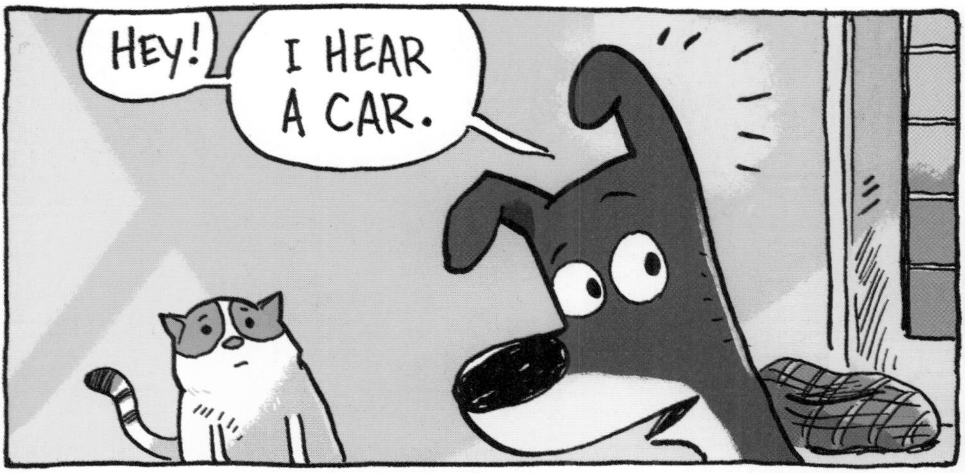
HEY!
I HEAR A CAR.

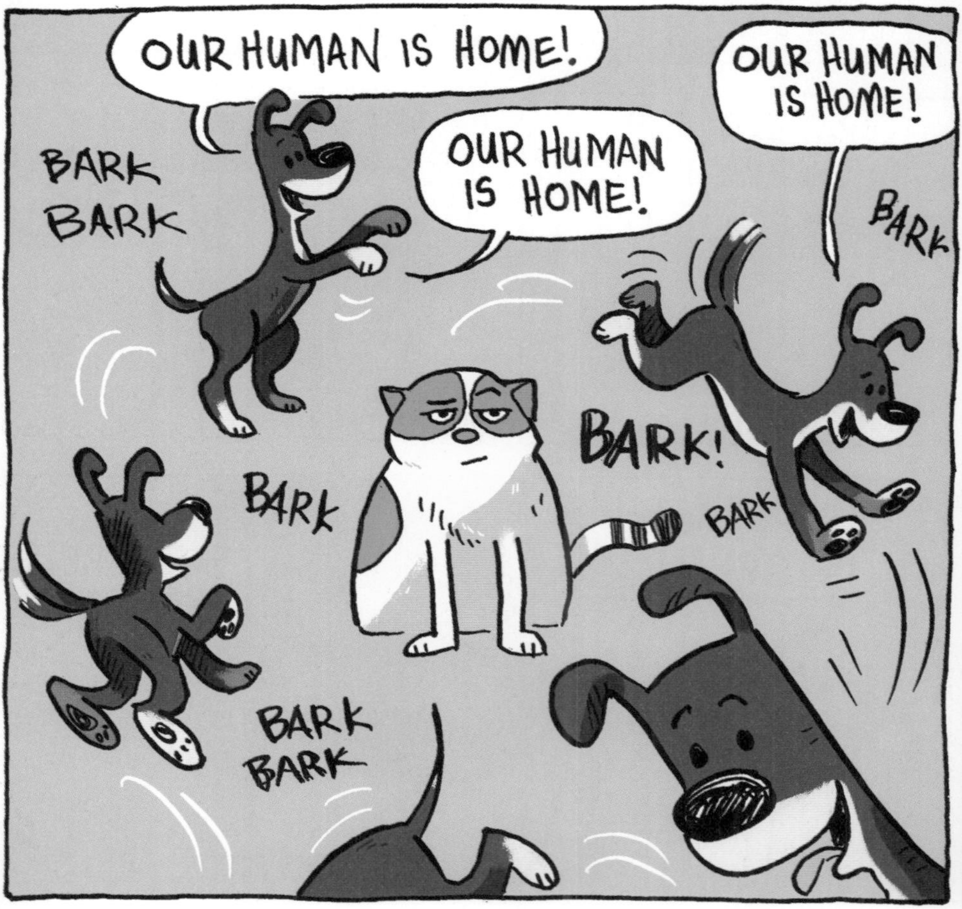
OUR HUMAN IS HOME!
BARK BARK
OUR HUMAN IS HOME!
OUR HUMAN IS HOME!
BARK
BARK!
BARK
BARK
BARK BARK

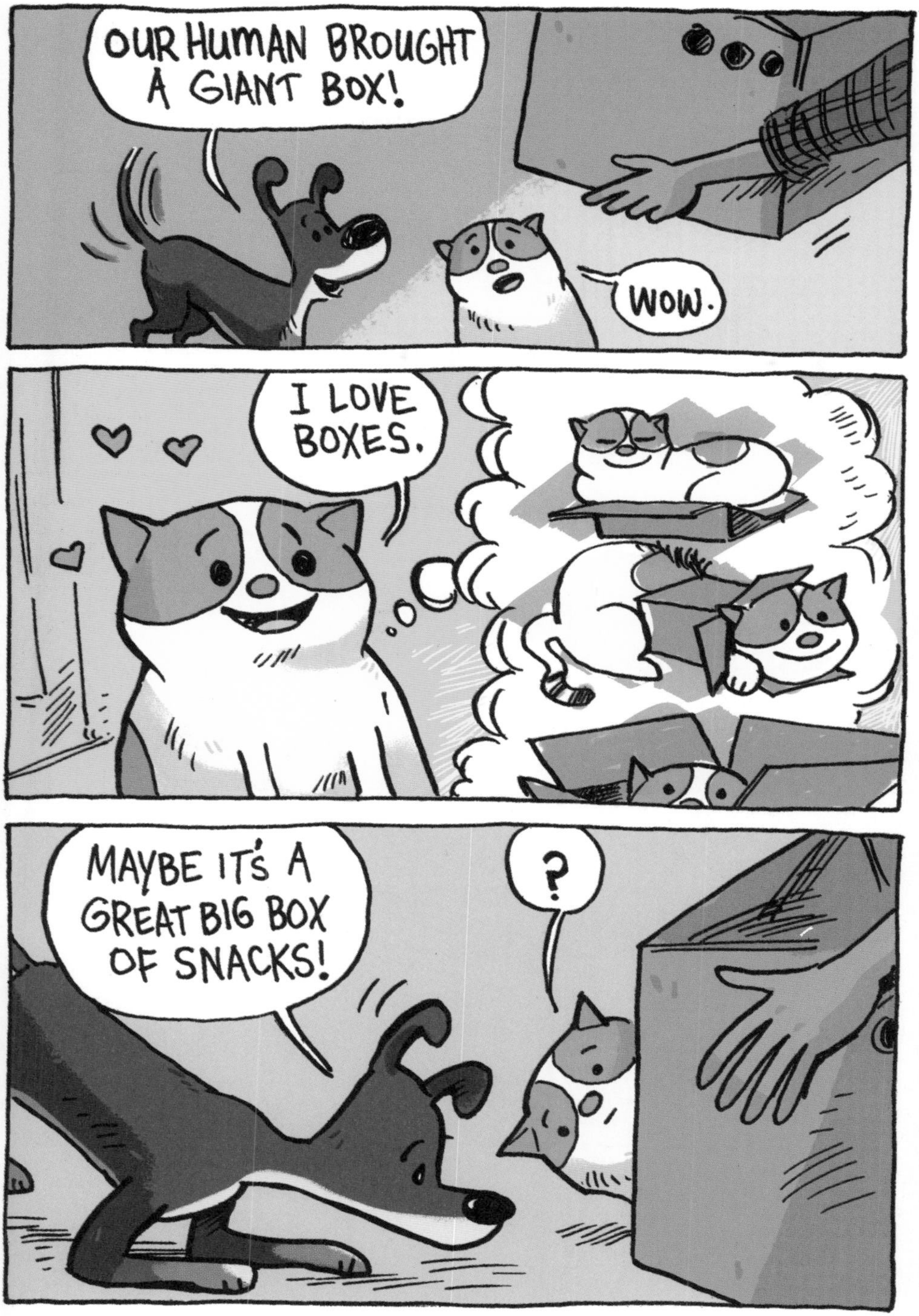
OUR HUMAN BROUGHT A GIANT BOX!
WOW.
I LOVE BOXES.
MAYBE IT'S A GREAT BIG BOX OF SNACKS!
?

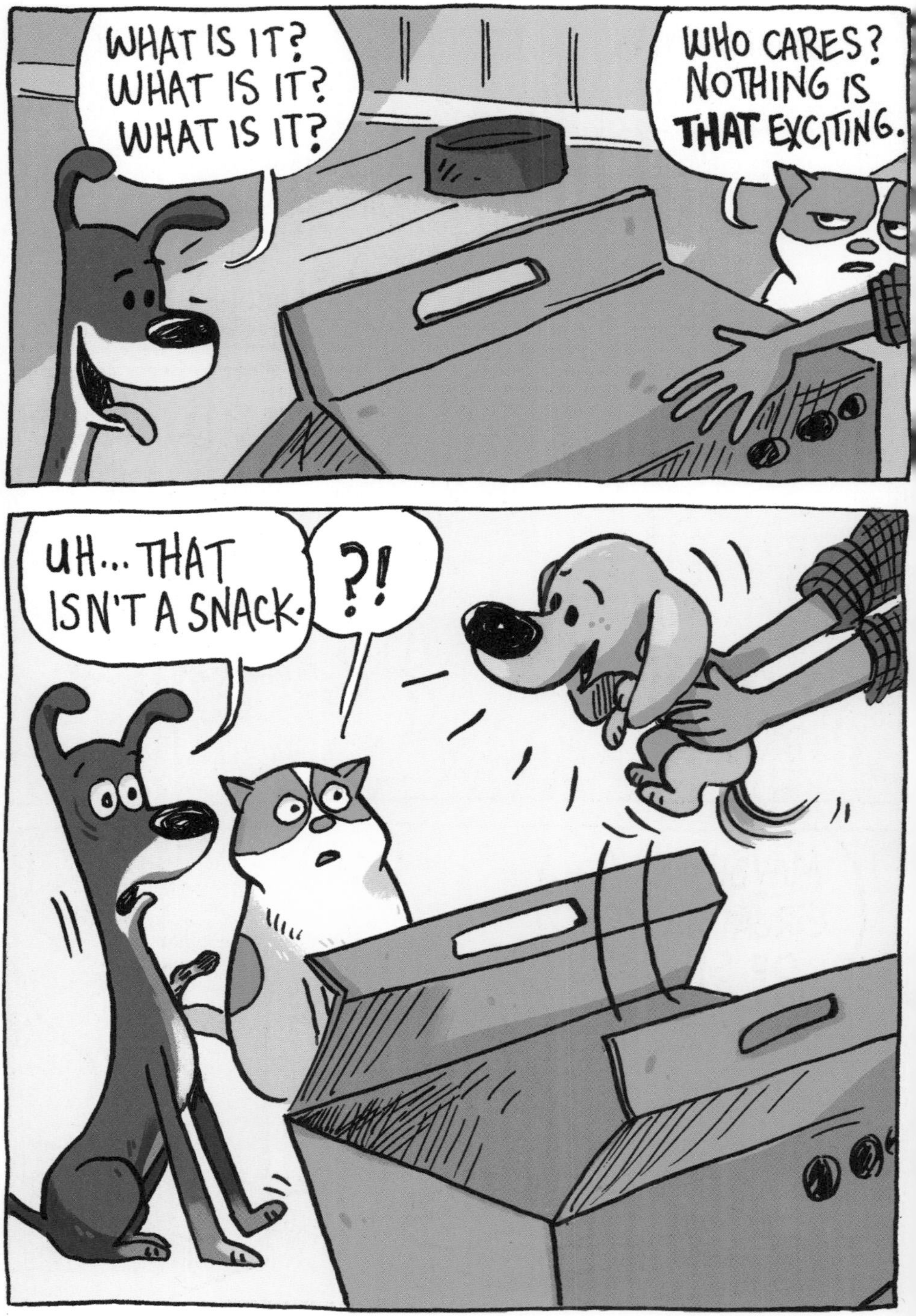
WHAT IS IT? WHAT IS IT? WHAT IS IT?
WHO CARES? NOTHING IS **THAT** EXCITING.
UH... THAT ISN'T A SNACK.
?!

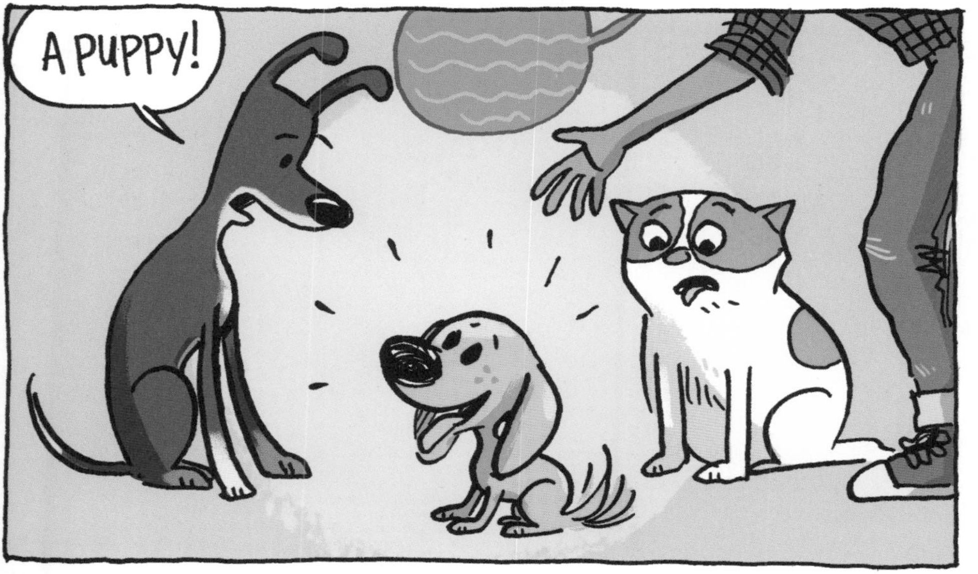
A PUPPY!

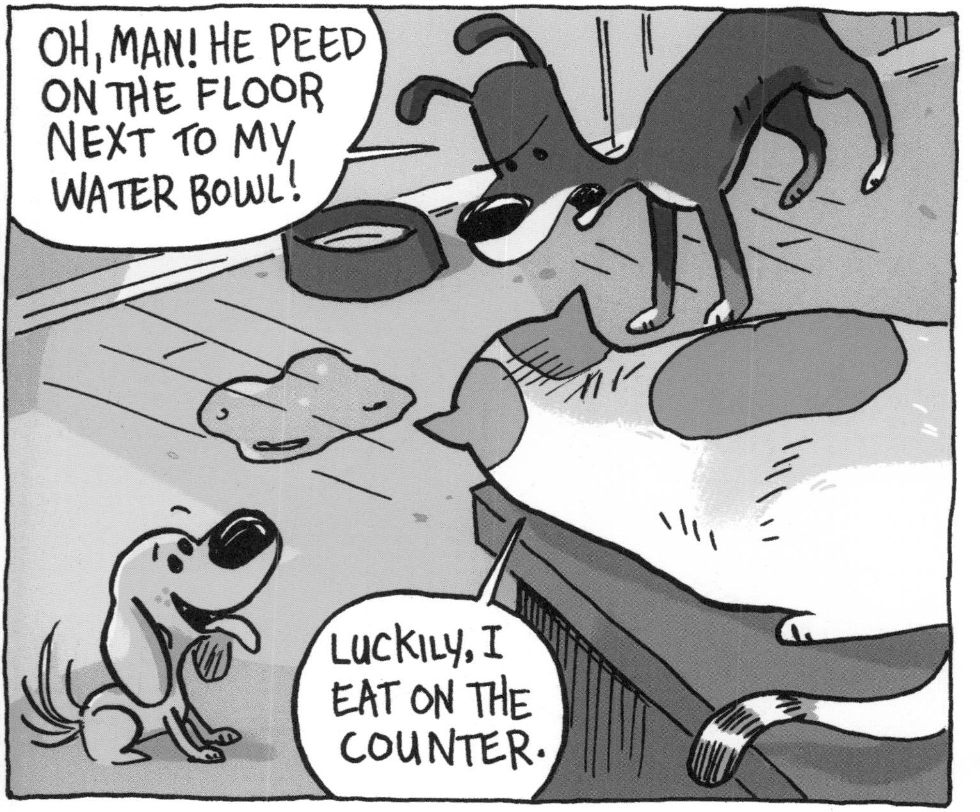
OH, MAN! HE PEED ON THE FLOOR NEXT TO MY WATER BOWL!
LUCKILY, I EAT ON THE COUNTER.

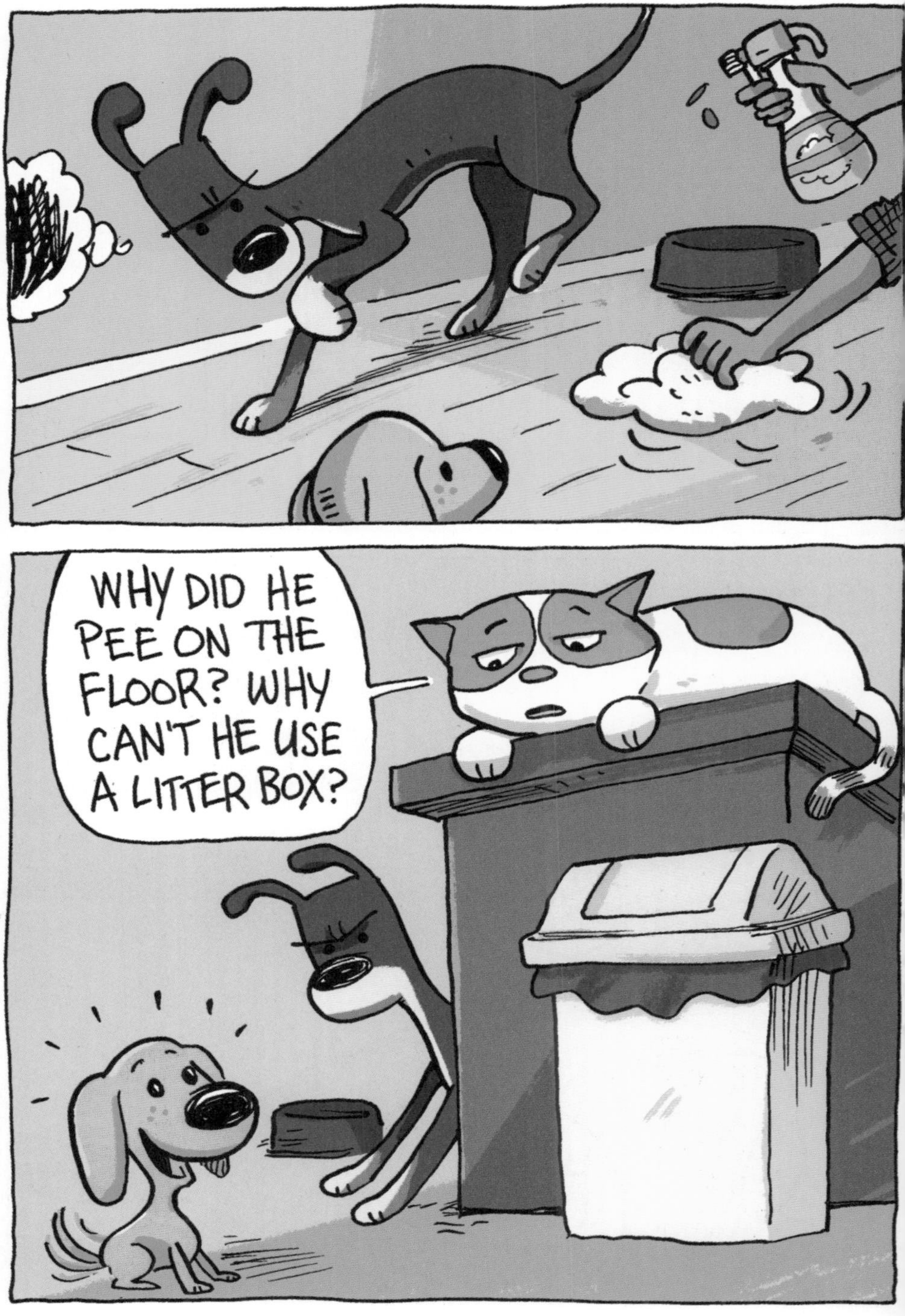
WHY DID HE PEE ON THE FLOOR? WHY CAN'T HE USE A LITTER BOX?

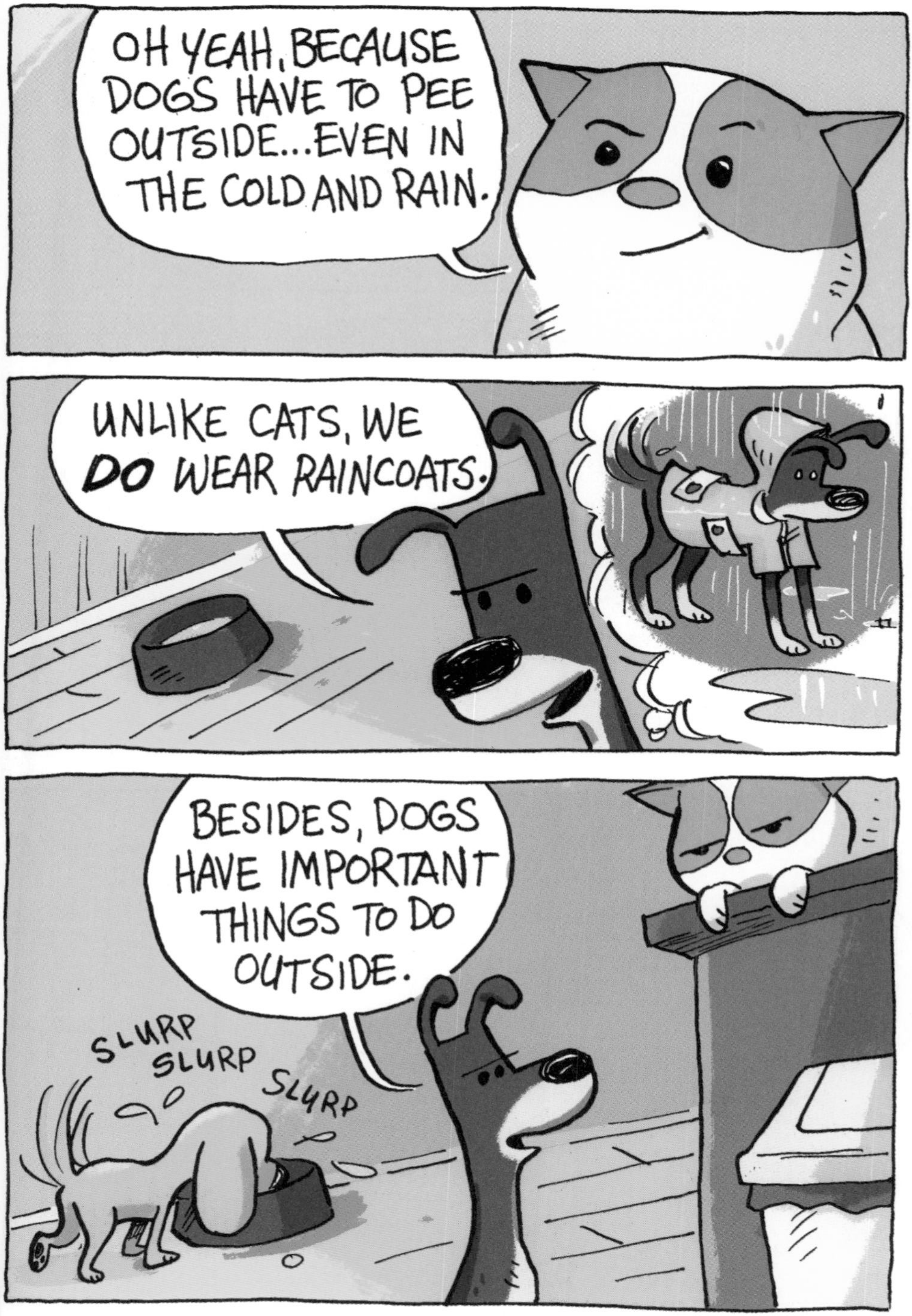

OH YEAH, BECAUSE DOGS HAVE TO PEE OUTSIDE...EVEN IN THE COLD AND RAIN.
UNLIKE CATS, WE **DO** WEAR RAINCOATS.
BESIDES, DOGS HAVE IMPORTANT THINGS TO DO OUTSIDE.
SLURP
SLURP
SLURP

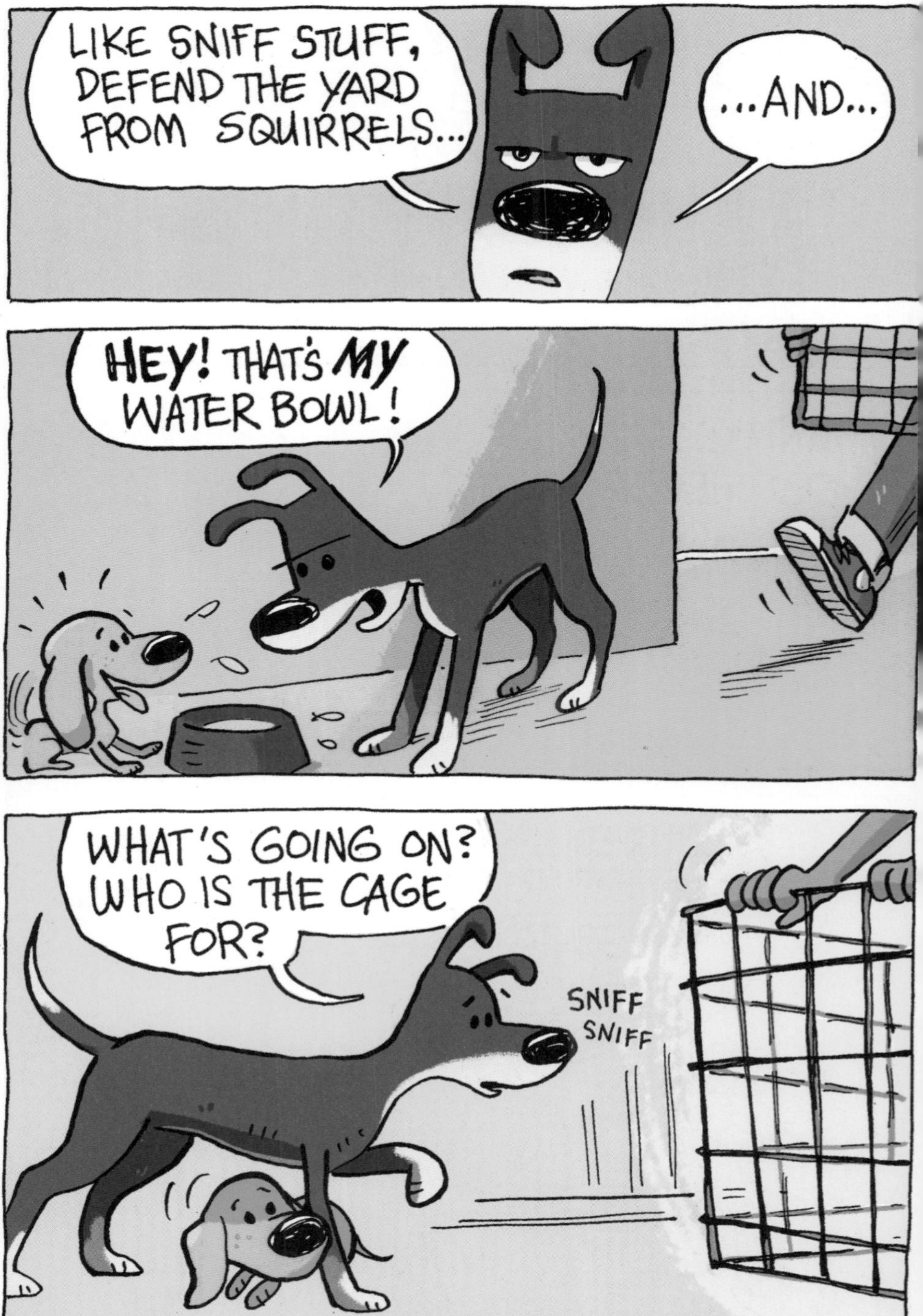
LIKE SNIFF STUFF, DEFEND THE YARD FROM SQUIRRELS...
...AND...
HEY! THAT'S MY WATER BOWL!
WHAT'S GOING ON? WHO IS THE CAGE FOR?
SNIFF SNIFF

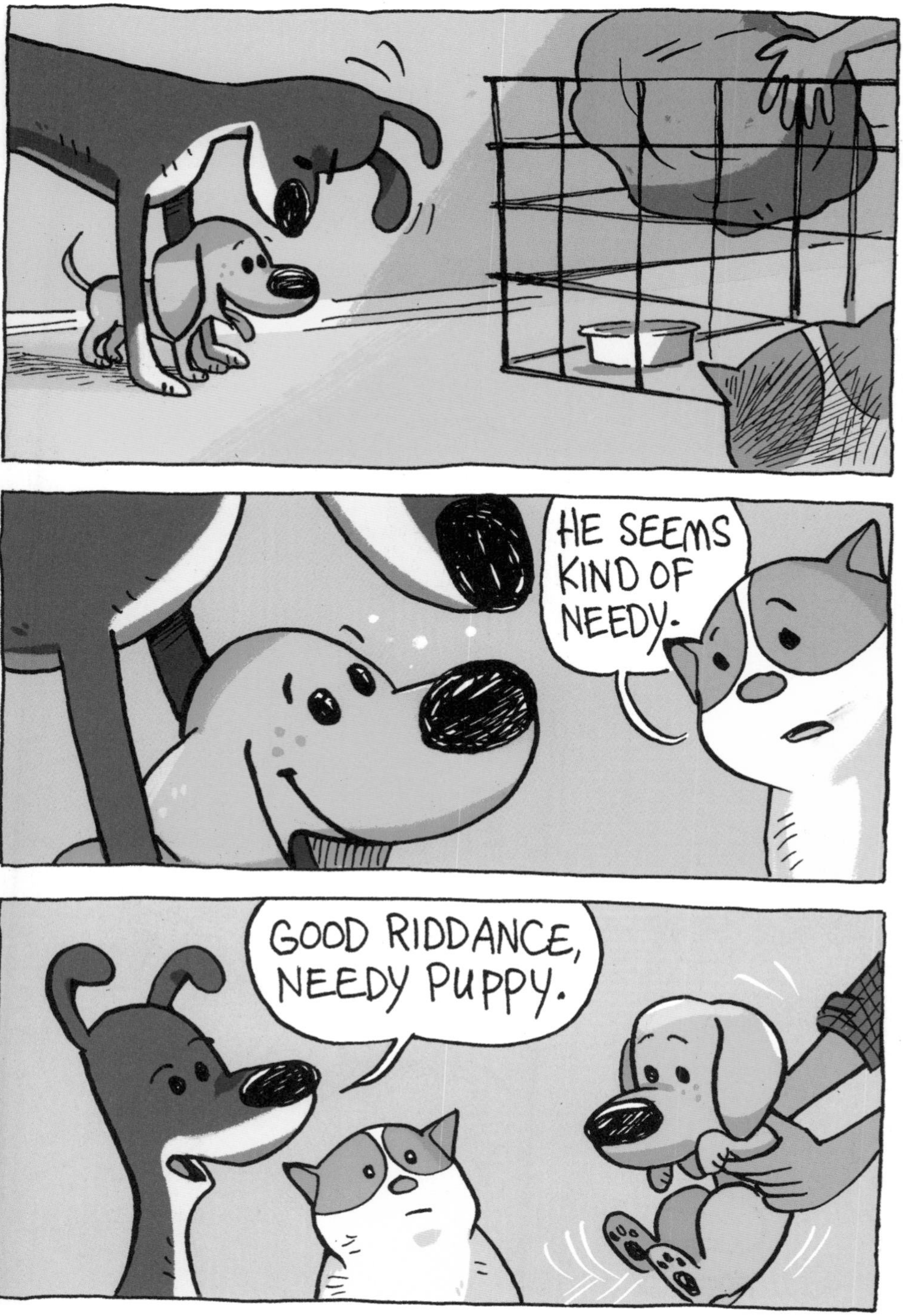
HE SEEMS KIND OF NEEDY.
GOOD RIDDANCE, NEEDY PUPPY.

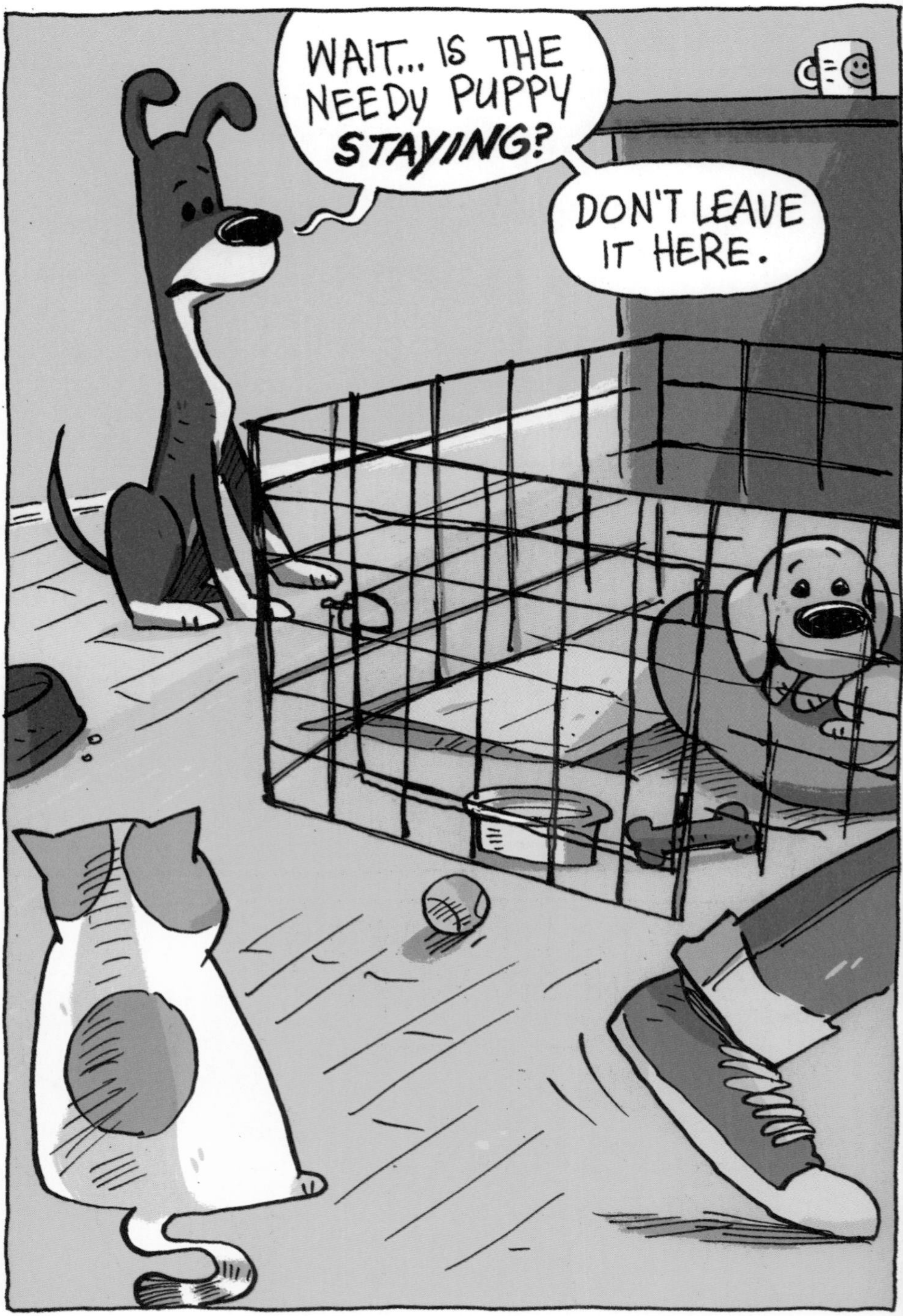
WAIT... IS THE NEEDY PUPPY *STAYING?*
DON'T LEAVE IT HERE.

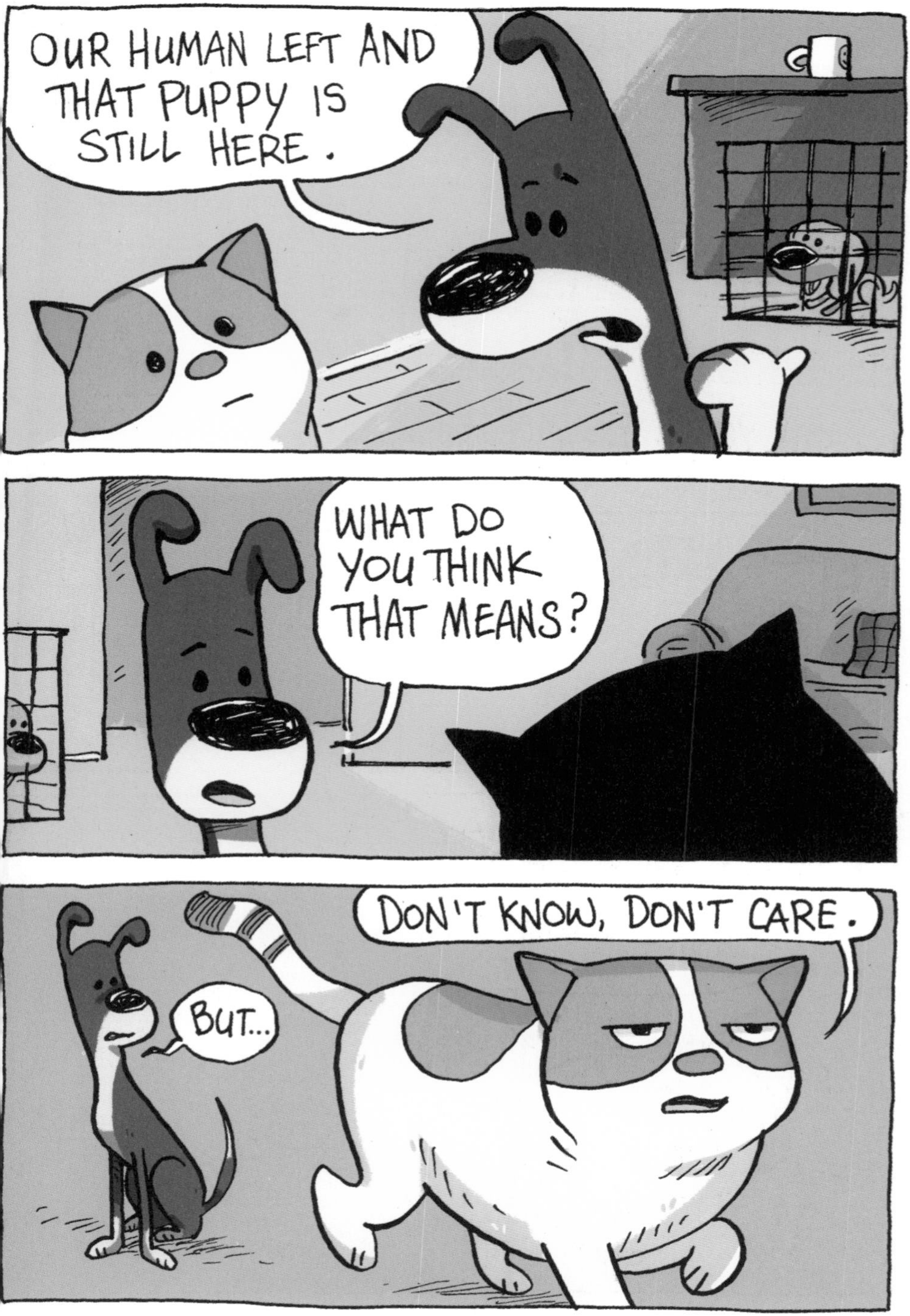
OUR HUMAN LEFT AND THAT PUPPY IS STILL HERE.
WHAT DO YOU THINK THAT MEANS?
DON'T KNOW, DON'T CARE.
BUT...

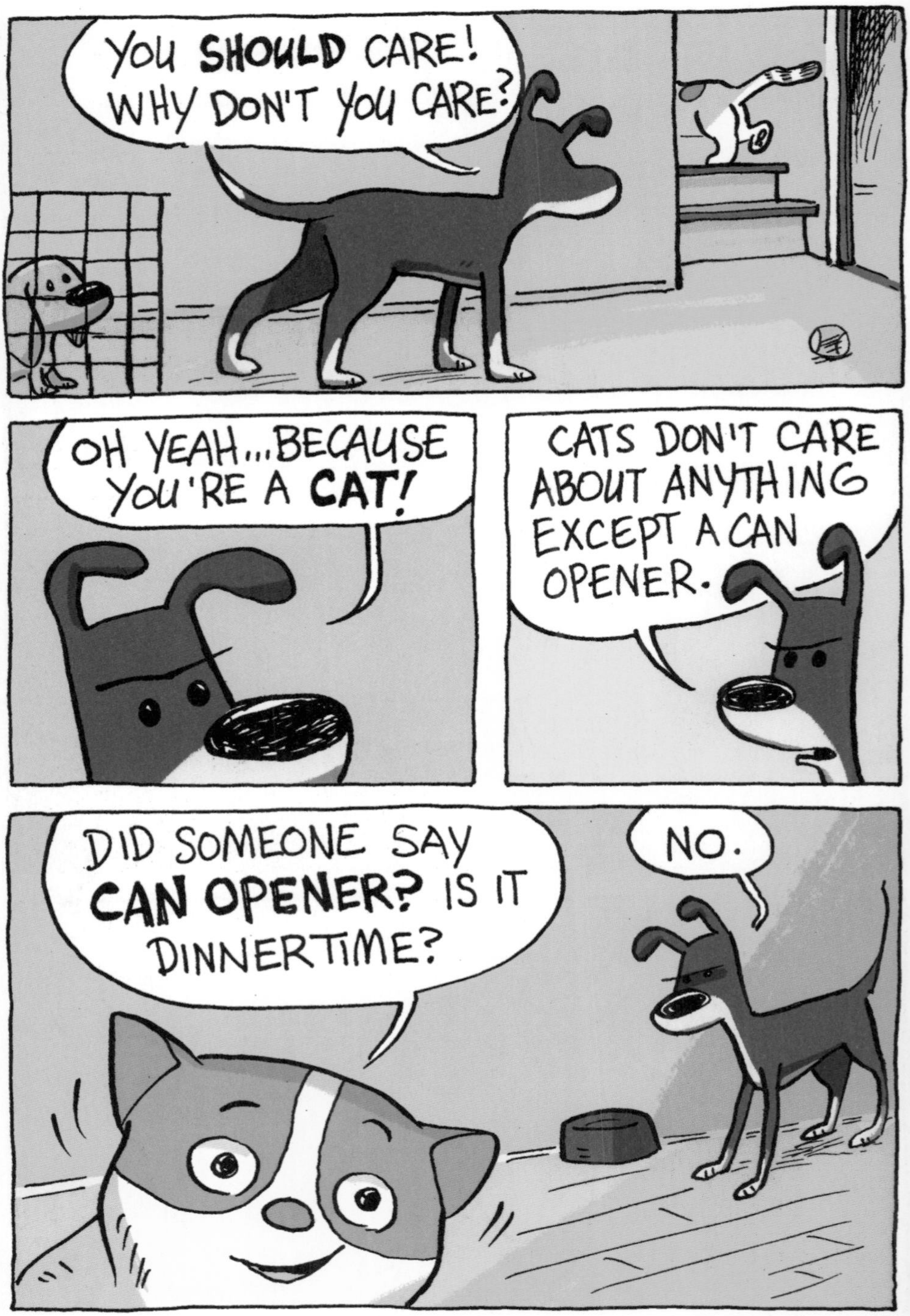
YOU SHOULD CARE! WHY DON'T YOU CARE?
OH YEAH... BECAUSE YOU'RE A CAT!
CATS DON'T CARE ABOUT ANYTHING EXCEPT A CAN OPENER.
DID SOMEONE SAY CAN OPENER? IS IT DINNERTIME?
NO.

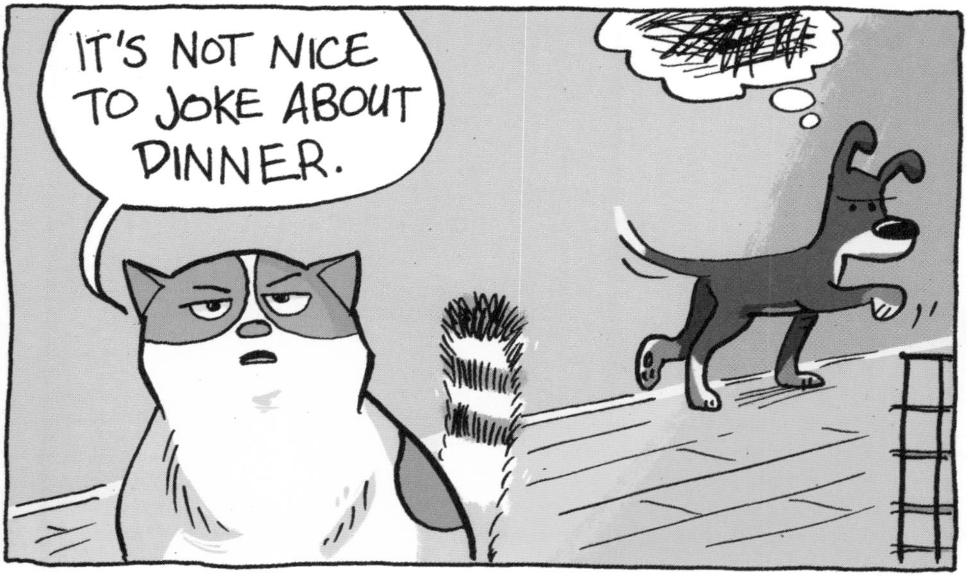
IT'S NOT NICE TO JOKE ABOUT DINNER.

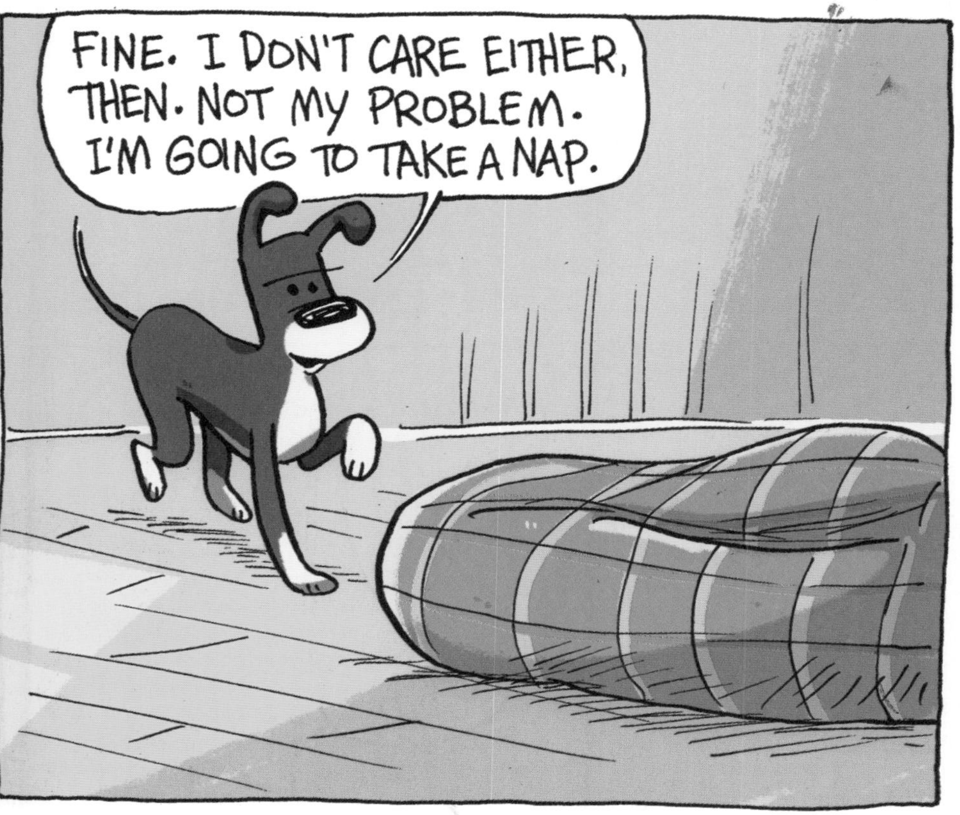
FINE. I DON'T CARE EITHER, THEN. NOT MY PROBLEM. I'M GOING TO TAKE A NAP.

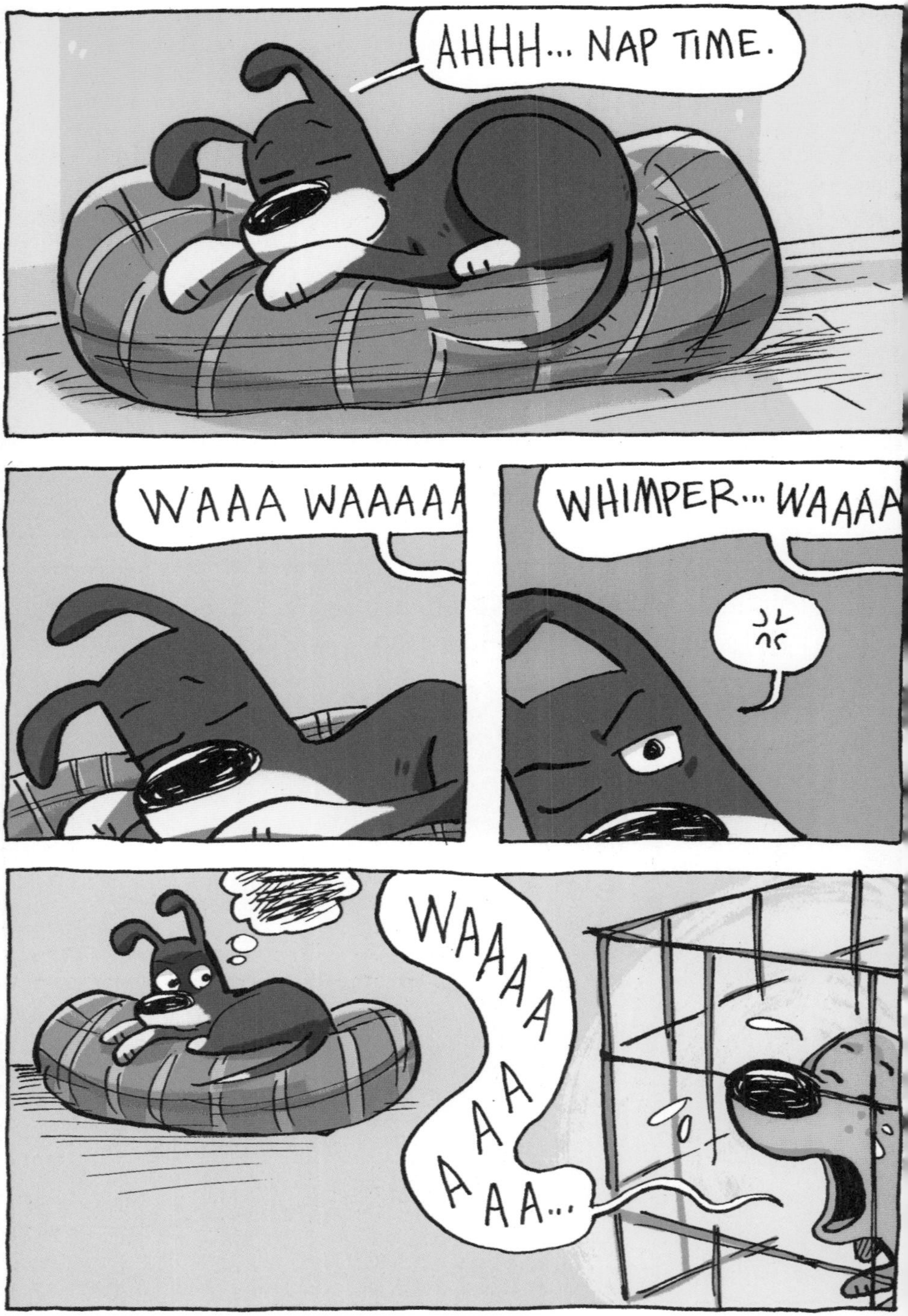
AHHH... NAP TIME.
WAAA WAAAAA
WHIMPER... WAAAA
WAAAAAAAAAA...

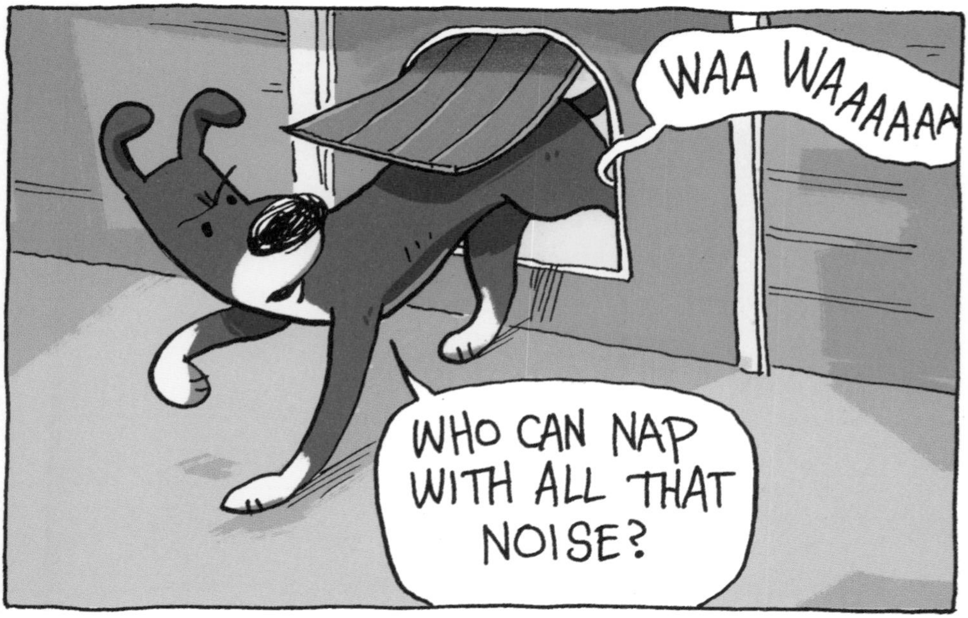
WAA WAAAAAA
WHO CAN NAP WITH ALL THAT NOISE?

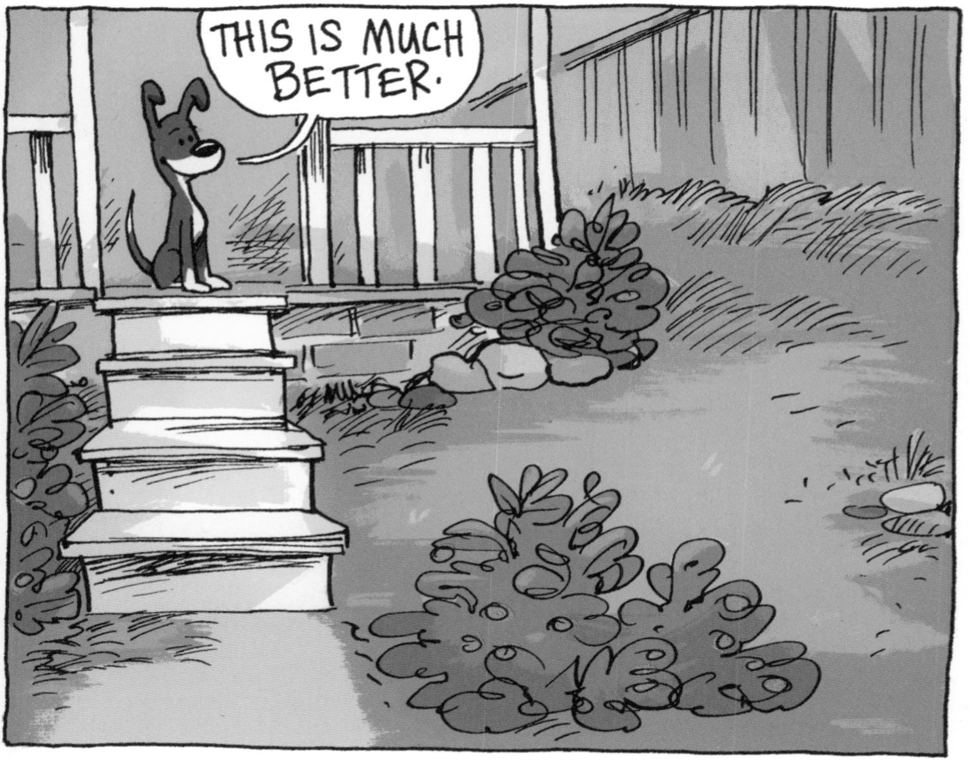
THIS IS MUCH BETTER.

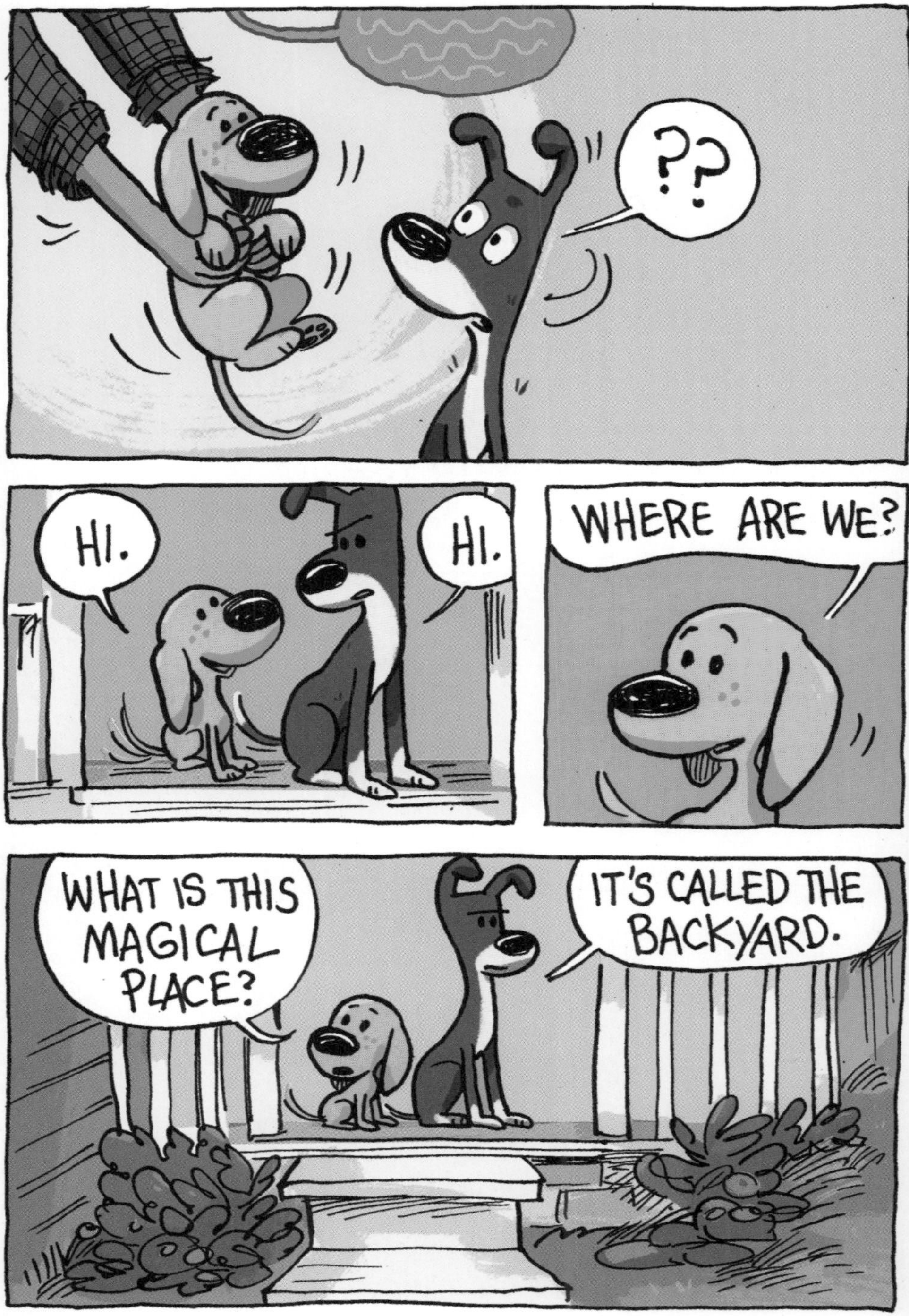
??
HI.
HI.
WHERE ARE WE?
WHAT IS THIS MAGICAL PLACE?
IT'S CALLED THE BACKYARD.

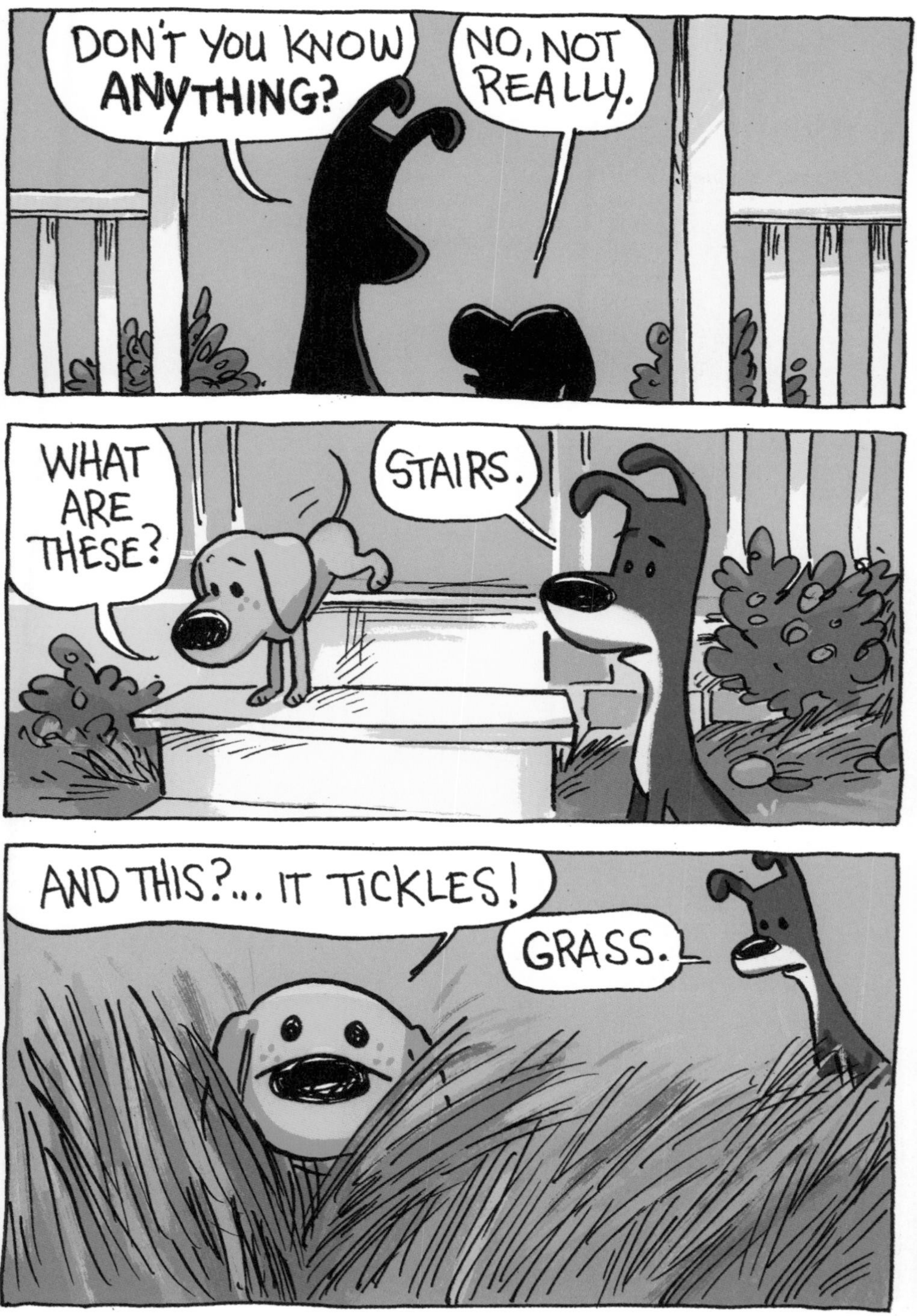
DON'T YOU KNOW ANYTHING?
NO, NOT REALLY.
WHAT ARE THESE?
STAIRS.
AND THIS?... IT TICKLES!
GRASS.

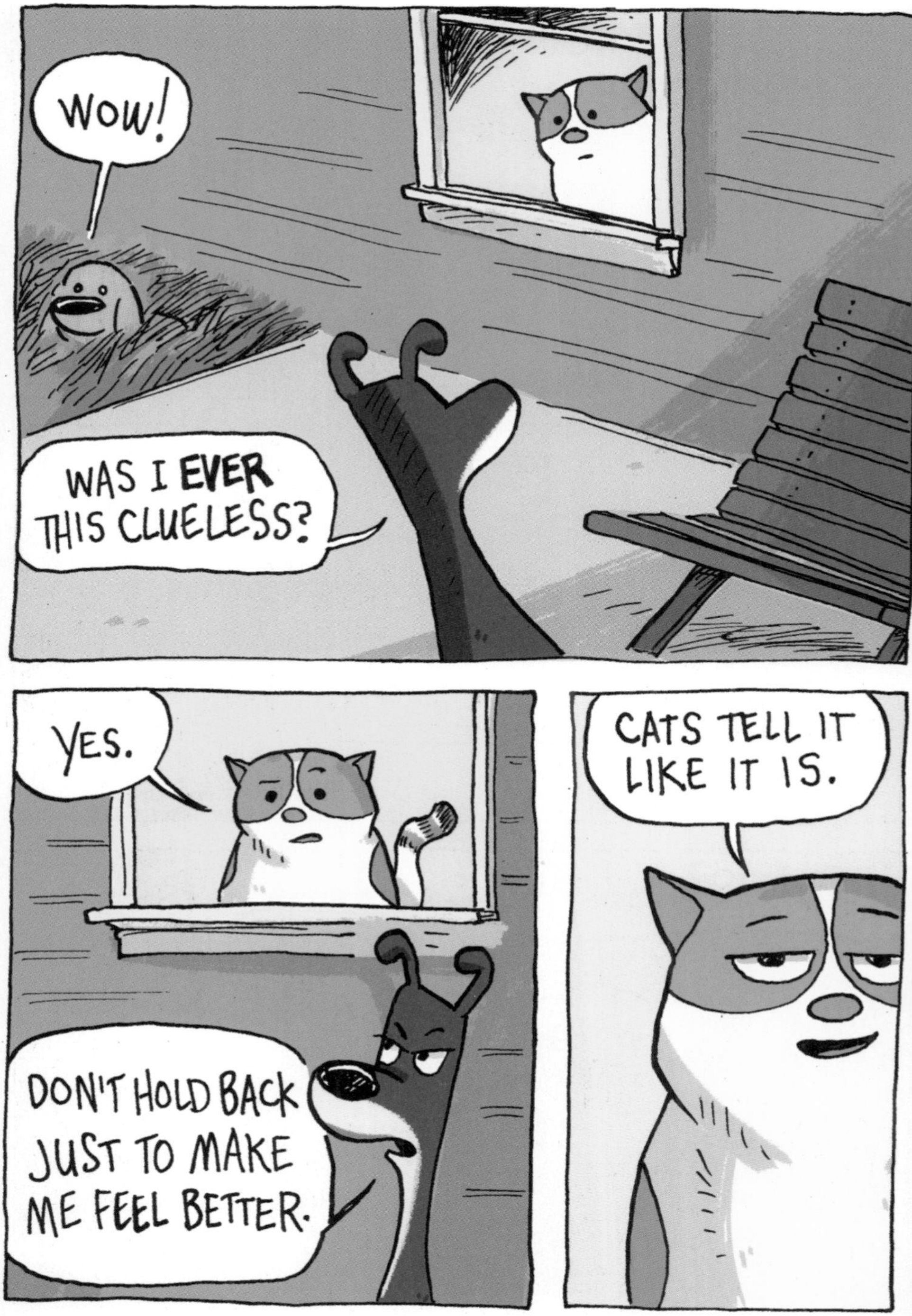
WOW!
WAS I **EVER** THIS CLUELESS?
YES.
DON'T HOLD BACK JUST TO MAKE ME FEEL BETTER.
CATS TELL IT LIKE IT IS.

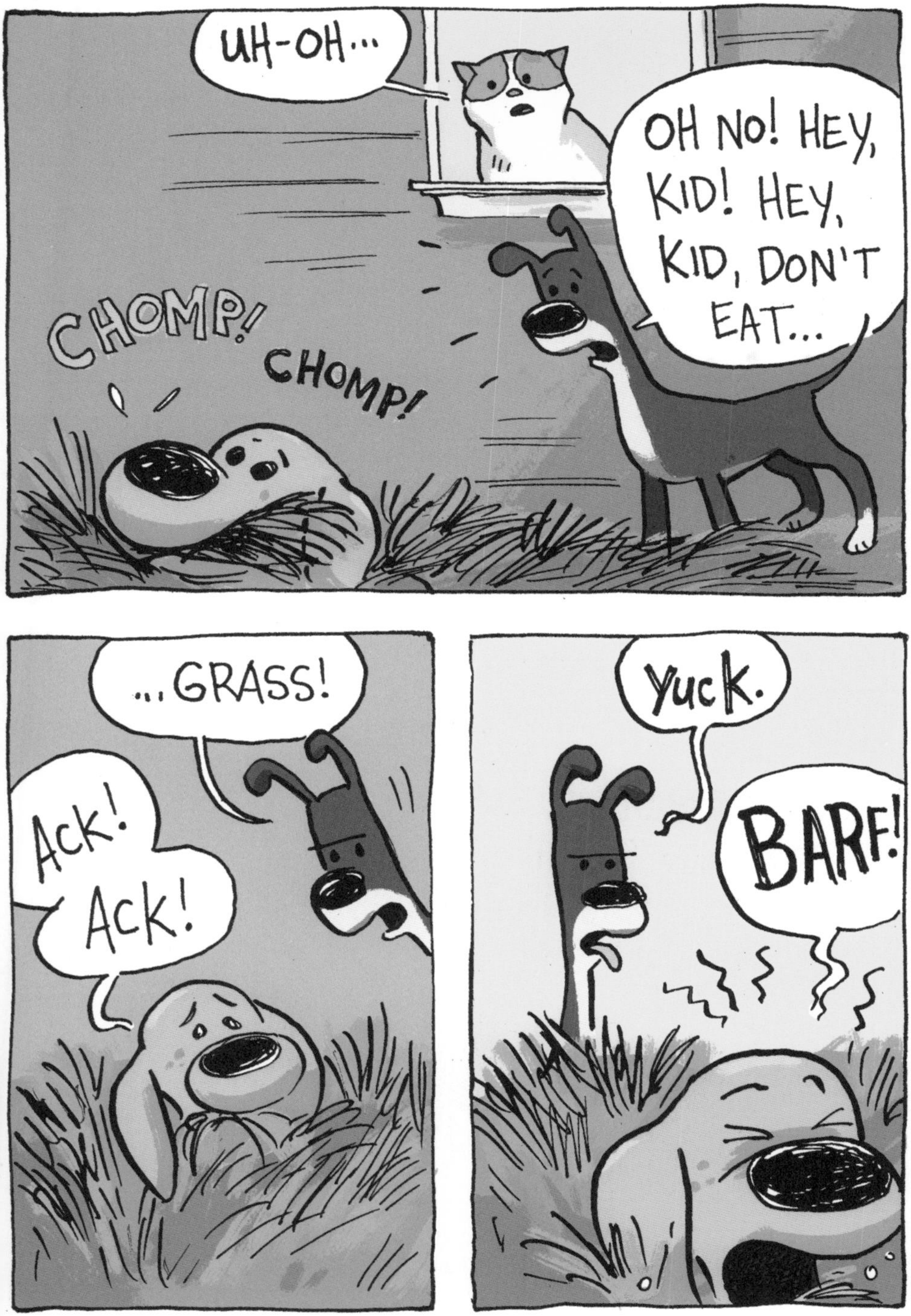
UH-OH...
OH NO! HEY, KID! HEY, KID, DON'T EAT...
CHOMP!
CHOMP!
...GRASS!
Ack! Ack!
yuck.
BARF!

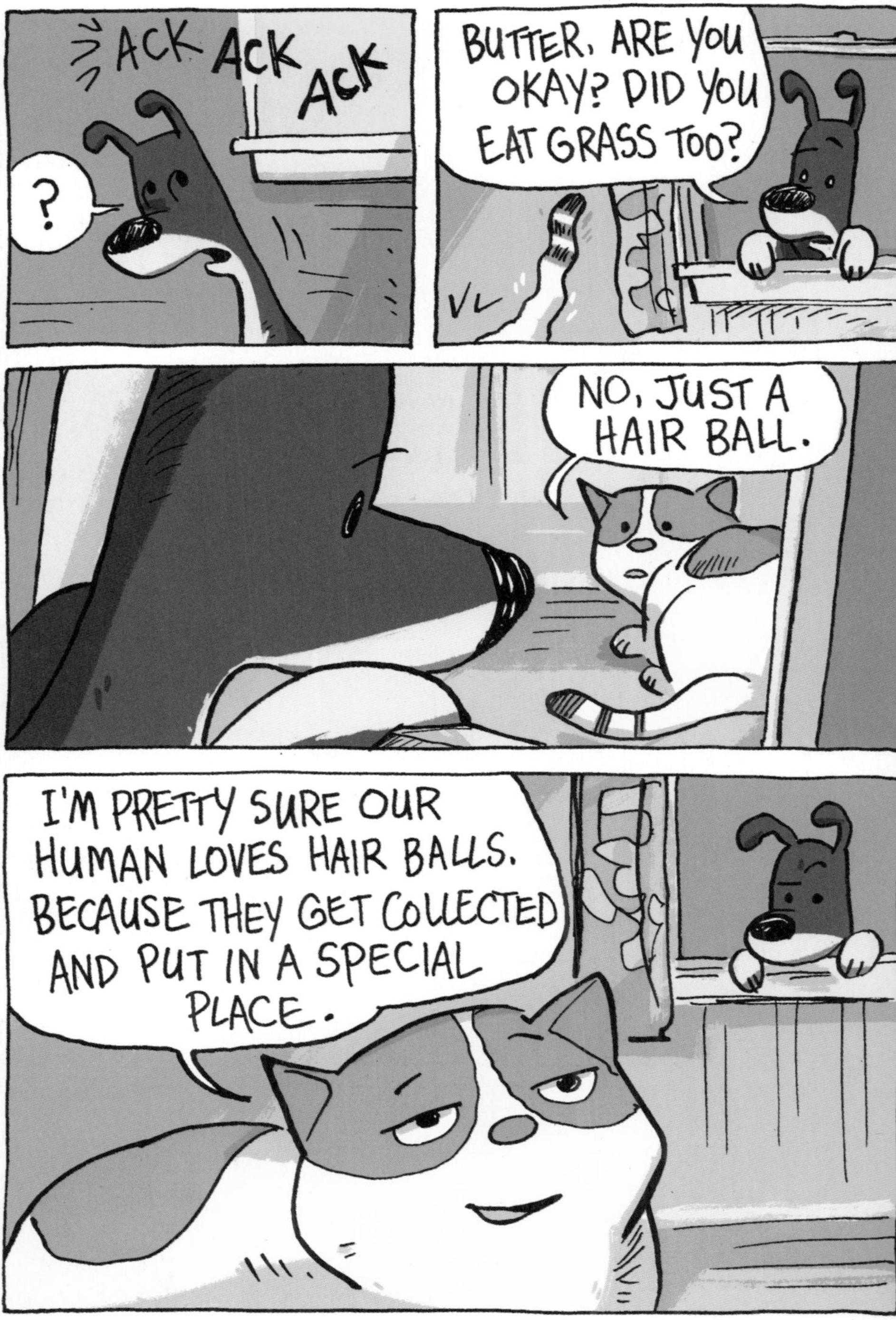
ACK ACK ACK
?
BUTTER, ARE YOU OKAY? DID YOU EAT GRASS TOO?
NO, JUST A HAIR BALL.
I'M PRETTY SURE OUR HUMAN LOVES HAIR BALLS. BECAUSE THEY GET COLLECTED AND PUT IN A SPECIAL PLACE.

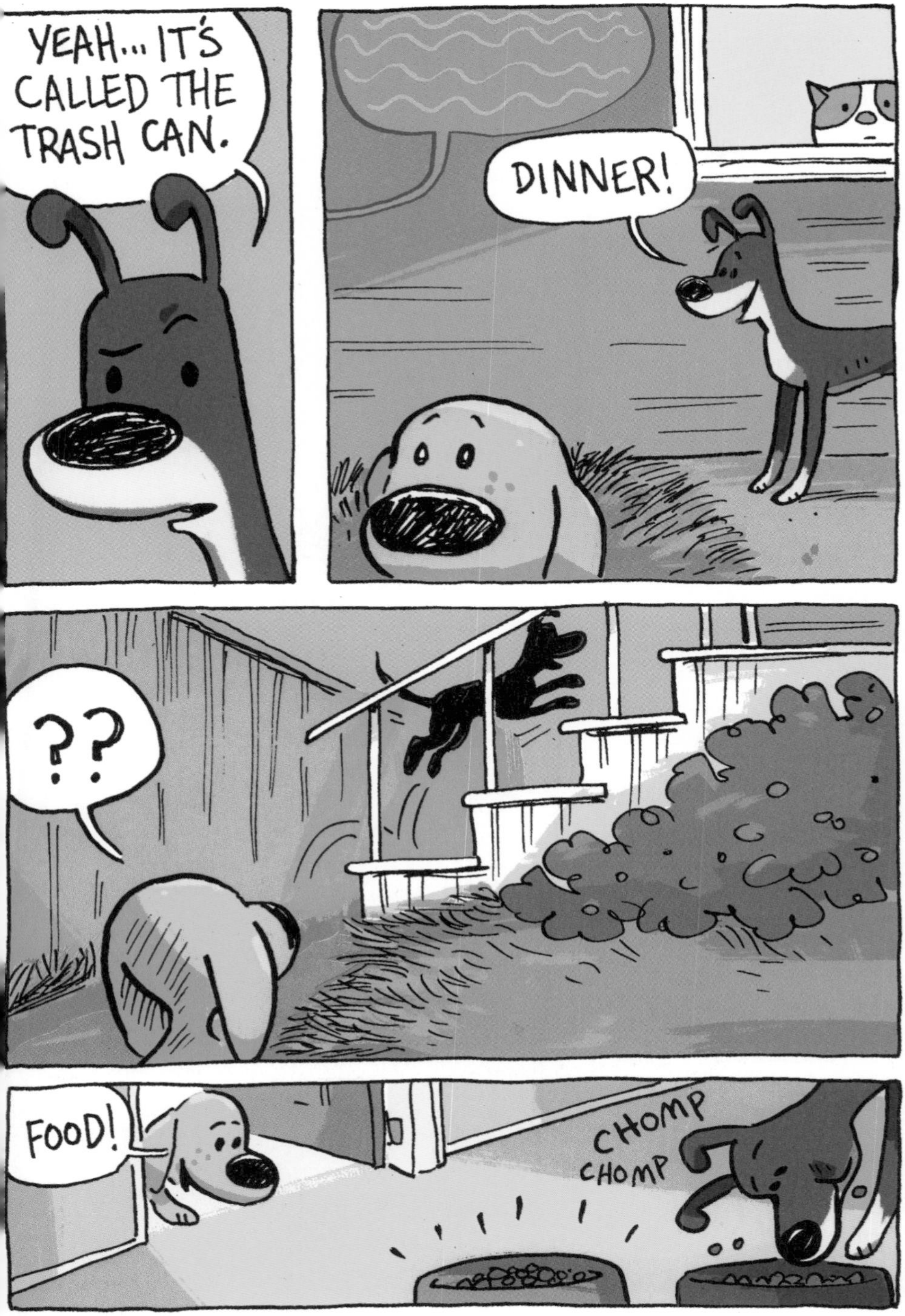
YEAH... IT'S CALLED THE TRASH CAN.
DINNER!
??
FOOD!
CHOMP
CHOMP

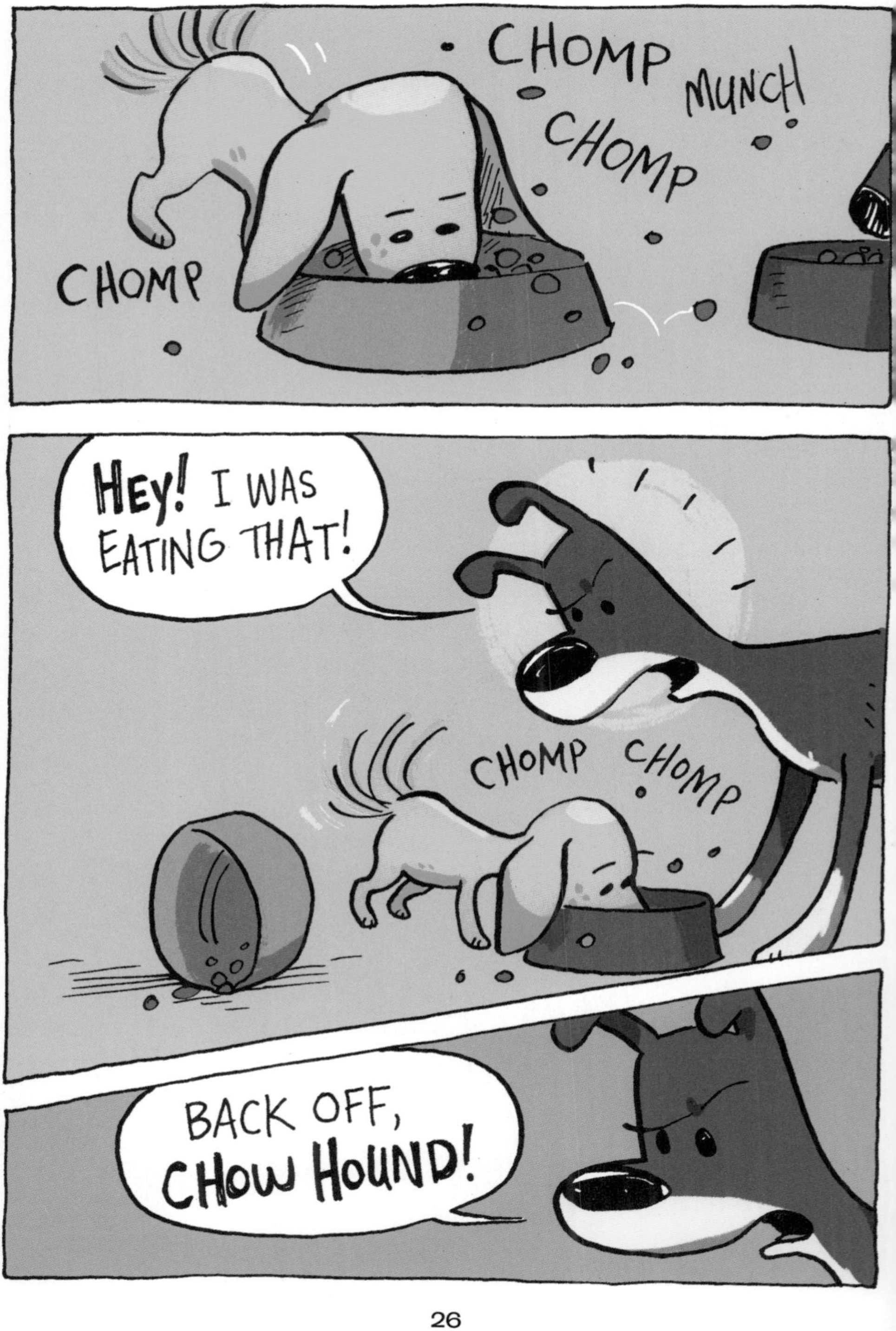
CHOMP
CHOMP
MUNCH
CHOMP
HEY! I WAS EATING THAT!
CHOMP CHOMP
BACK OFF, CHOW HOUND!

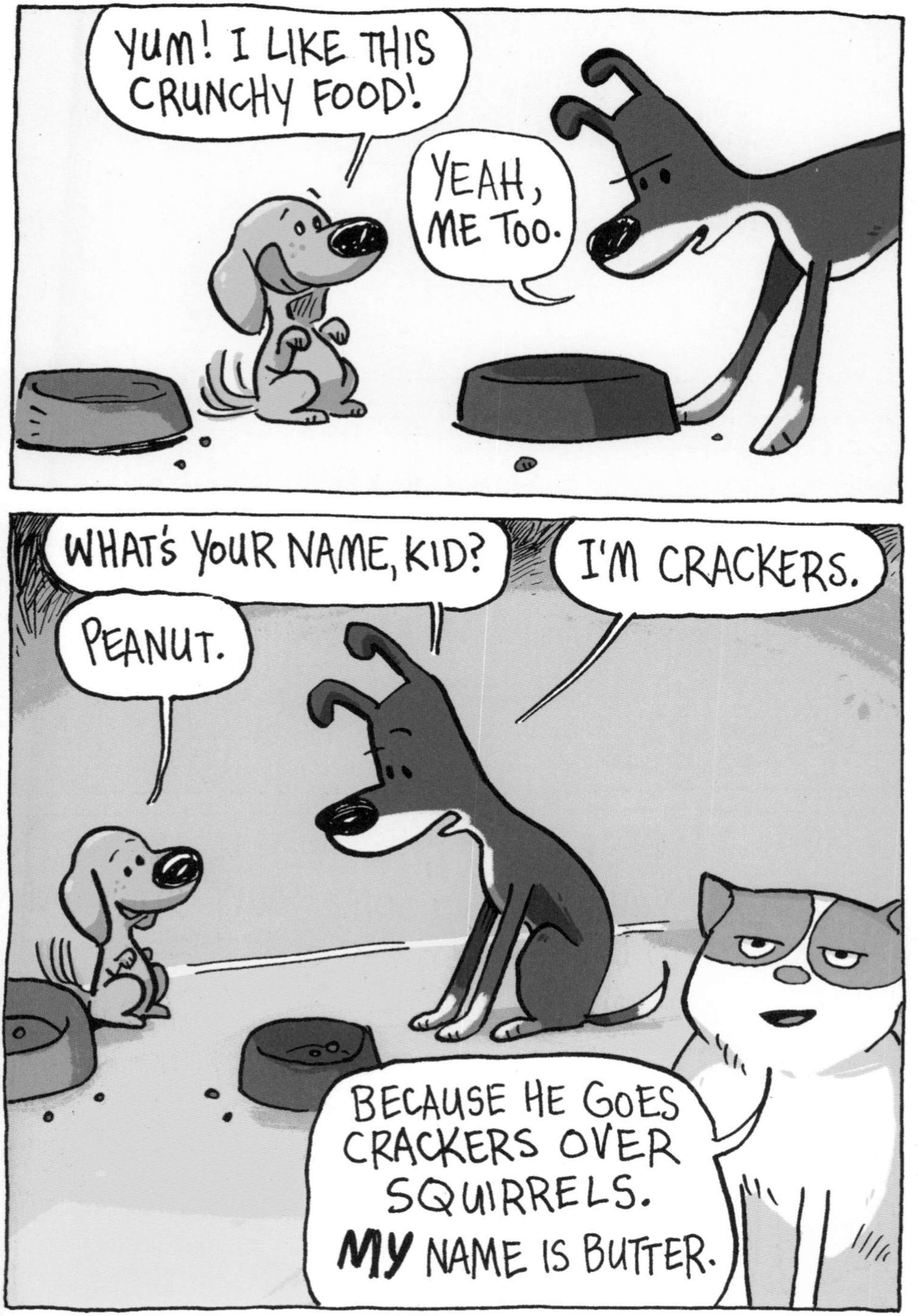
YUM! I LIKE THIS CRUNCHY FOOD!
YEAH, ME TOO.
WHAT'S YOUR NAME, KID?
PEANUT.
I'M CRACKERS.
BECAUSE HE GOES CRACKERS OVER SQUIRRELS.
MY NAME IS BUTTER.

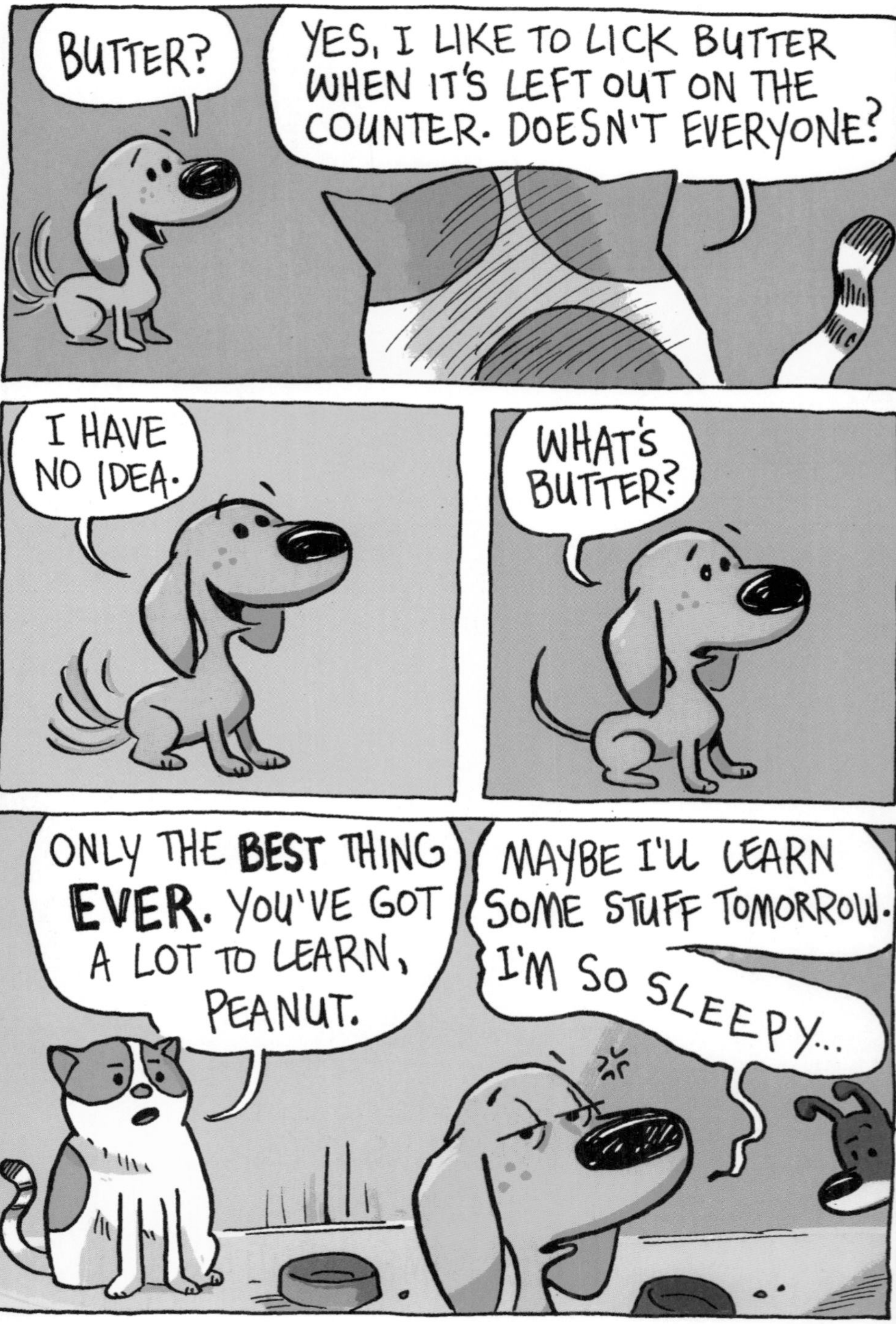
BUTTER?
YES, I LIKE TO LICK BUTTER WHEN IT'S LEFT OUT ON THE COUNTER. DOESN'T EVERYONE?
I HAVE NO IDEA.
WHAT'S BUTTER?
ONLY THE **BEST** THING **EVER**. YOU'VE GOT A LOT TO LEARN, PEANUT.
MAYBE I'LL LEARN SOME STUFF TOMORROW.
I'M SO SLEEPY...

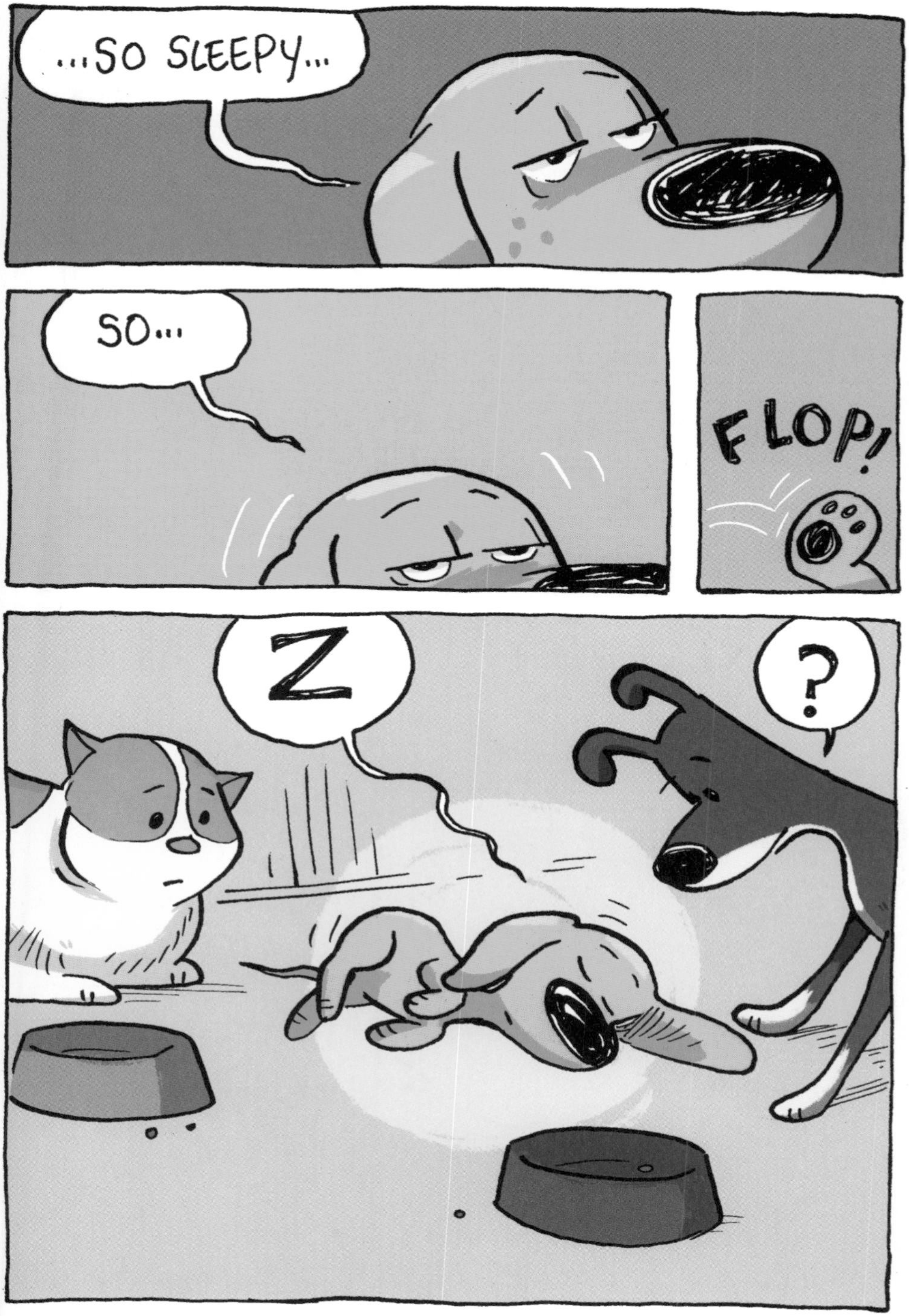
...SO SLEEPY...
SO...
FLOP!
Z
?

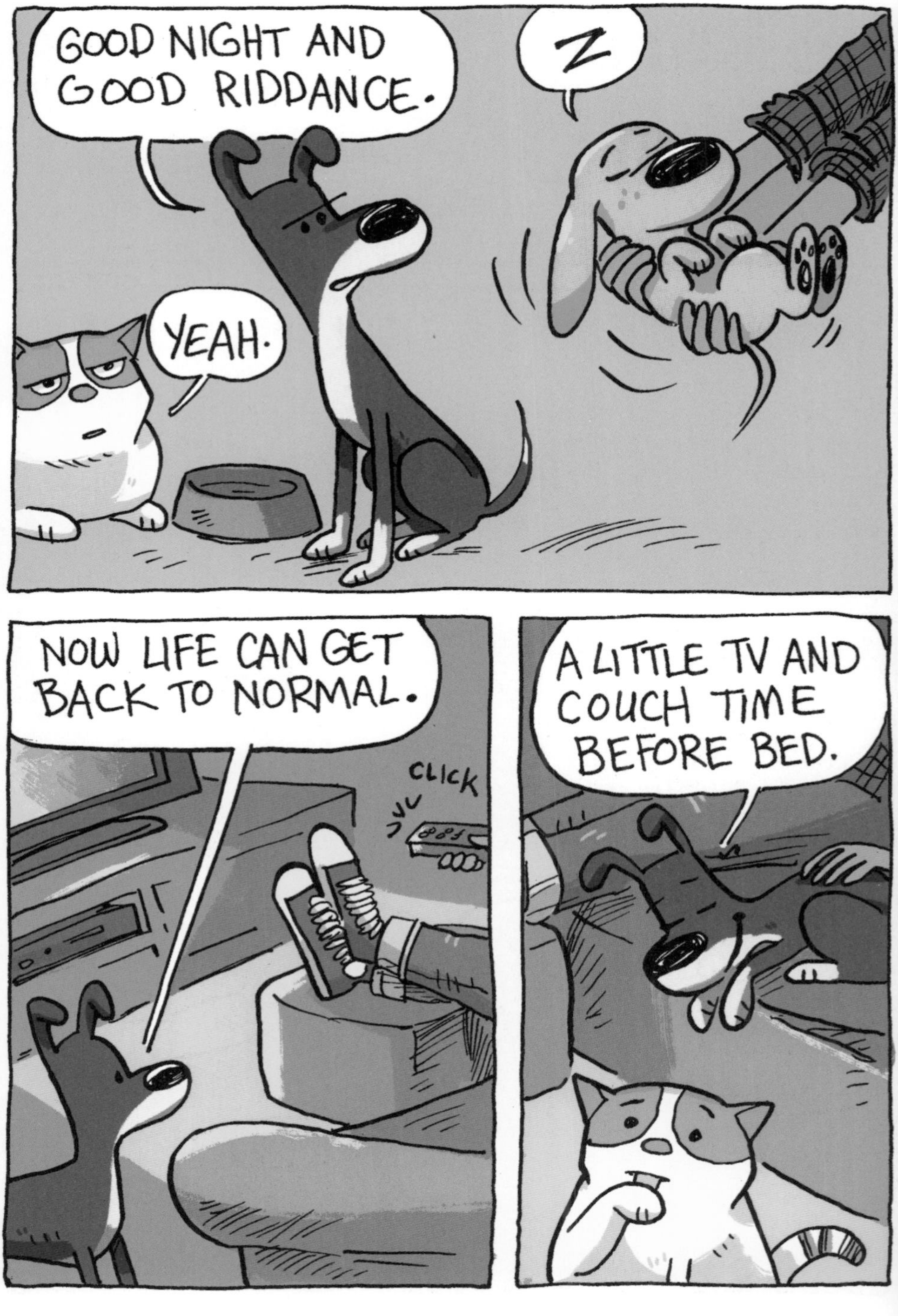
GOOD NIGHT AND GOOD RIDDANCE.
Z
YEAH.
NOW LIFE CAN GET BACK TO NORMAL.
CLICK
A LITTLE TV AND COUCH TIME BEFORE BED.

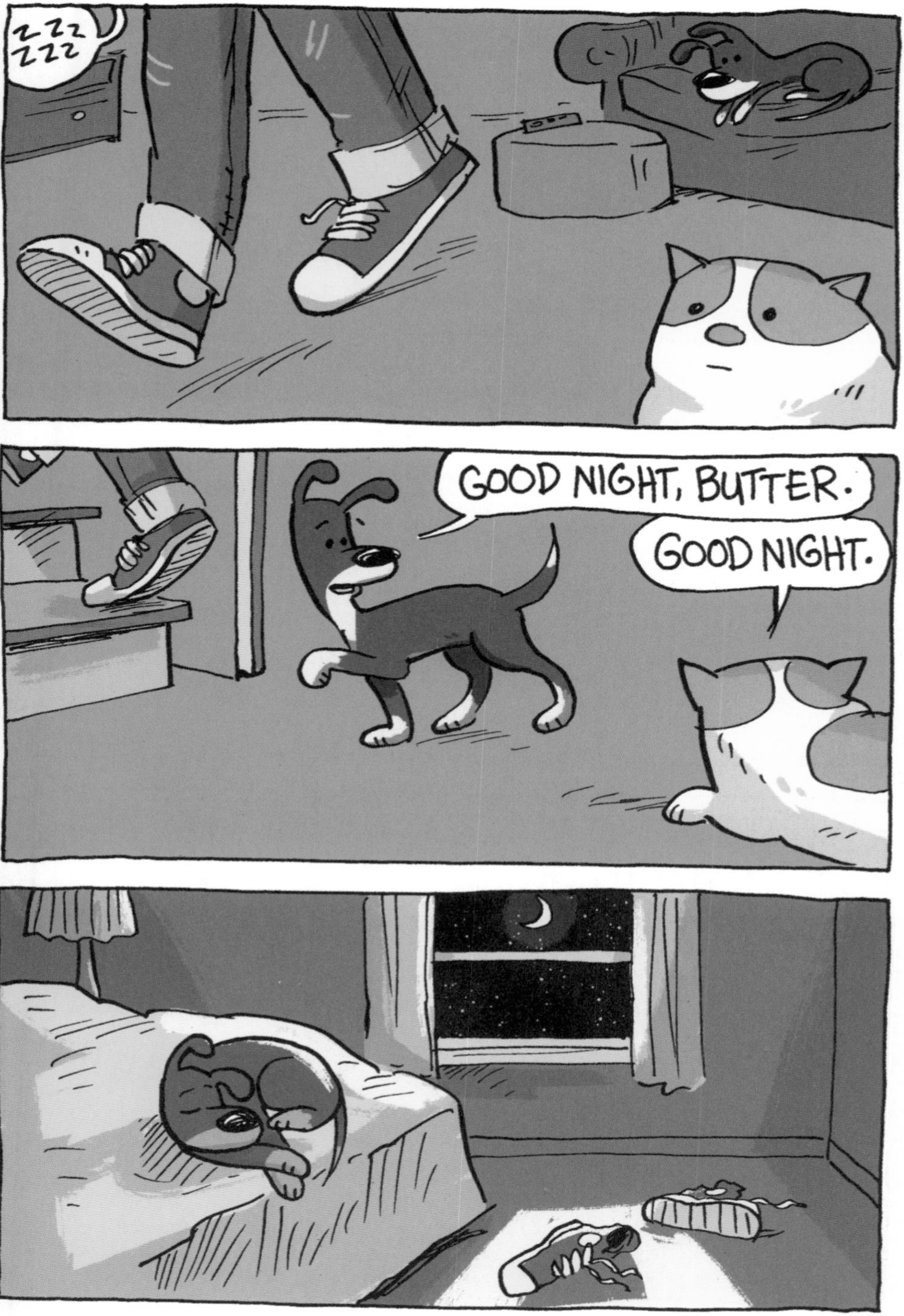
ZZZ
ZZZ
GOOD NIGHT, BUTTER.
GOOD NIGHT.

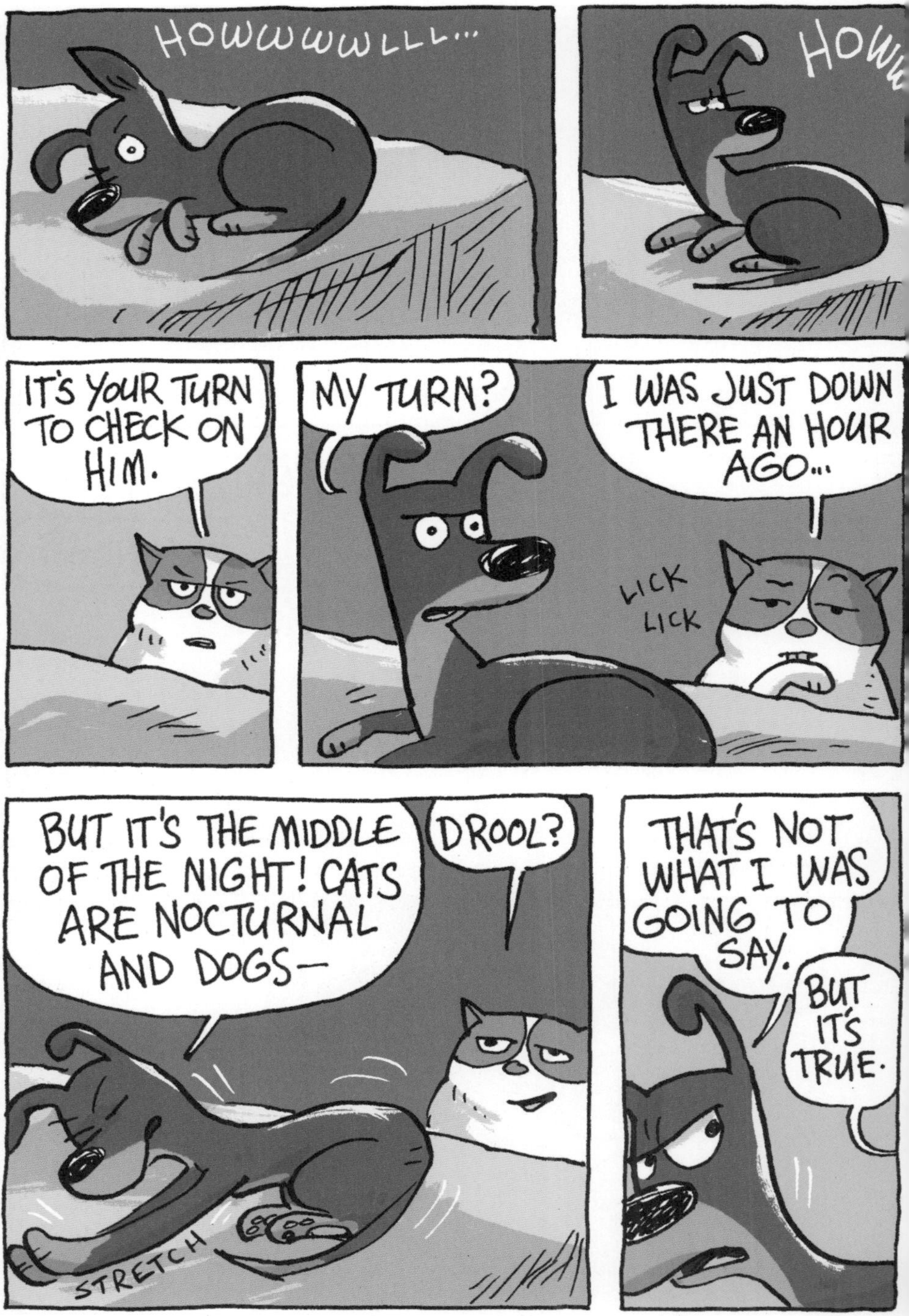
HOWWWWLLL...
HOWW
IT'S YOUR TURN TO CHECK ON HIM.
MY TURN?
I WAS JUST DOWN THERE AN HOUR AGO...
LICK LICK
BUT IT'S THE MIDDLE OF THE NIGHT! CATS ARE NOCTURNAL AND DOGS—
DROOL?
STRETCH
THAT'S NOT WHAT I WAS GOING TO SAY.
BUT IT'S TRUE.

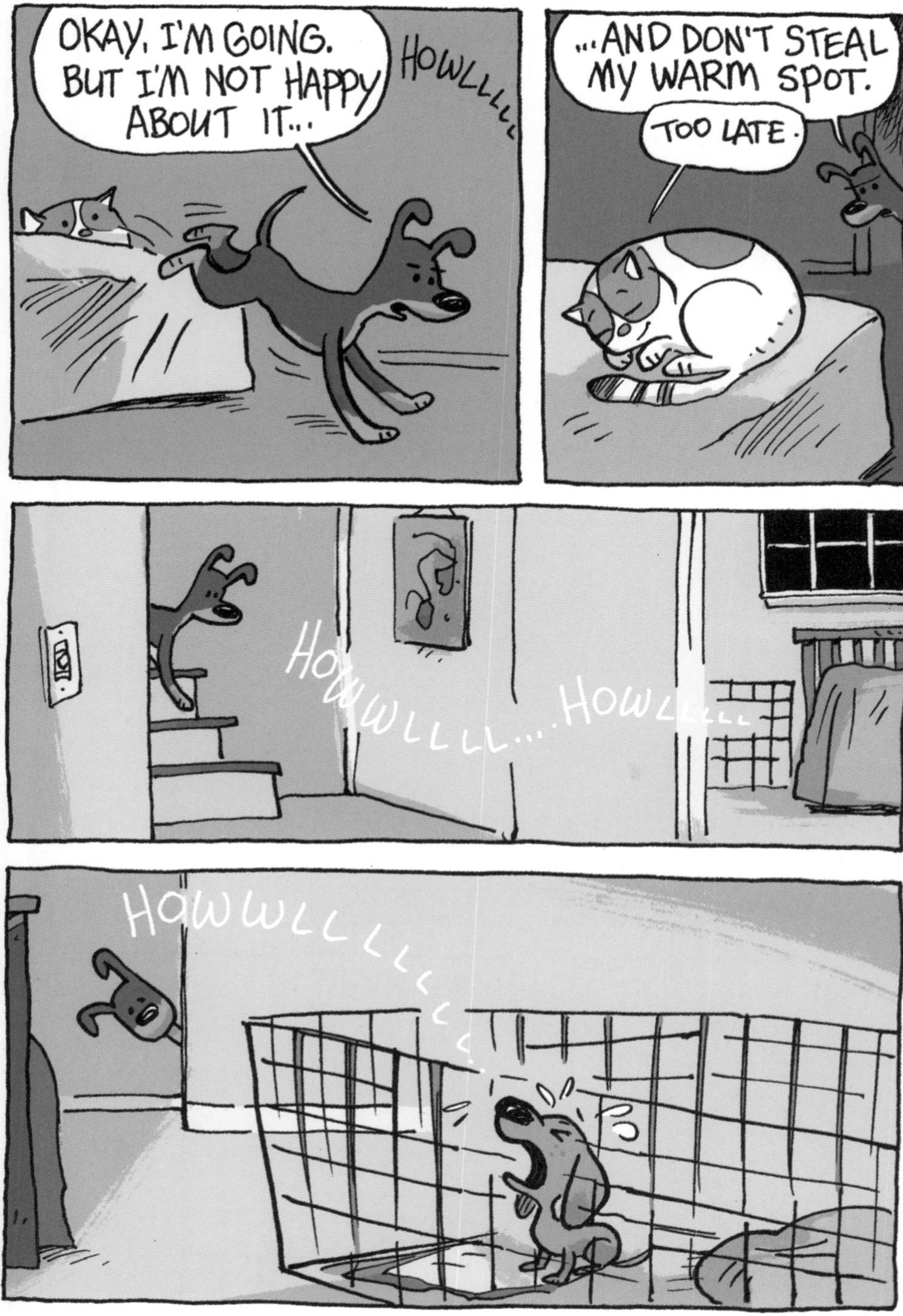
OKAY, I'M GOING. BUT I'M NOT HAPPY ABOUT IT...
HOWLLLLL
...AND DON'T STEAL MY WARM SPOT.
TOO LATE.
HOWWLLLLL....HOWLLLLL
HOWWLLLLLLLL

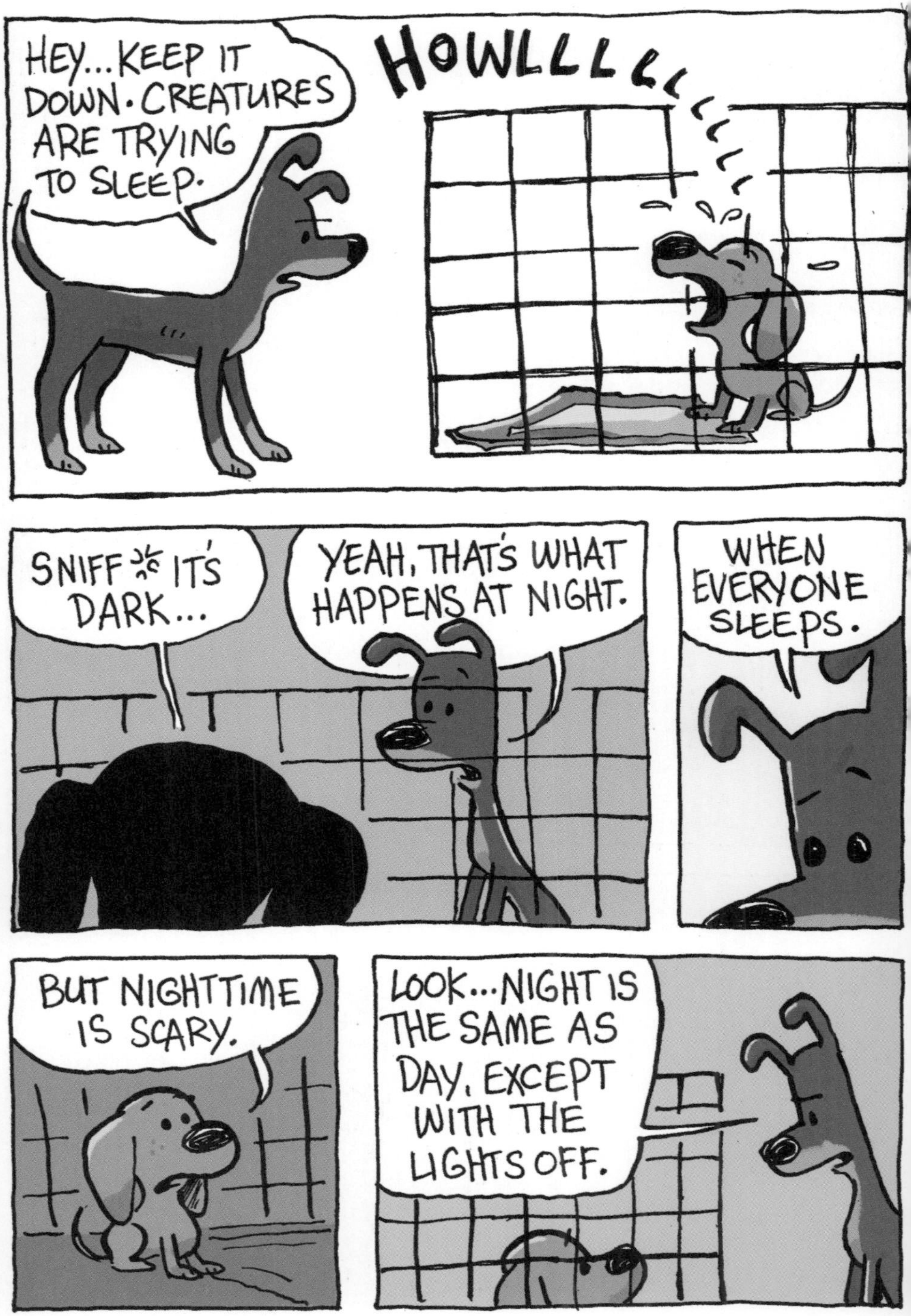
HEY... KEEP IT DOWN. CREATURES ARE TRYING TO SLEEP.
HOWLLLLLLLLLLLL
SNIFF IT'S DARK...
YEAH, THAT'S WHAT HAPPENS AT NIGHT.
WHEN EVERYONE SLEEPS.
BUT NIGHTTIME IS SCARY.
LOOK... NIGHT IS THE SAME AS DAY, EXCEPT WITH THE LIGHTS OFF.

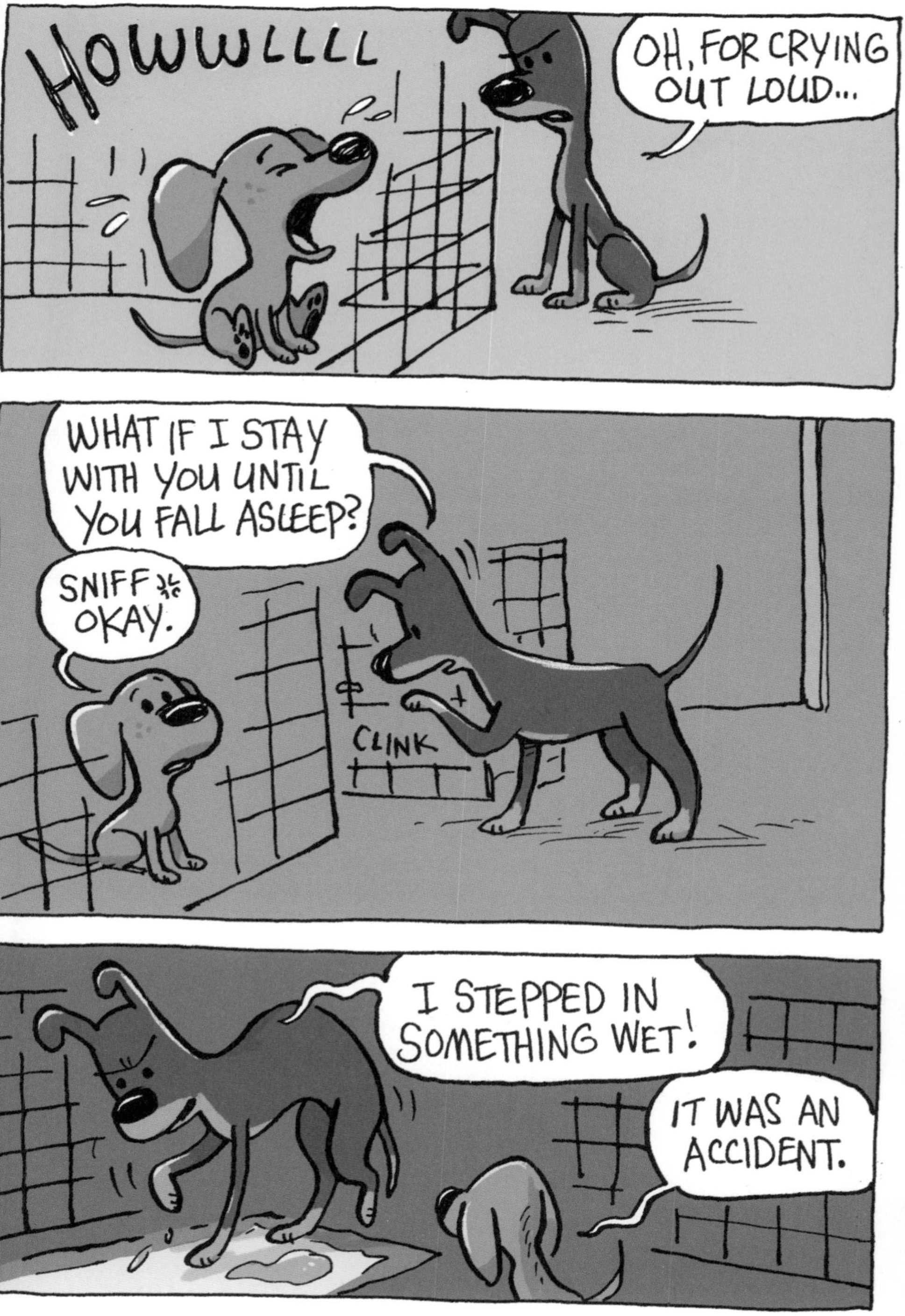
HOWWLLLL
OH, FOR CRYING OUT LOUD...
WHAT IF I STAY WITH YOU UNTIL YOU FALL ASLEEP?
SNIFF OKAY.
CLINK
I STEPPED IN SOMETHING WET!
IT WAS AN ACCIDENT.

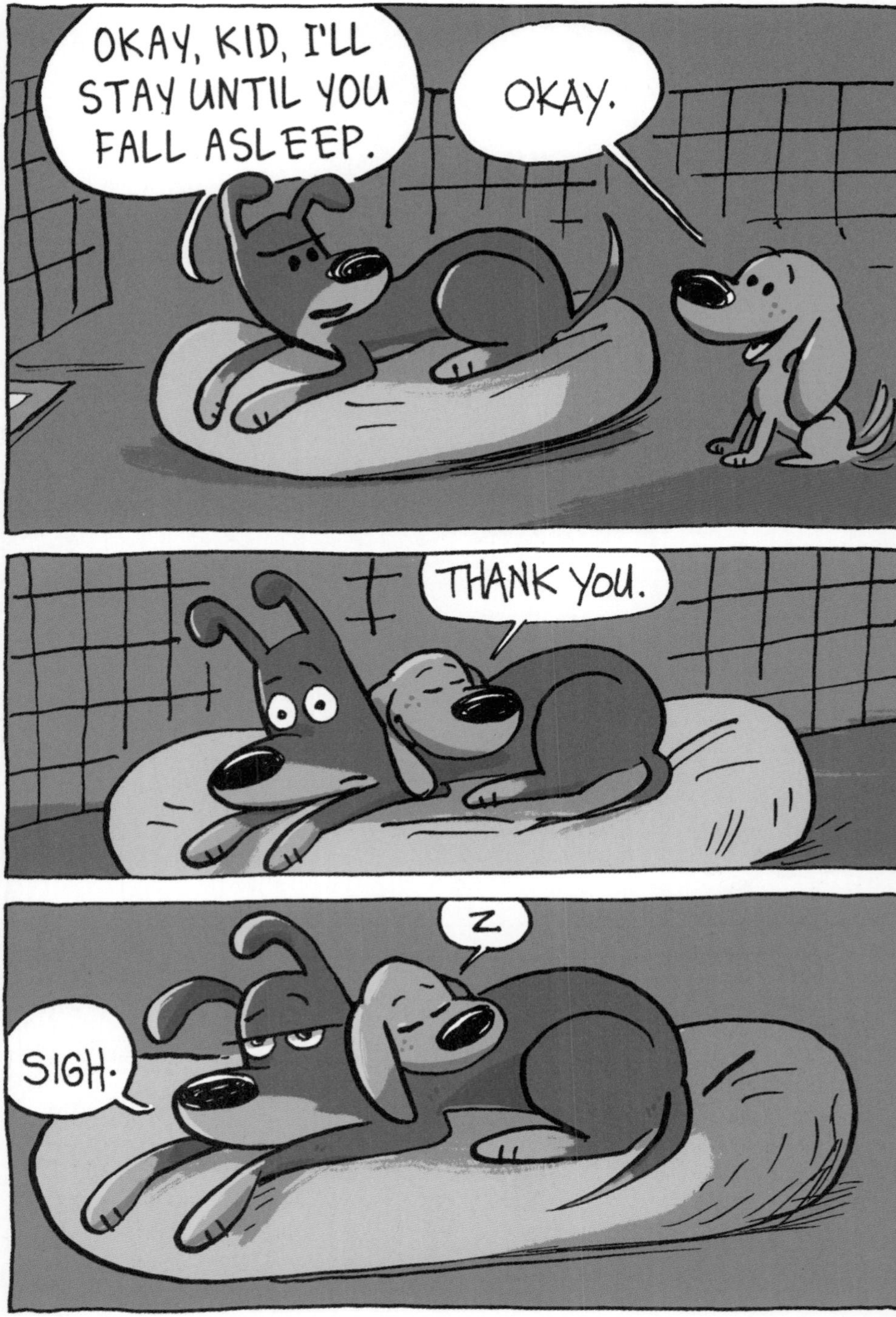
OKAY, KID, I'LL STAY UNTIL YOU FALL ASLEEP.
OKAY.
THANK YOU.
Z
SIGH.

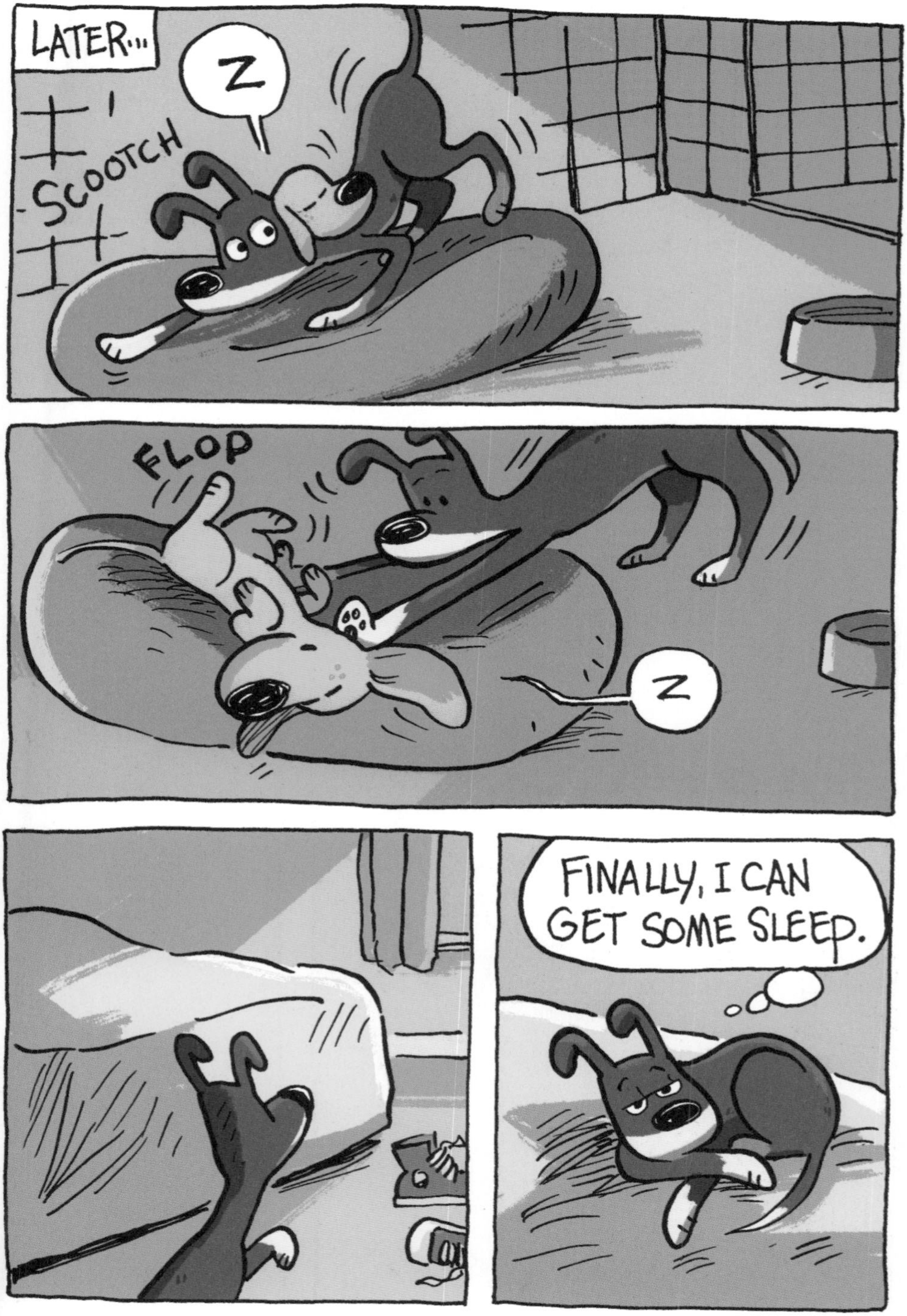

LATER...
SCOOTCH
Z
FLOP
Z
FINALLY, I CAN GET SOME SLEEP.

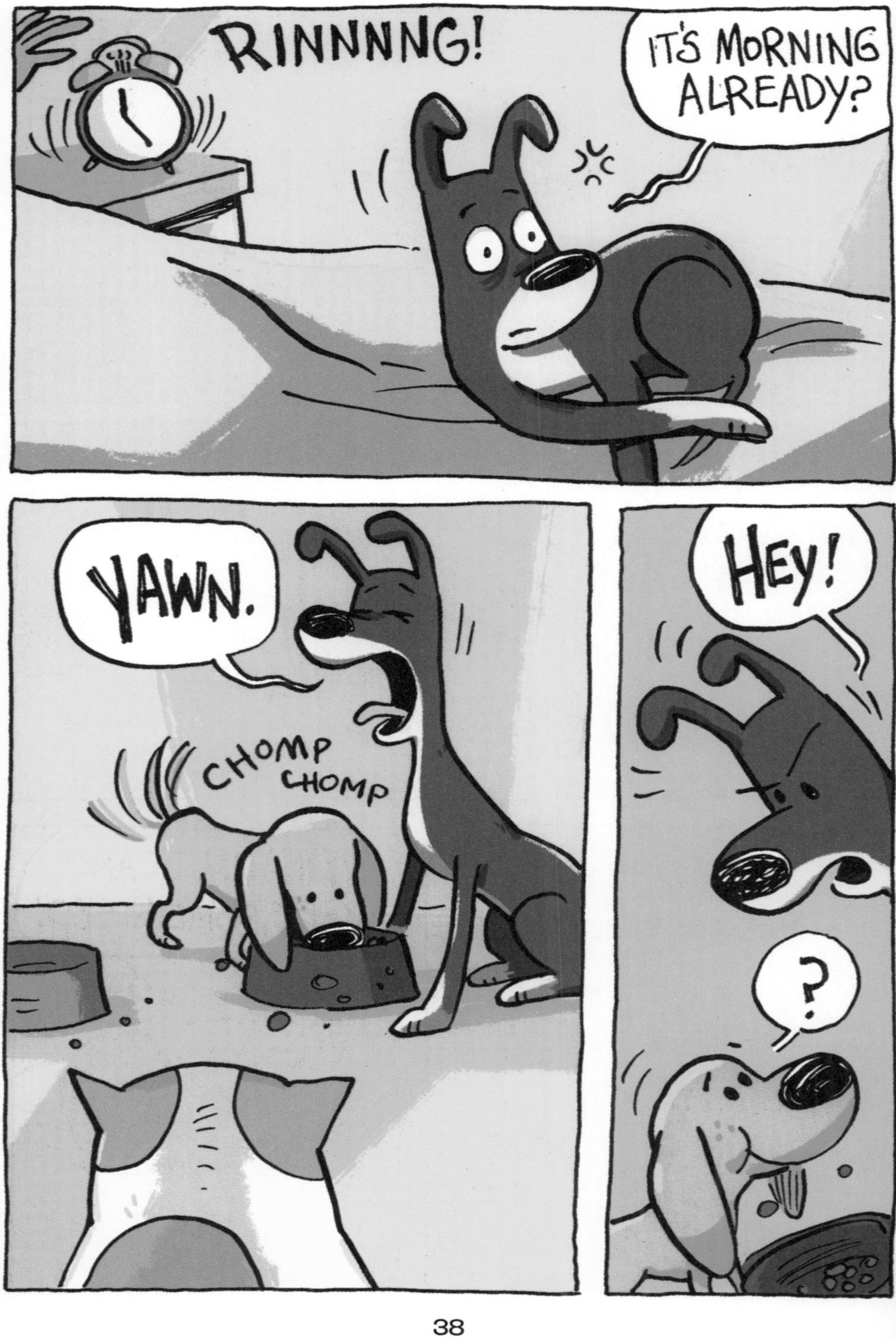
RINNNNG!
IT'S MORNING ALREADY?
YAWN.
CHOMP CHOMP
HEY!
?

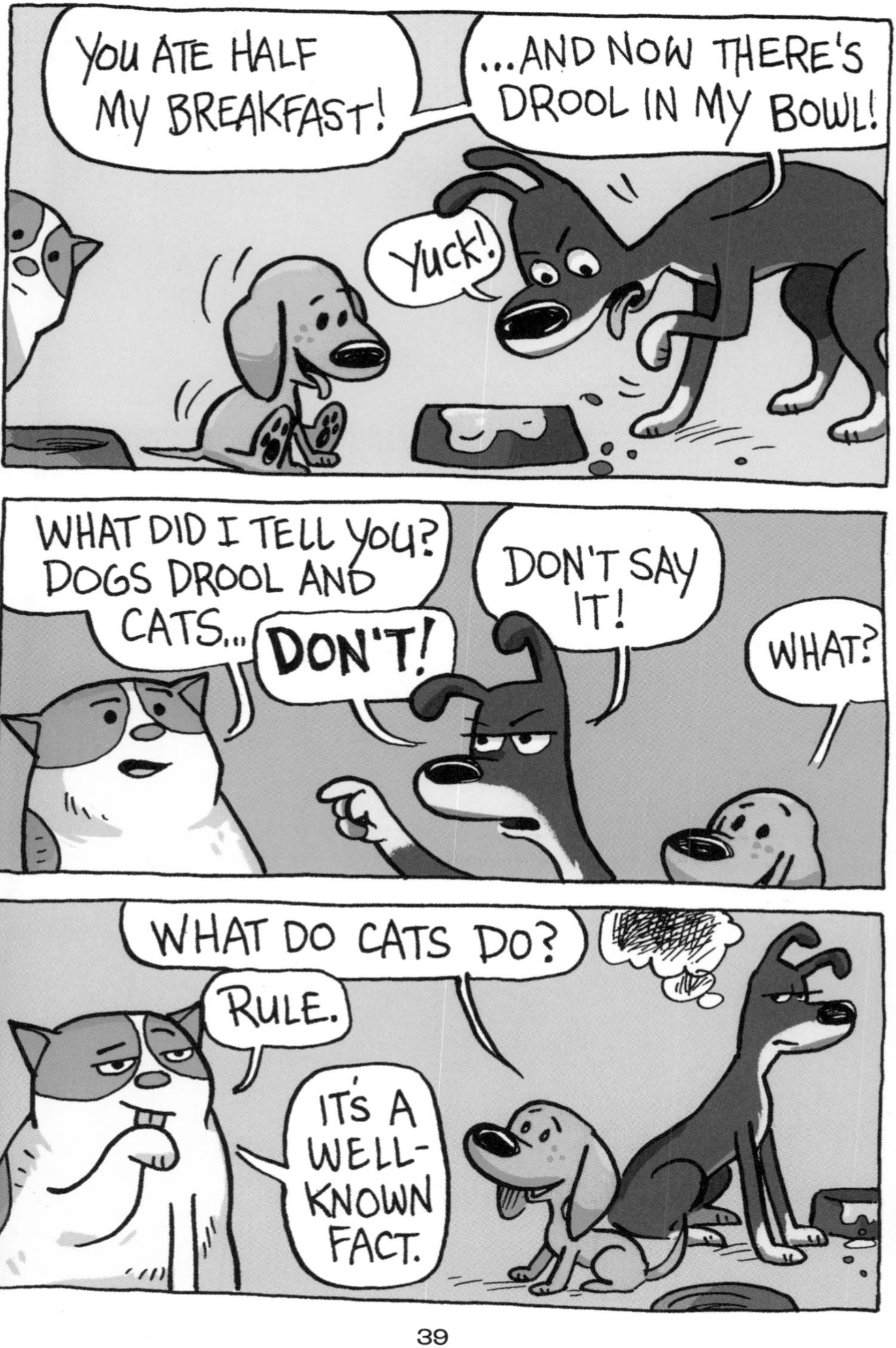
YOU ATE HALF MY BREAKFAST!
...AND NOW THERE'S DROOL IN MY BOWL!
YUCK!
WHAT DID I TELL YOU? DOGS DROOL AND CATS...
DON'T!
DON'T SAY IT!
WHAT?
WHAT DO CATS DO?
RULE.
IT'S A WELL-KNOWN FACT.

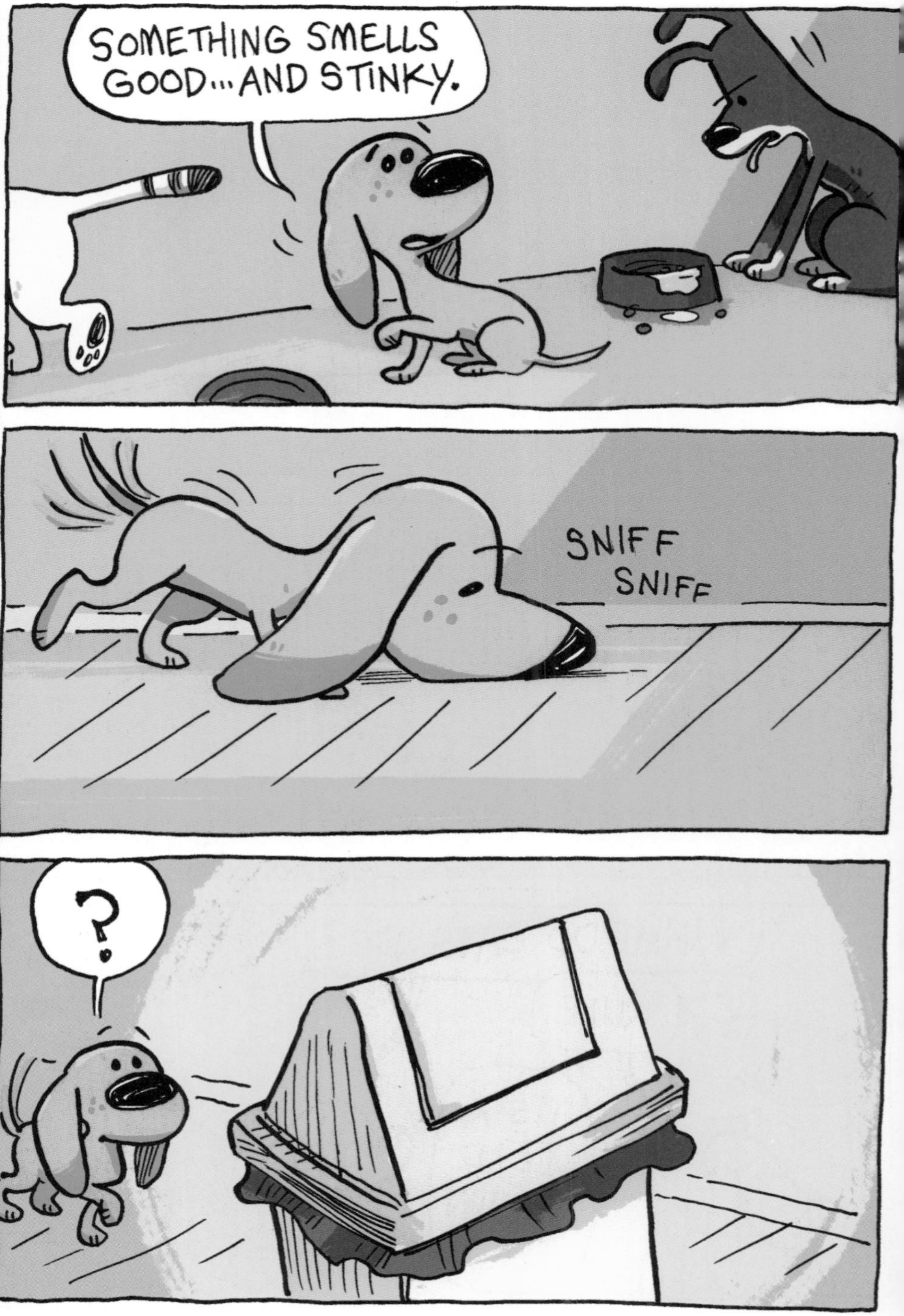
SOMETHING SMELLS GOOD... AND STINKY.
SNIFF
SNIFF
?

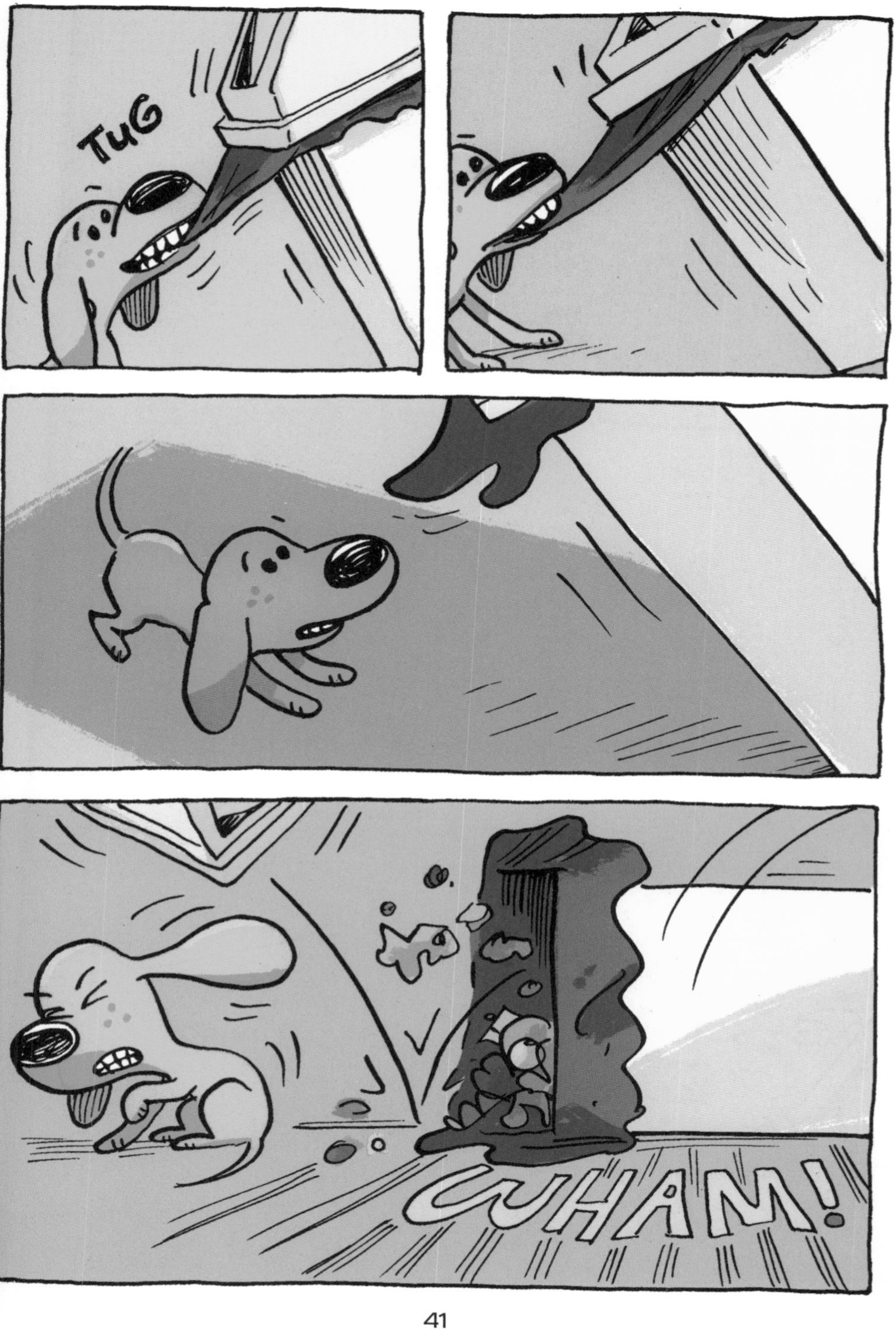
TUG
CHAM!

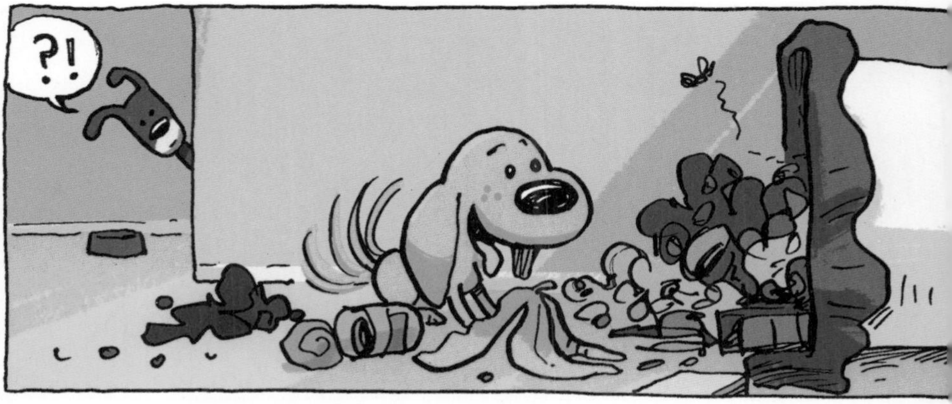
?!

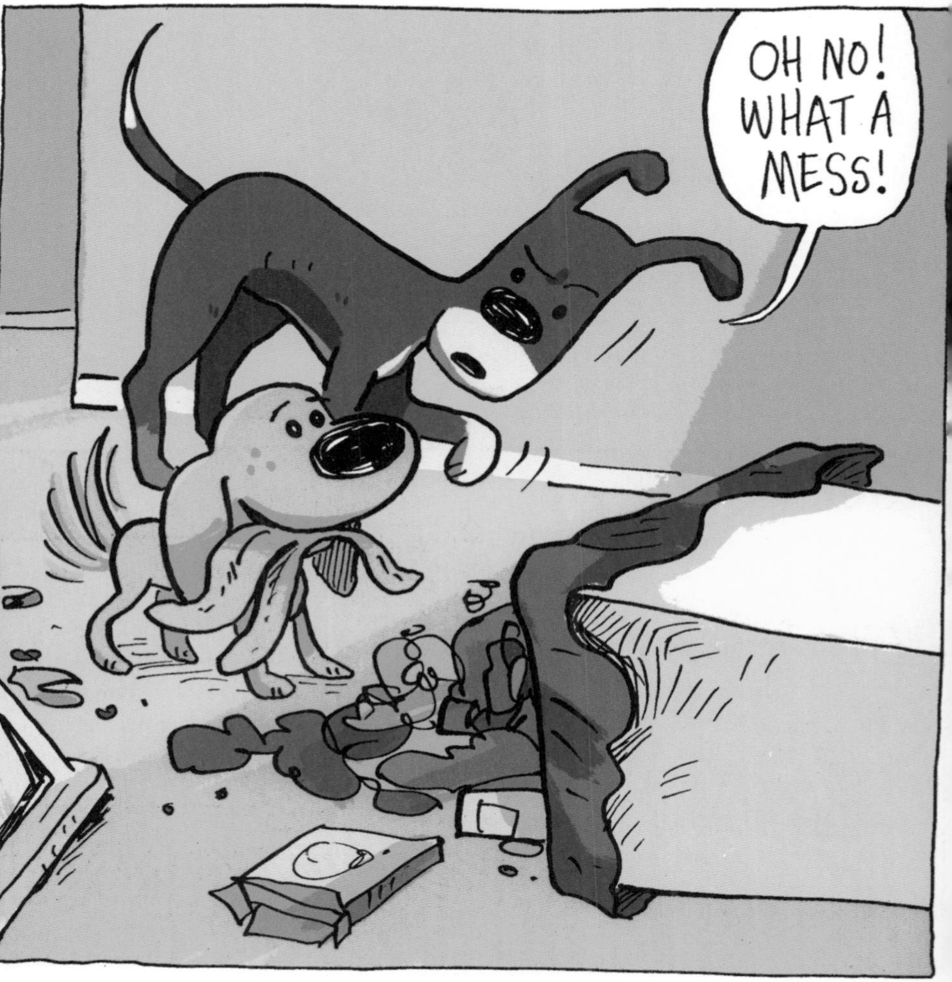
OH NO! WHAT A MESS!

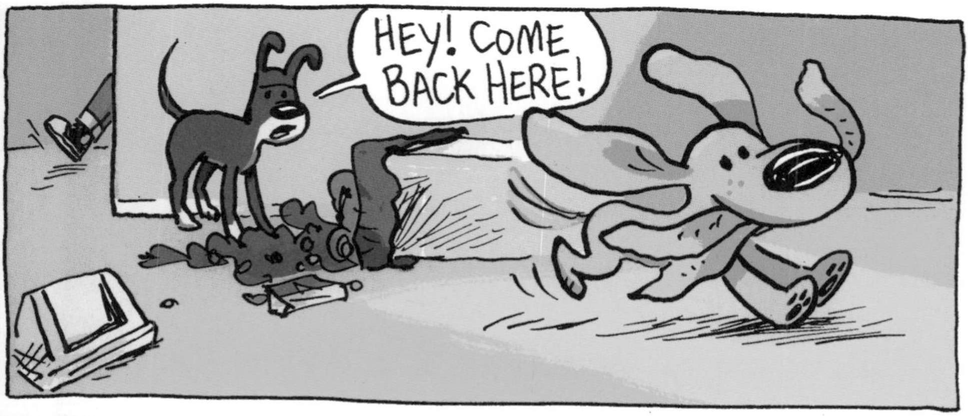
HEY! COME BACK HERE!

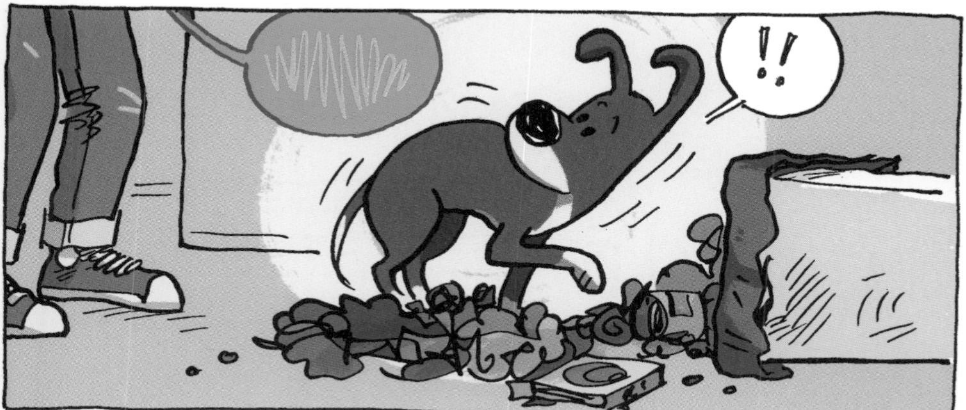
!!

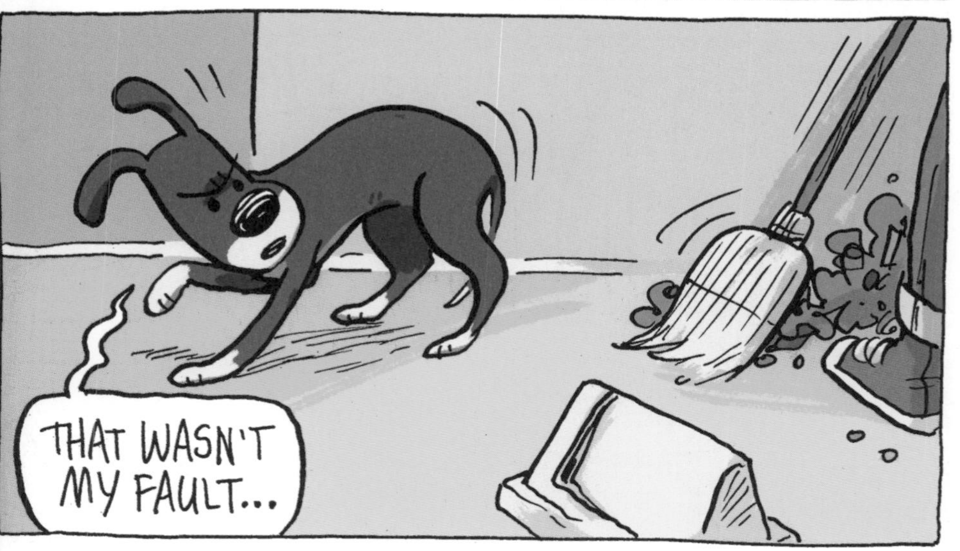
THAT WASN'T MY FAULT...

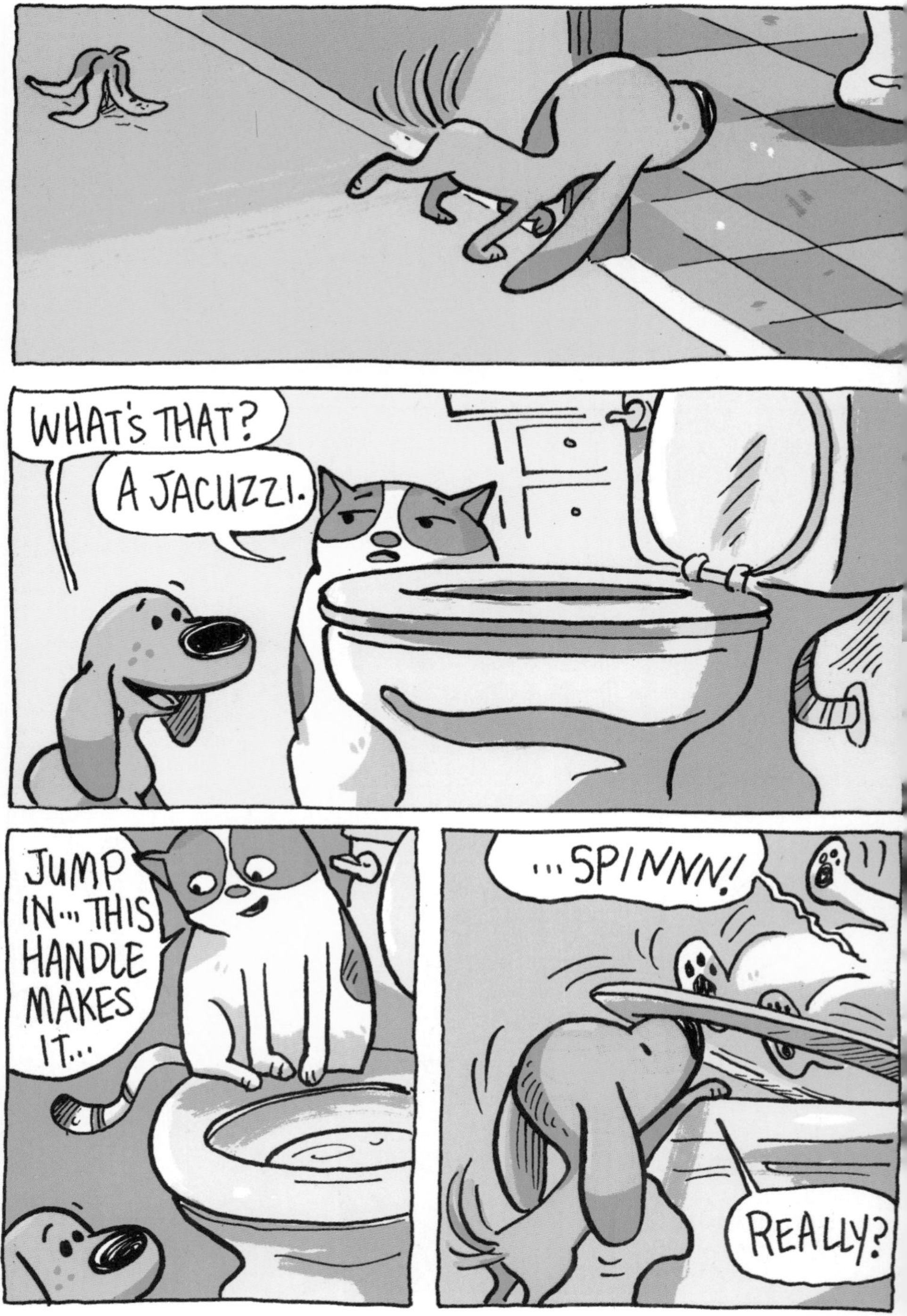
WHAT'S THAT?
A JACUZZI.
JUMP IN... THIS HANDLE MAKES IT...
...SPINNN!
REALLY?

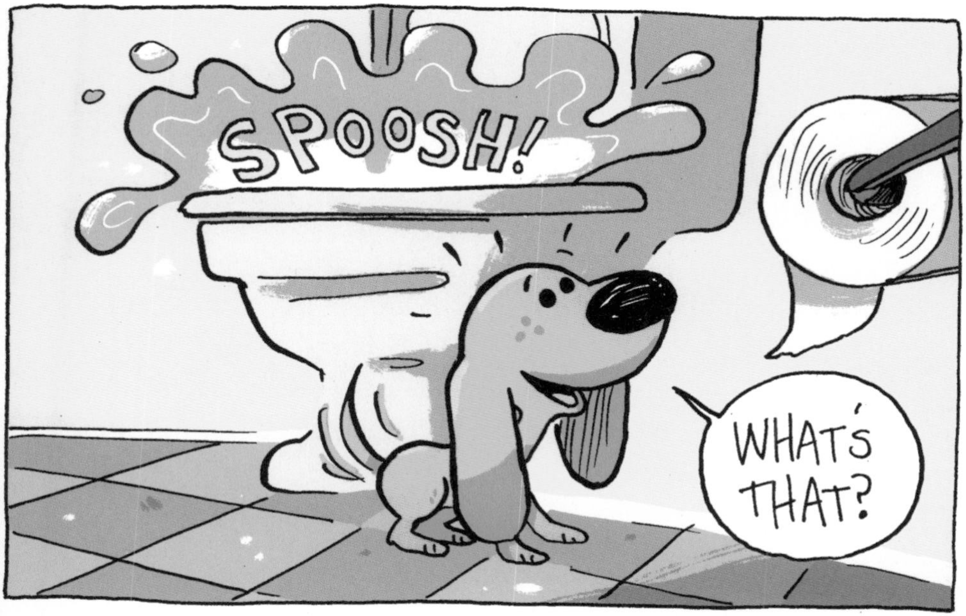
SPOOSH!
WHAT'S THAT?

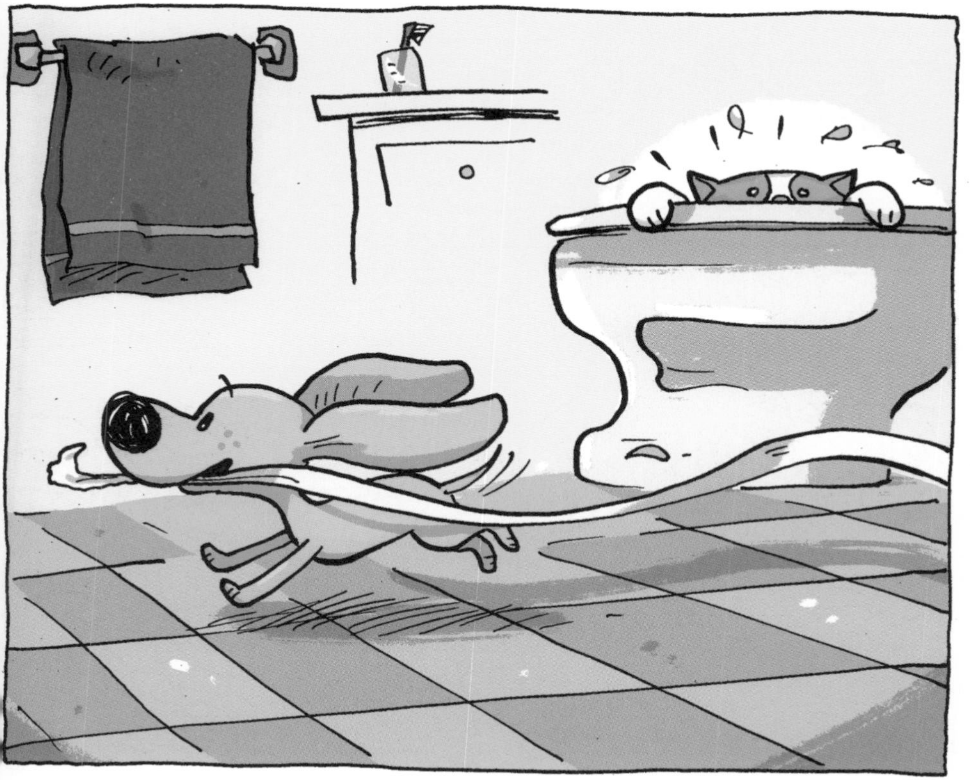

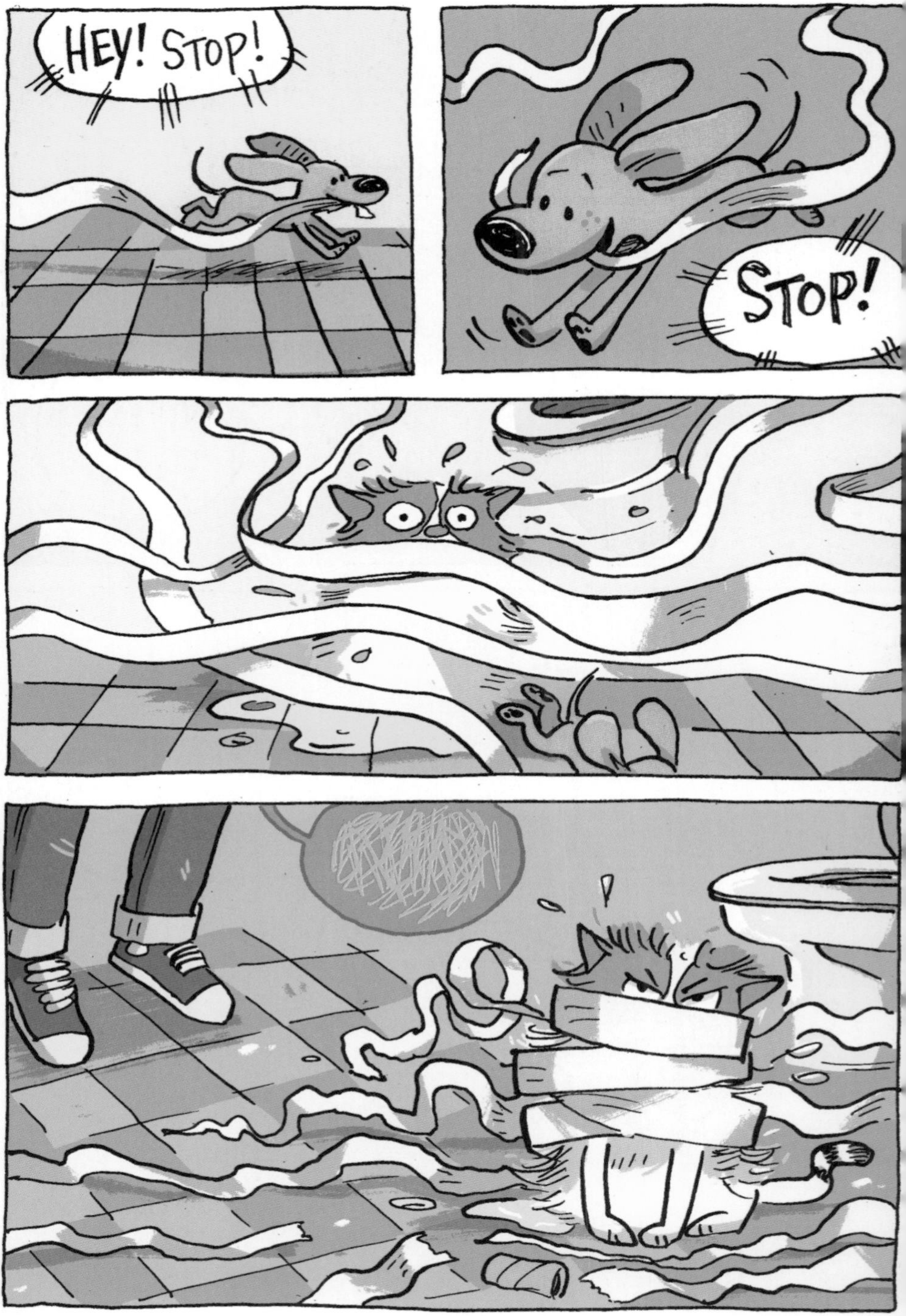
HEY! STOP!
STOP!

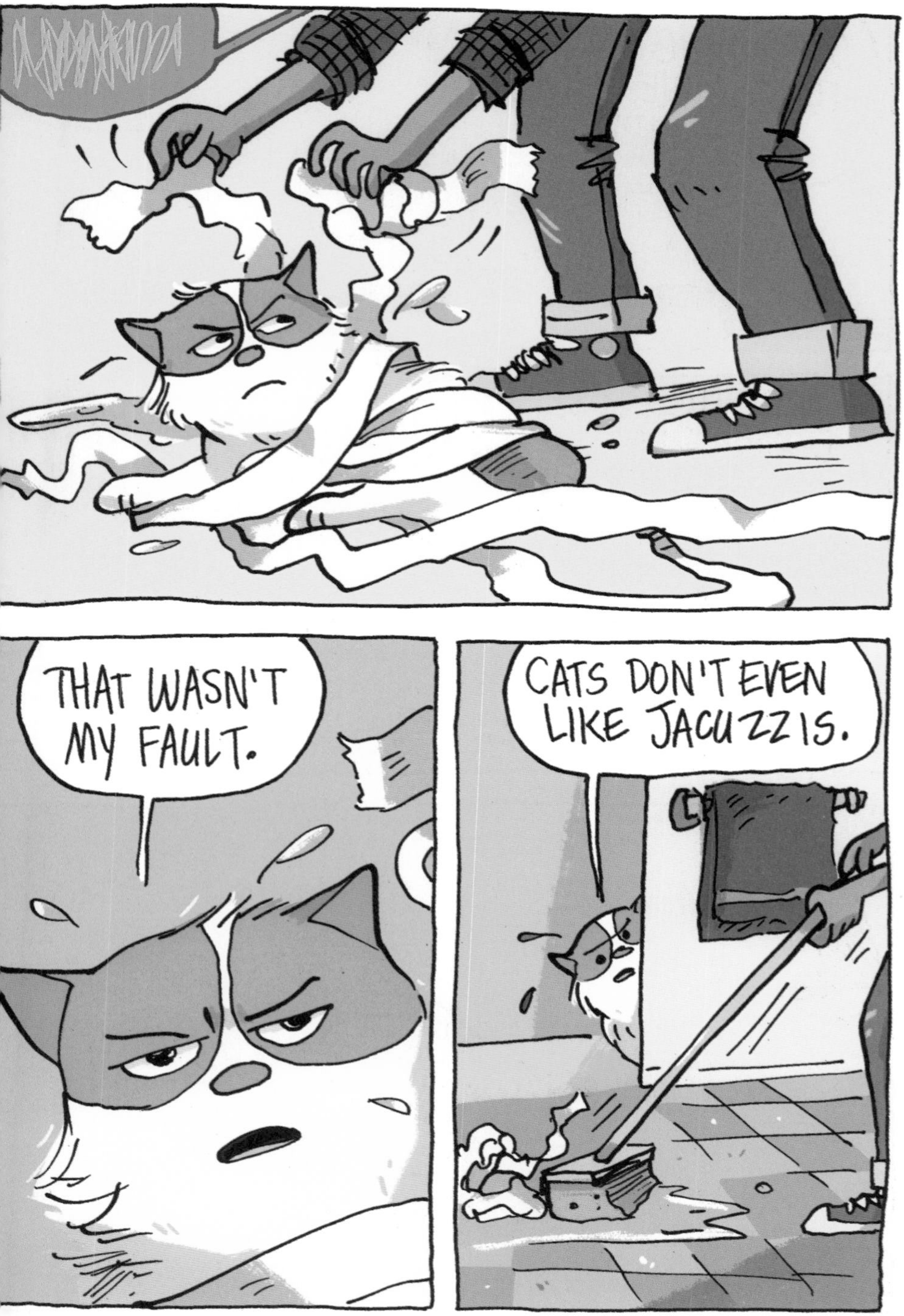
THAT WASN'T MY FAULT.
CATS DON'T EVEN LIKE JACUZZIS.

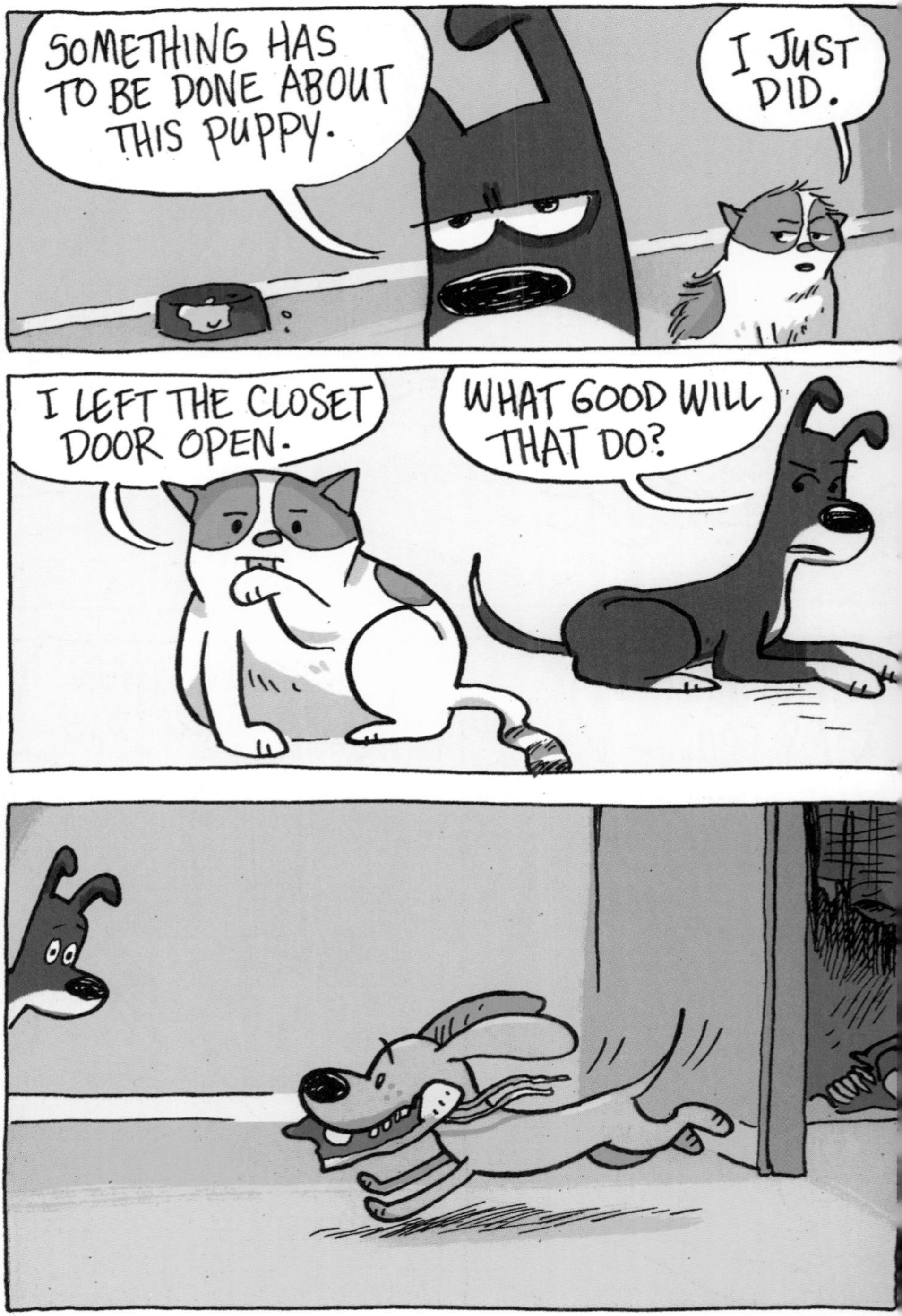
SOMETHING HAS TO BE DONE ABOUT THIS PUPPY.
I JUST DID.
I LEFT THE CLOSET DOOR OPEN.
WHAT GOOD WILL THAT DO?

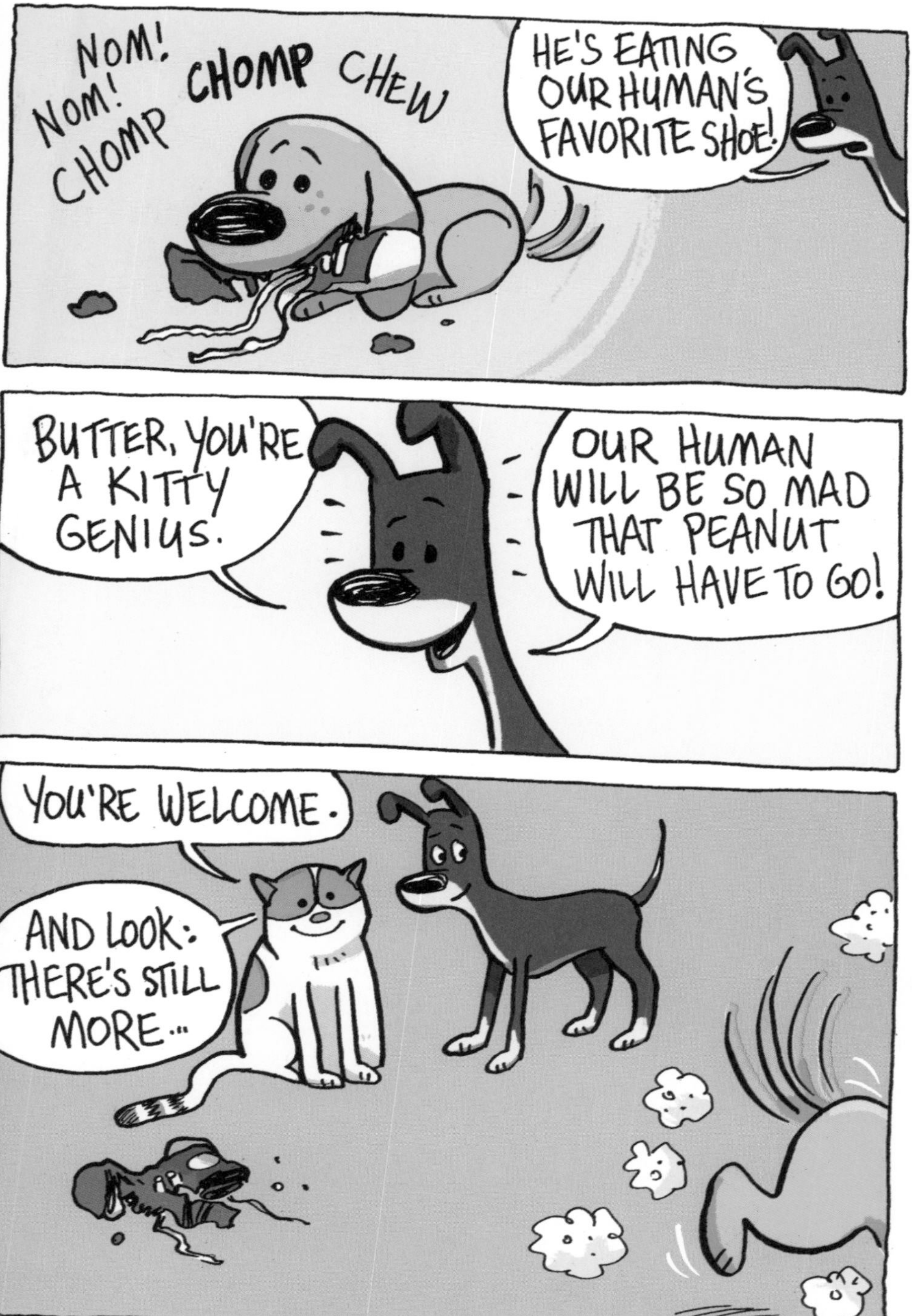
NOM! NOM! CHOMP CHOMP CHEW
HE'S EATING OUR HUMAN'S FAVORITE SHOE!
BUTTER, YOU'RE A KITTY GENIUS.
OUR HUMAN WILL BE SO MAD THAT PEANUT WILL HAVE TO GO!
YOU'RE WELCOME.
AND LOOK: THERE'S STILL MORE...

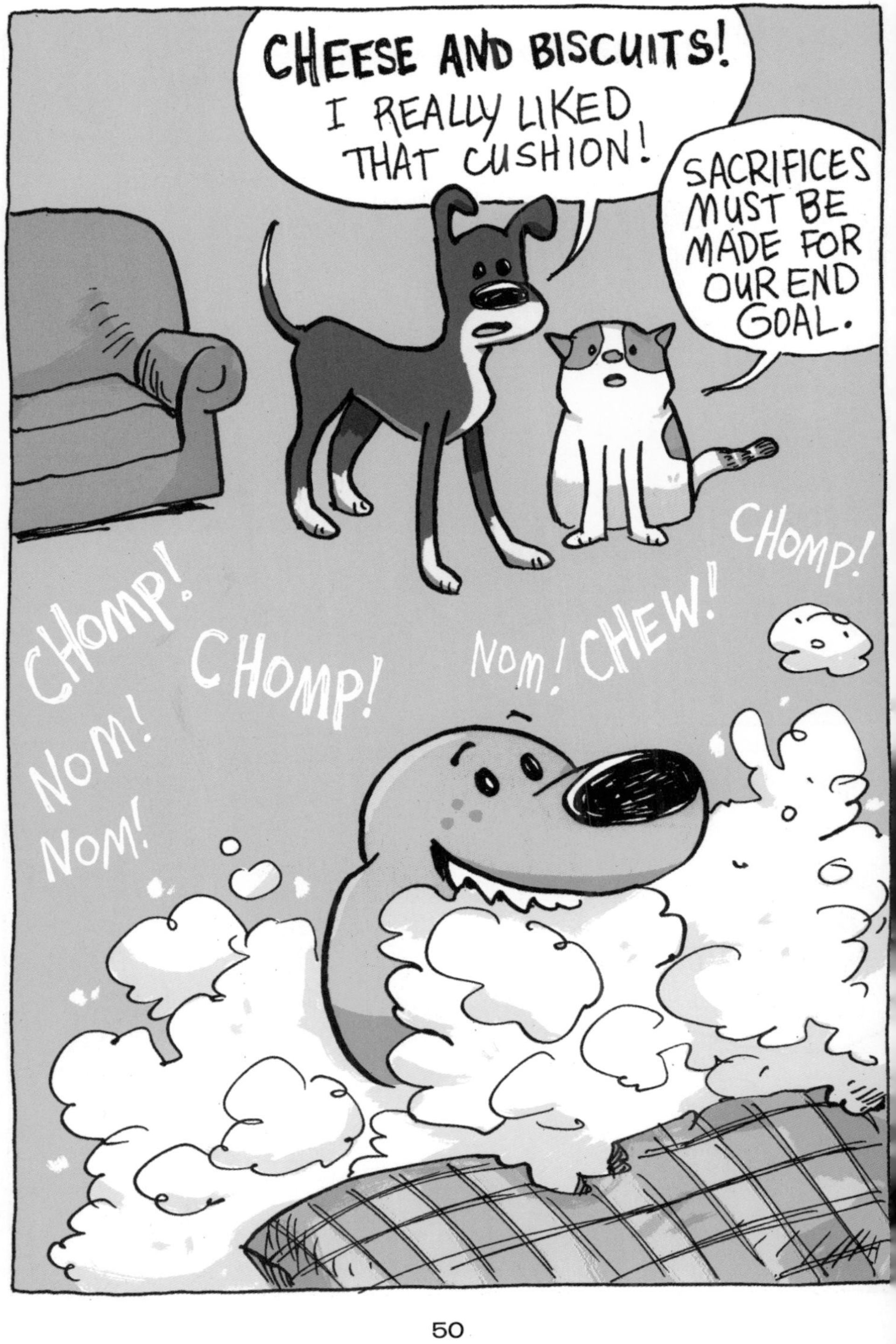
CHEESE AND BISCUITS! I REALLY LIKED THAT CUSHION!
SACRIFICES MUST BE MADE FOR OUR END GOAL.
CHOMP! NOM! NOM!
CHOMP!
NOM! CHEW!
CHOMP!

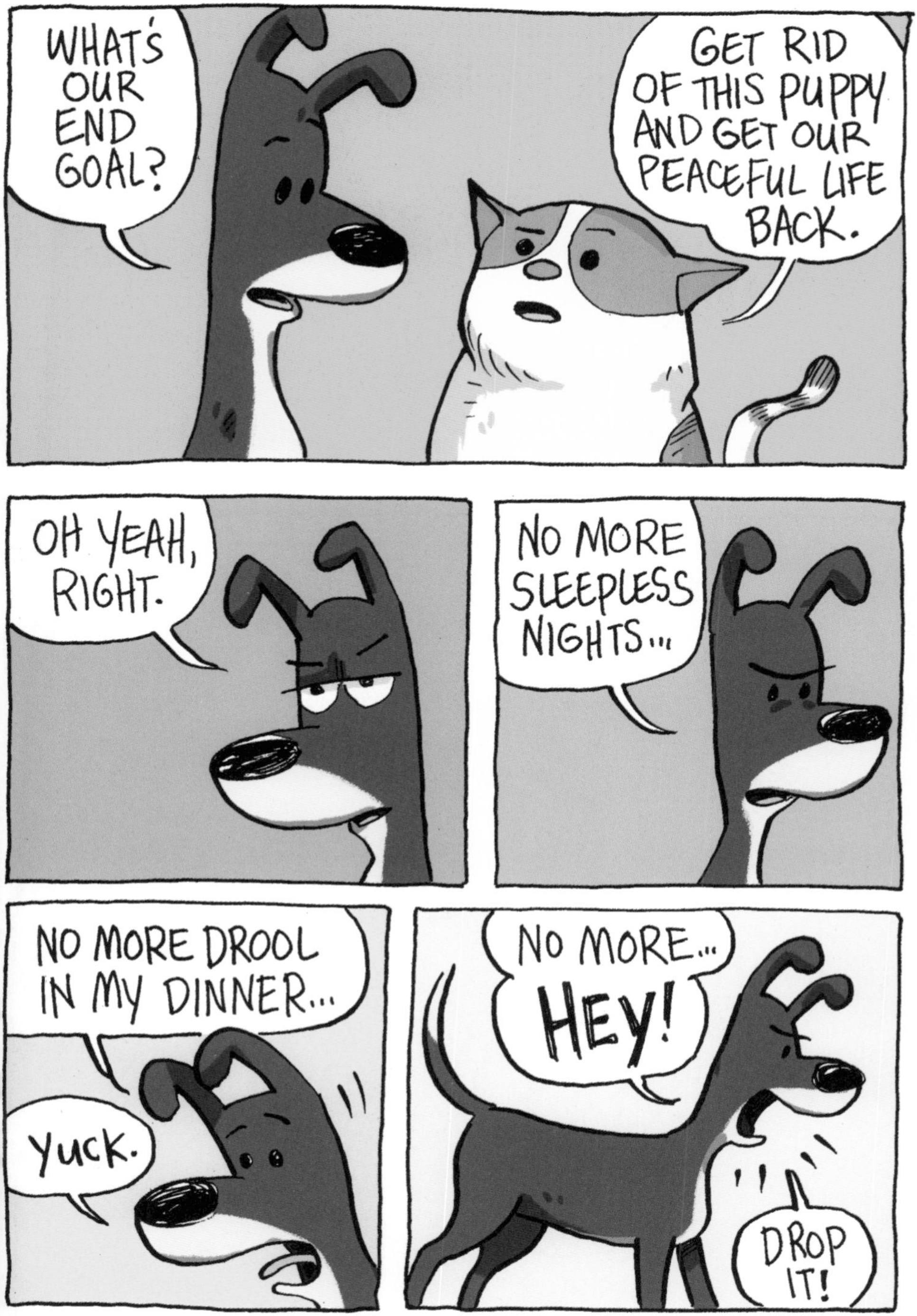
WHAT'S OUR END GOAL?
GET RID OF THIS PUPPY AND GET OUR PEACEFUL LIFE BACK.
OH YEAH, RIGHT.
NO MORE SLEEPLESS NIGHTS...
NO MORE DROOL IN MY DINNER...
YUCK.
NO MORE...
HEY!
DROP IT!

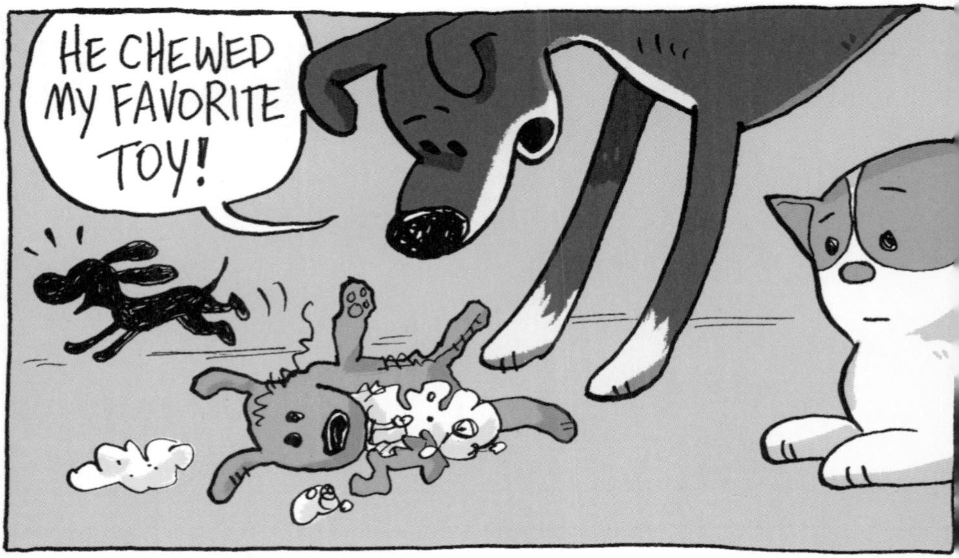
HE CHEWED MY FAVORITE TOY!

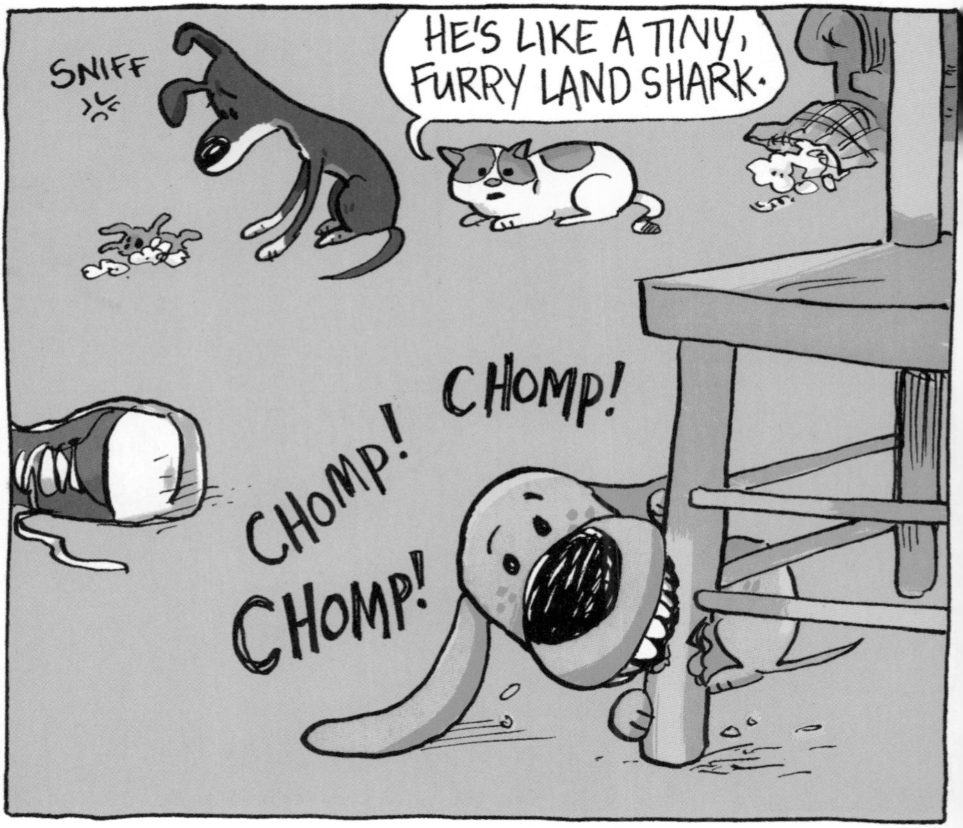
SNIFF
HE'S LIKE A TINY, FURRY LAND SHARK.
CHOMP!
CHOMP!
CHOMP!

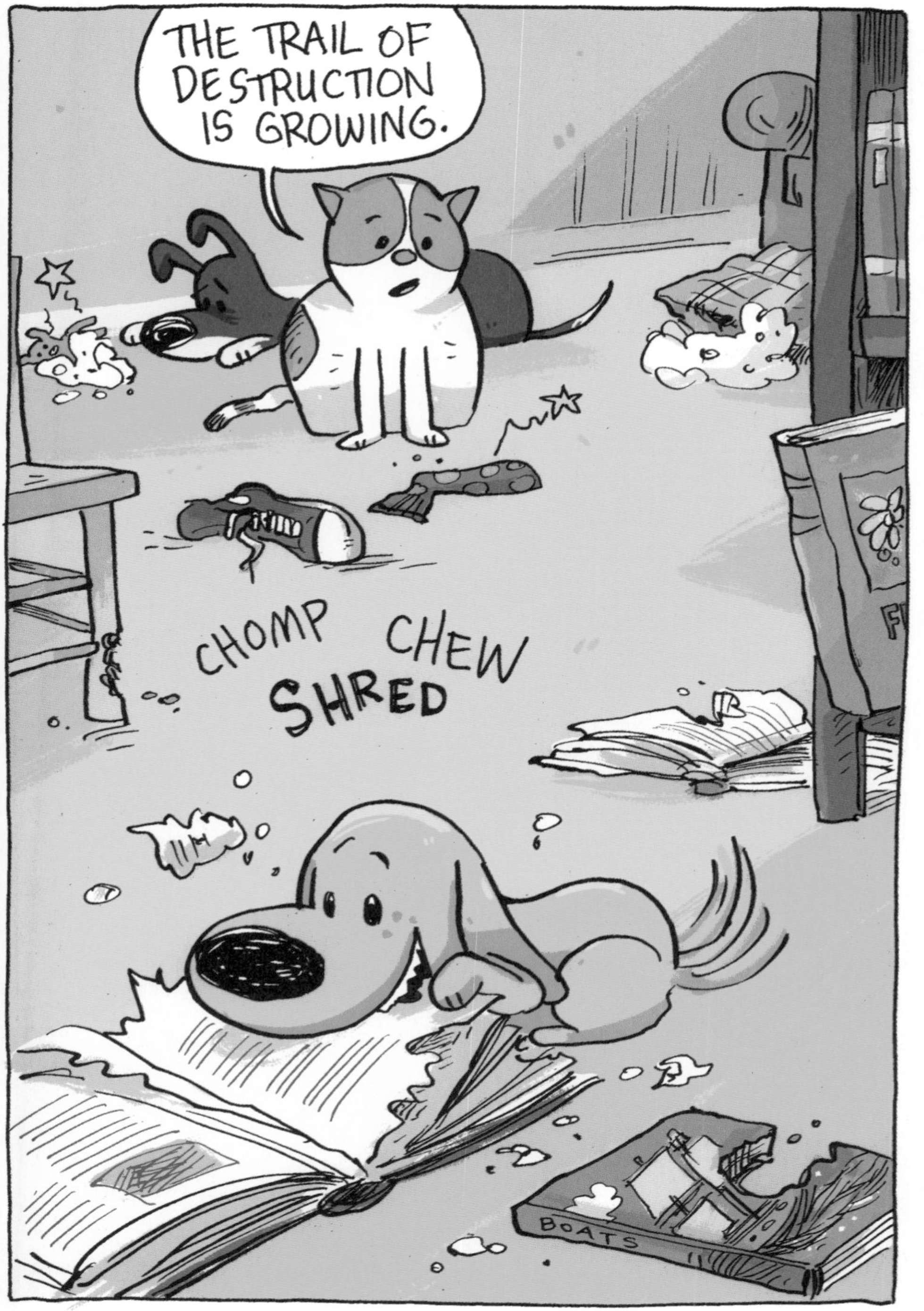
THE TRAIL OF DESTRUCTION IS GROWING.
CHOMP
CHEW
SHRED
BOATS

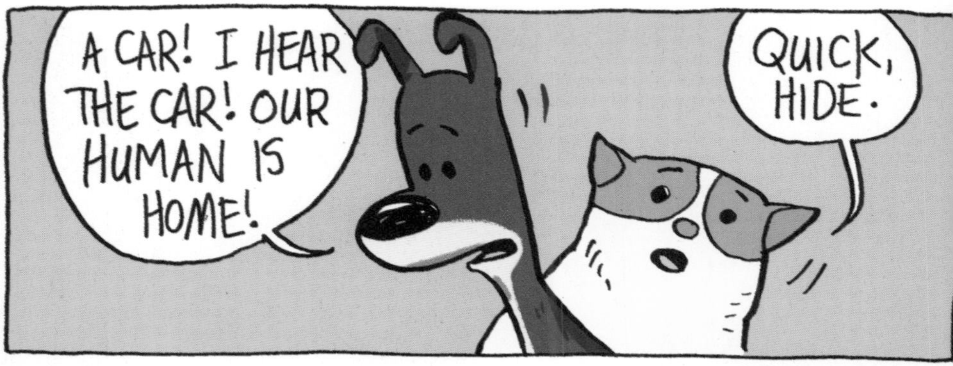
A CAR! I HEAR THE CAR! OUR HUMAN IS HOME!
QUICK, HIDE.

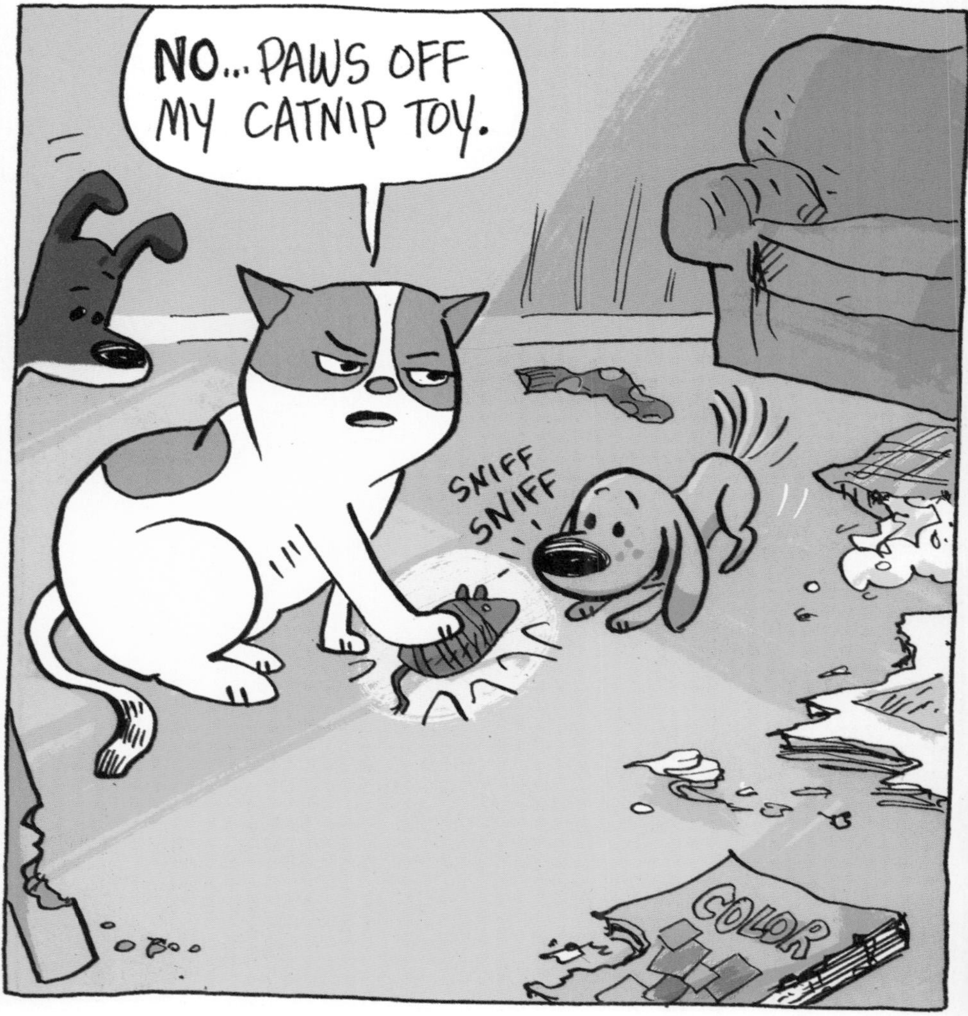
NO... PAWS OFF MY CATNIP TOY.
SNIFF SNIFF
COLOR

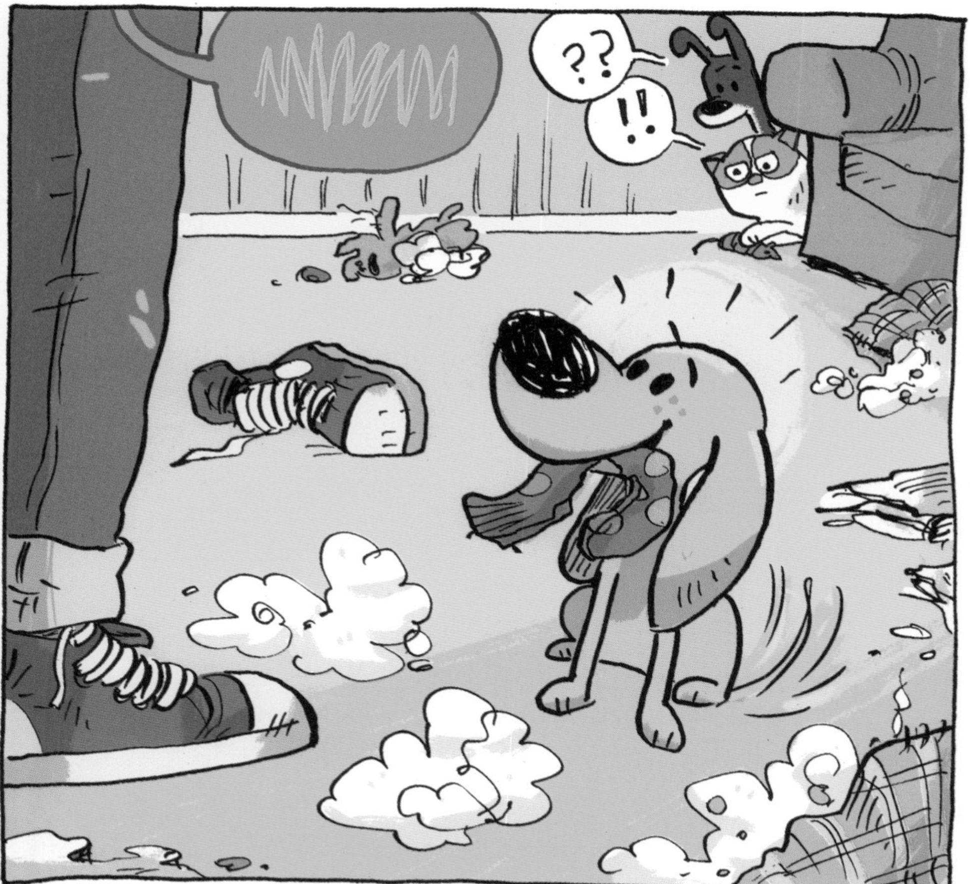
??
!!

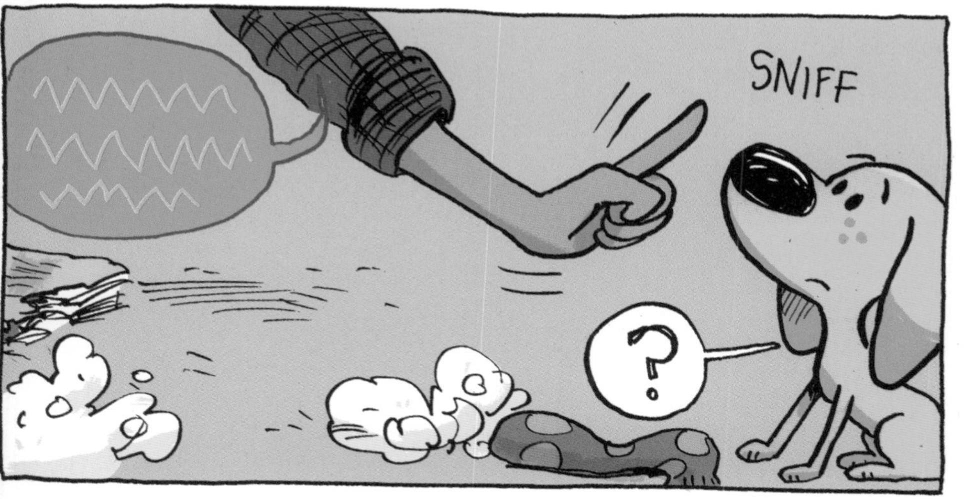
SNIFF
?

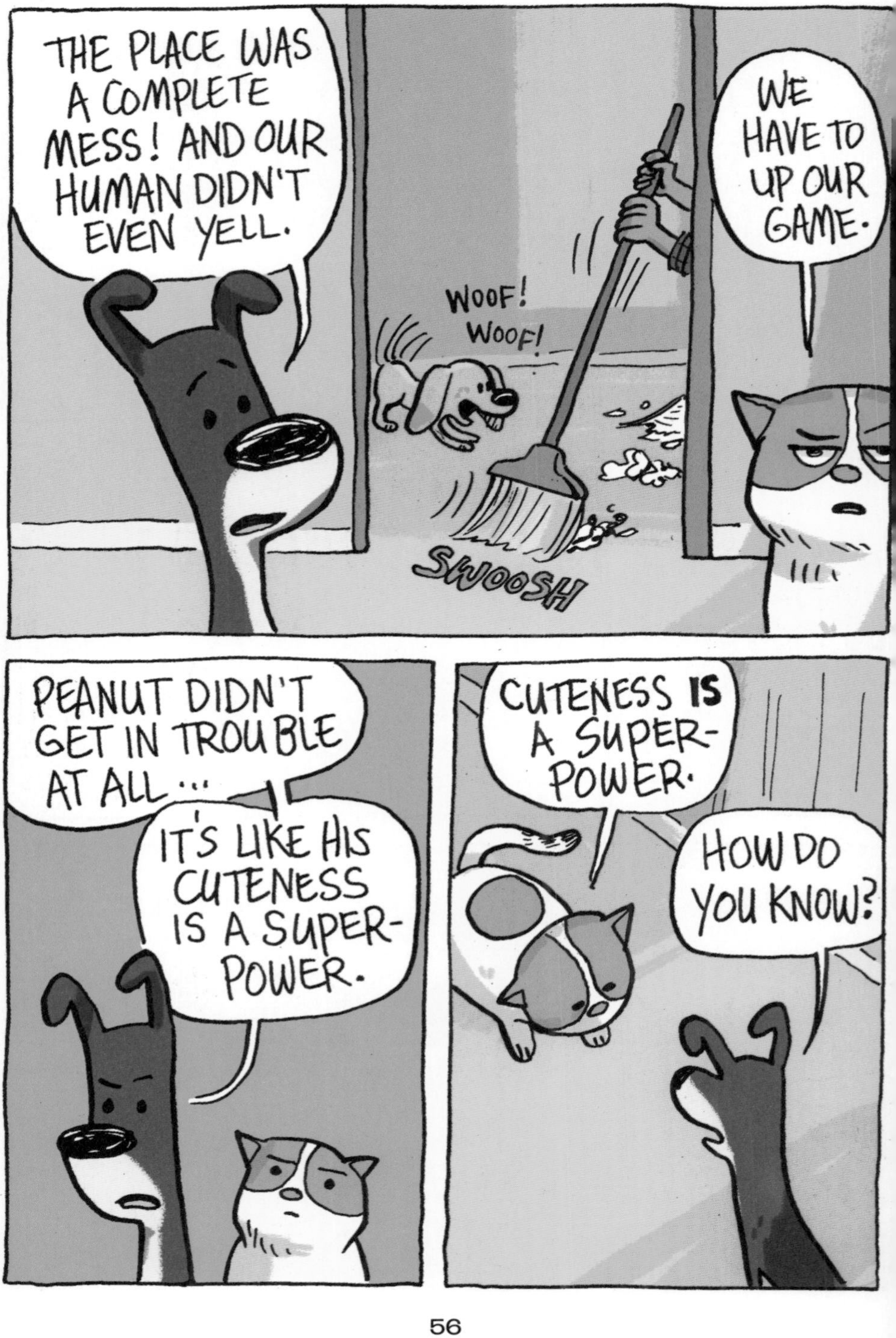
THE PLACE WAS A COMPLETE MESS! AND OUR HUMAN DIDN'T EVEN YELL.
WOOF! WOOF!
SWOOSH
WE HAVE TO UP OUR GAME.
PEANUT DIDN'T GET IN TROUBLE AT ALL...
IT'S LIKE HIS CUTENESS IS A SUPER-POWER.
CUTENESS IS A SUPER-POWER.
HOW DO YOU KNOW?

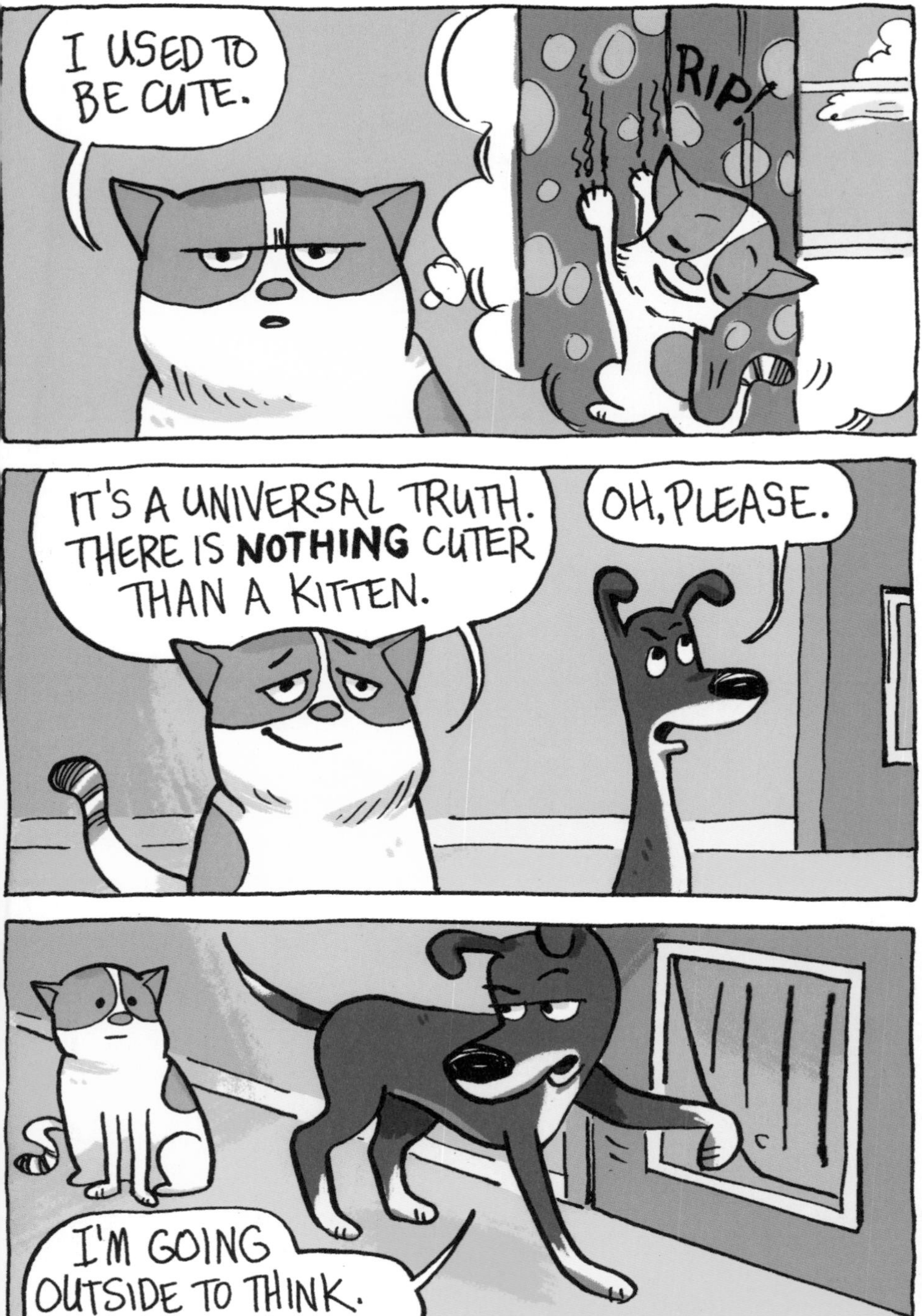
I USED TO BE CUTE.
RIP!
IT'S A UNIVERSAL TRUTH. THERE IS **NOTHING** CUTER THAN A KITTEN.
OH, PLEASE.
I'M GOING OUTSIDE TO THINK.

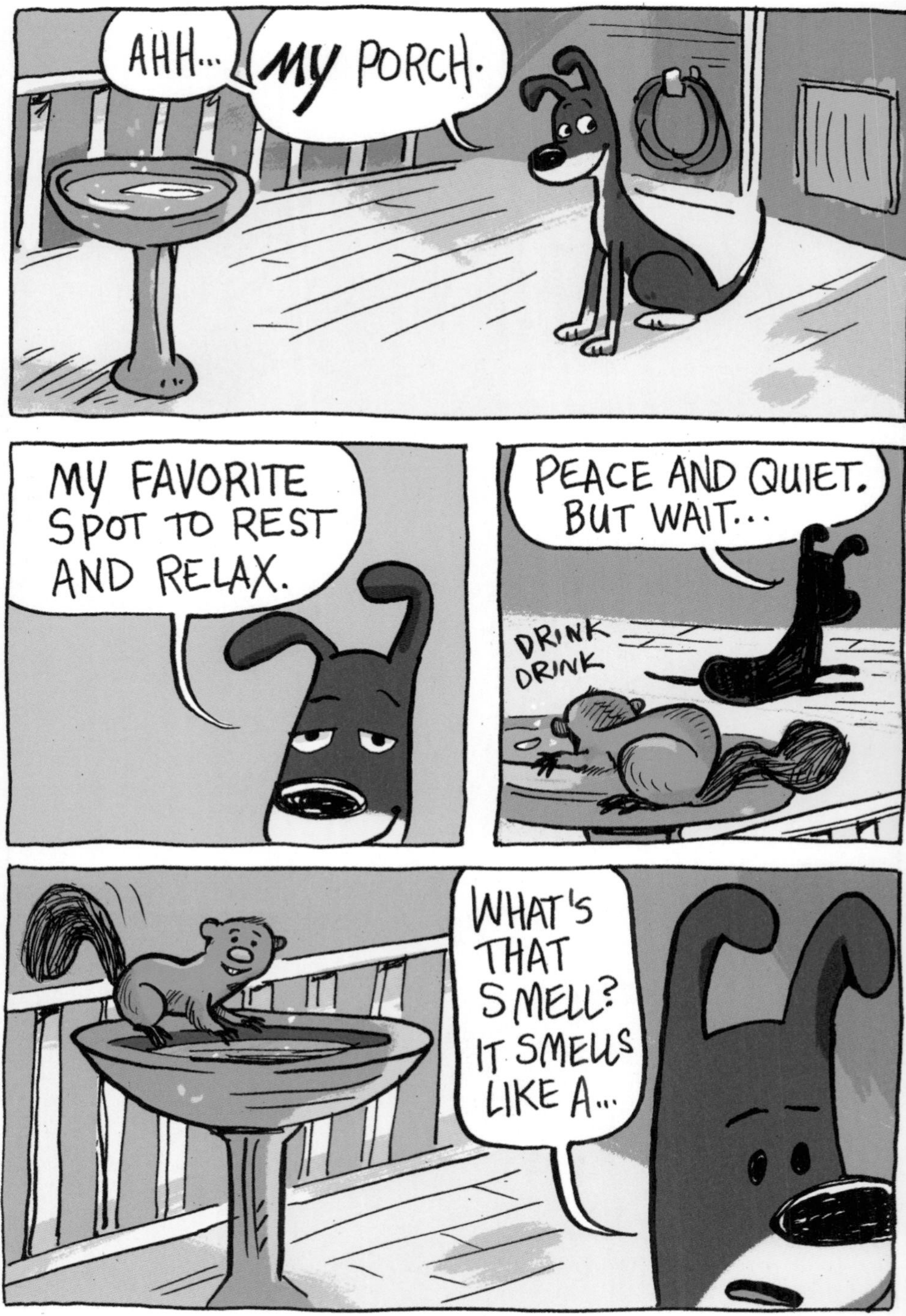
AHH...
MY PORCH.
MY FAVORITE SPOT TO REST AND RELAX.
PEACE AND QUIET. BUT WAIT...
DRINK DRINK
WHAT'S THAT SMELL? IT SMELLS LIKE A...

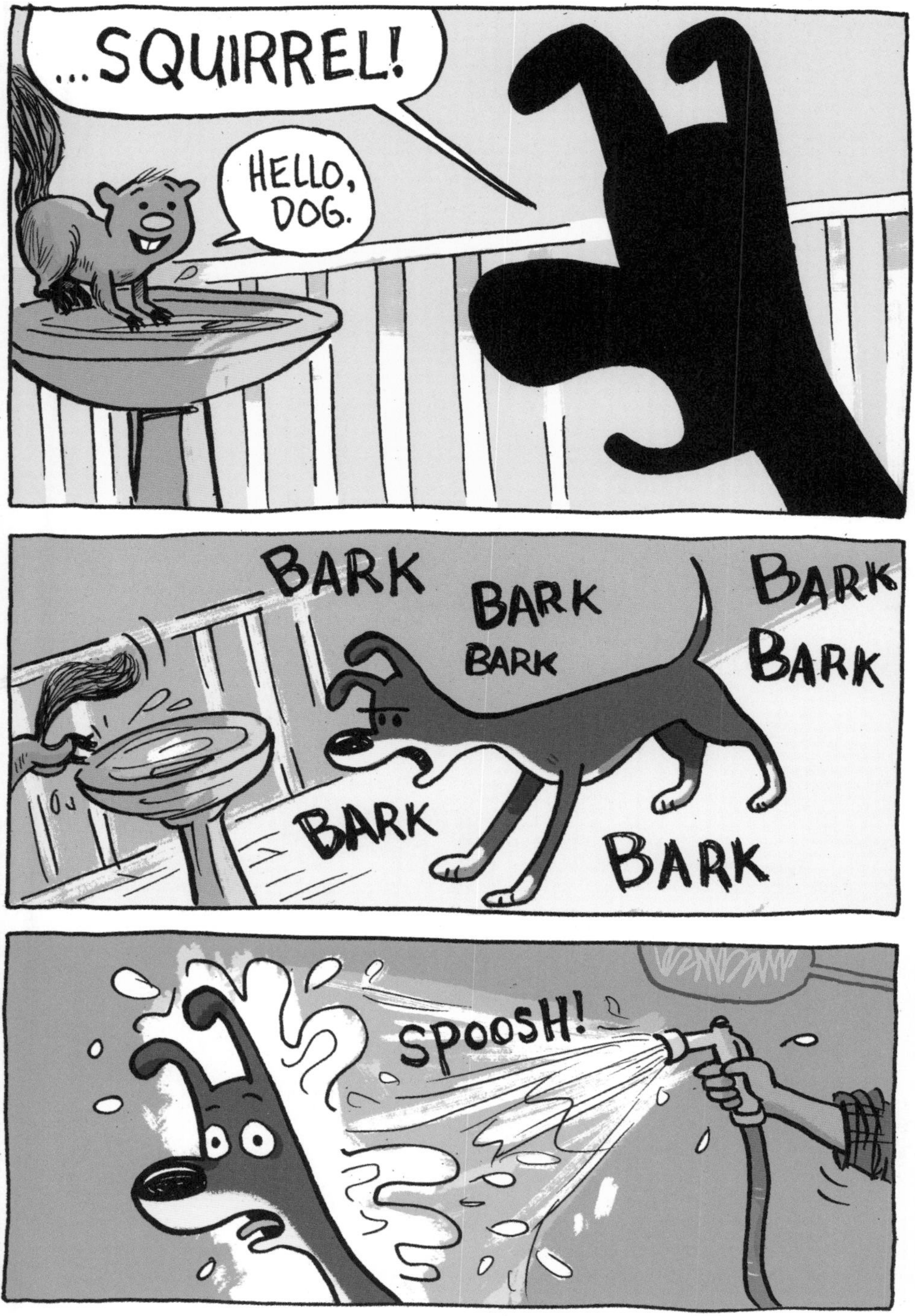
...SQUIRREL!
HELLO, DOG.
BARK
BARK
BARK
BARK
BARK
BARK
BARK
SPOOSH!

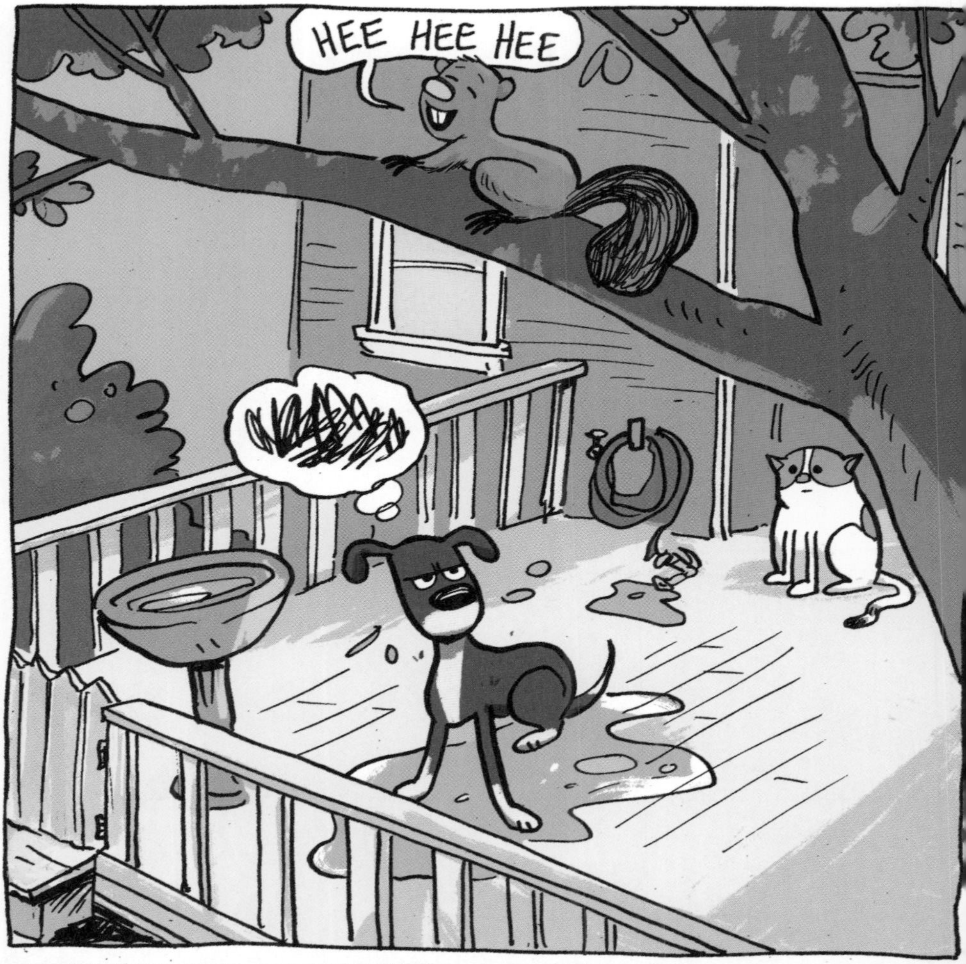
HEE HEE HEE

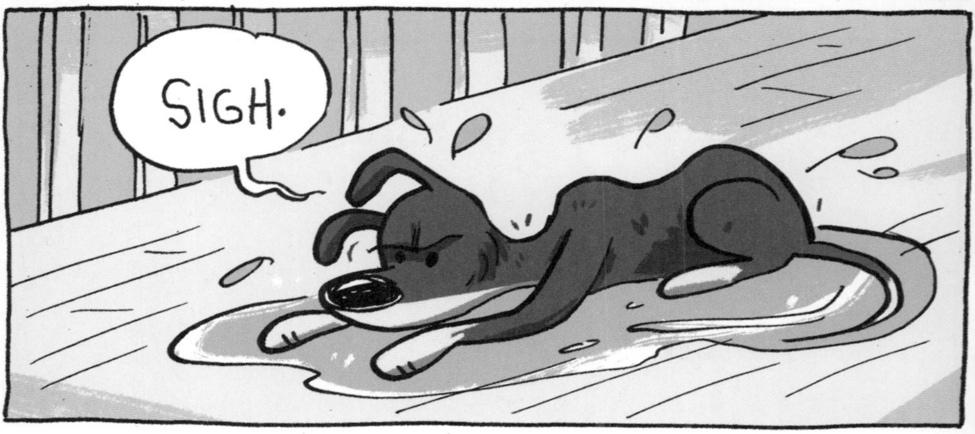
SIGH.

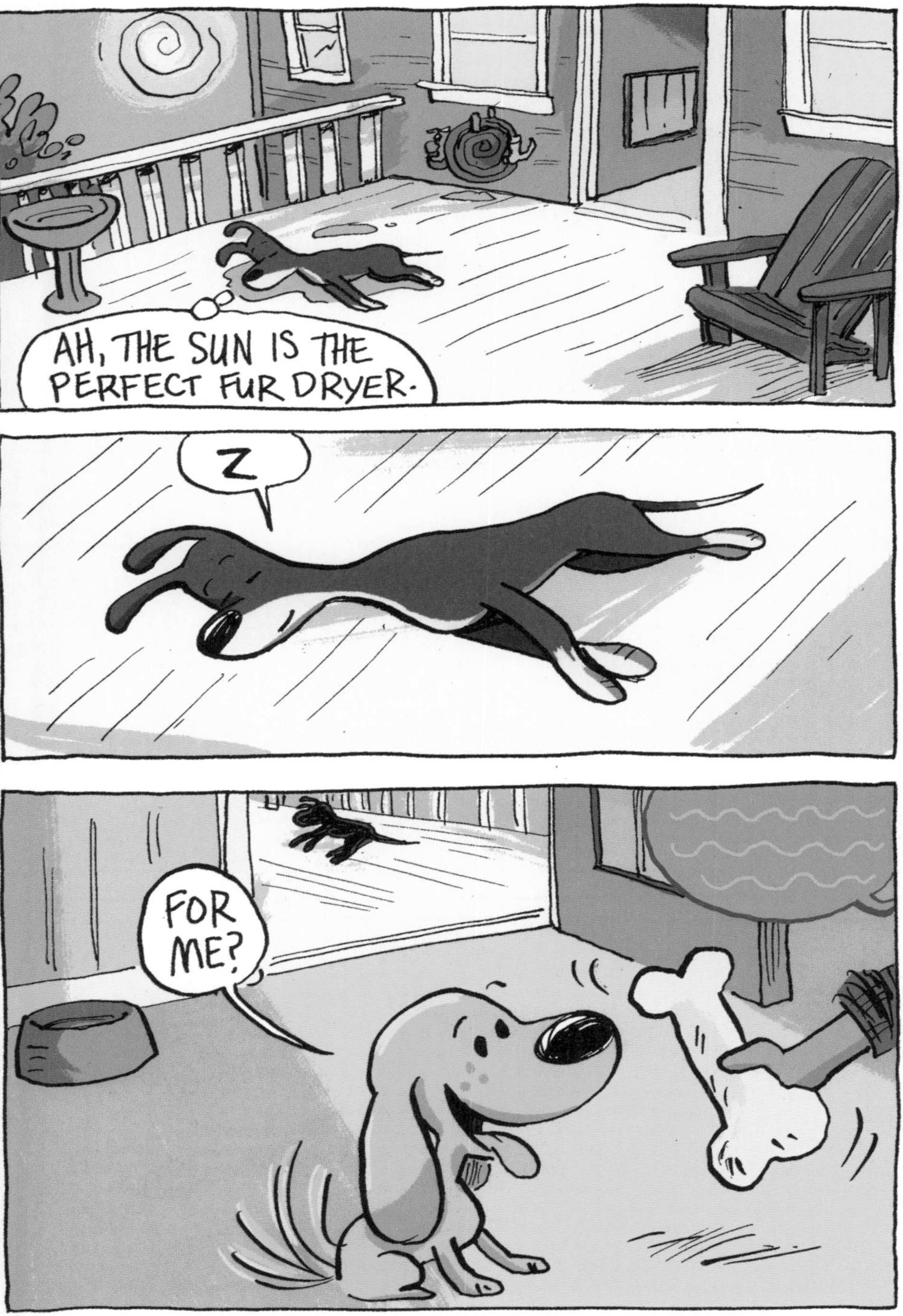
AH, THE SUN IS THE PERFECT FUR DRYER.
Z
FOR ME?

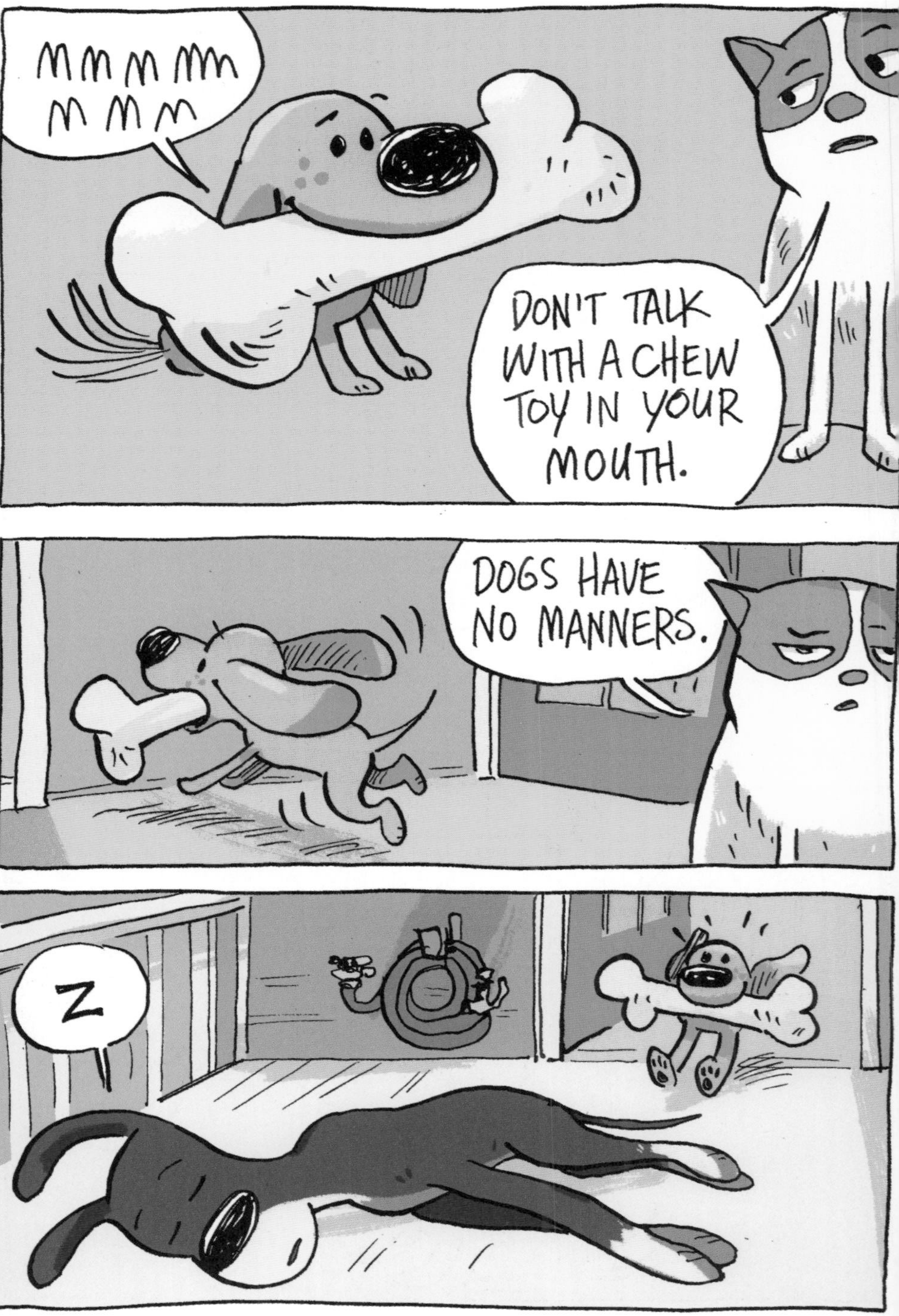
MMMMM MMM
DON'T TALK WITH A CHEW TOY IN YOUR MOUTH.
DOGS HAVE NO MANNERS.
Z

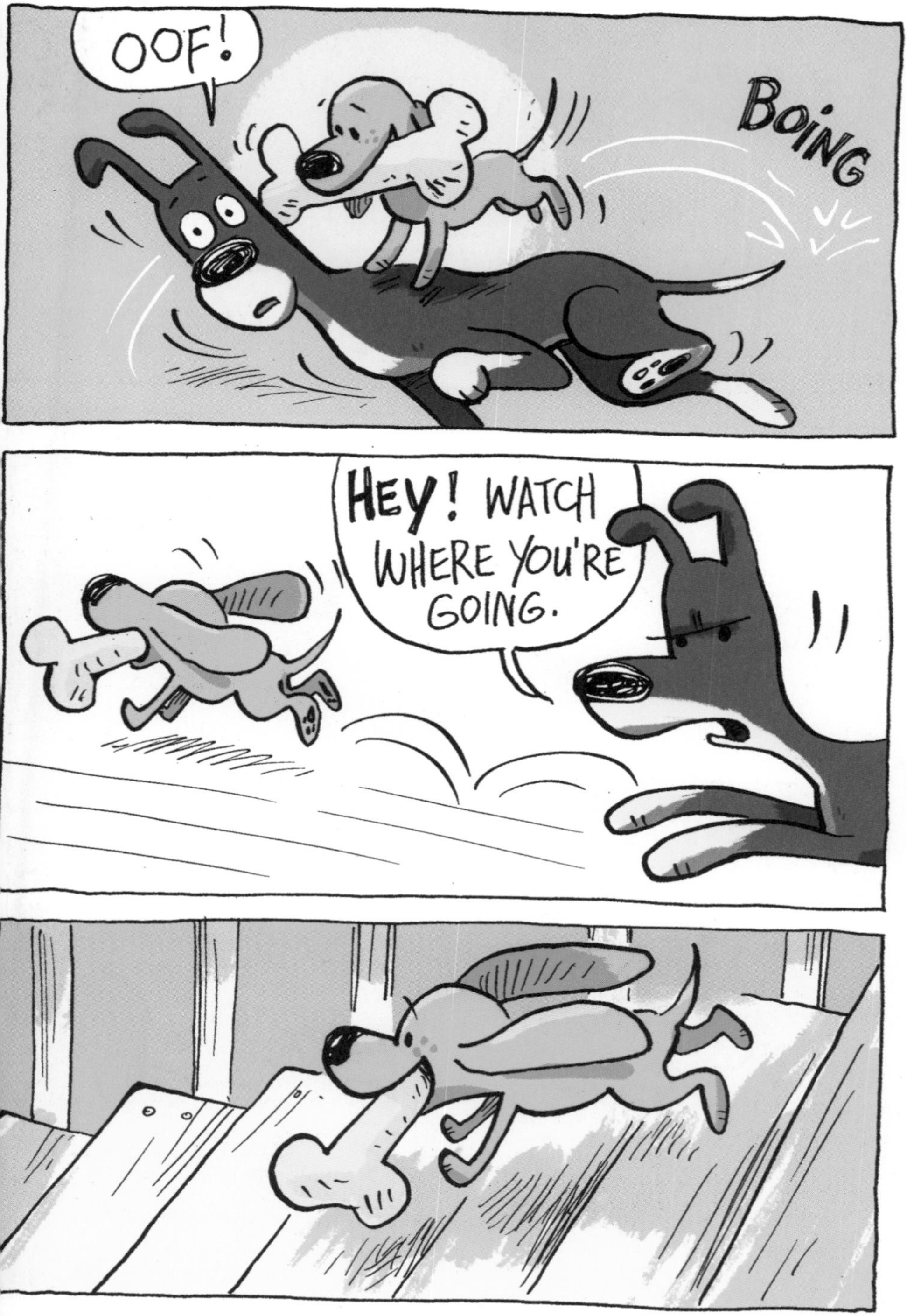
OOF!
BOING
HEY! WATCH WHERE YOU'RE GOING.

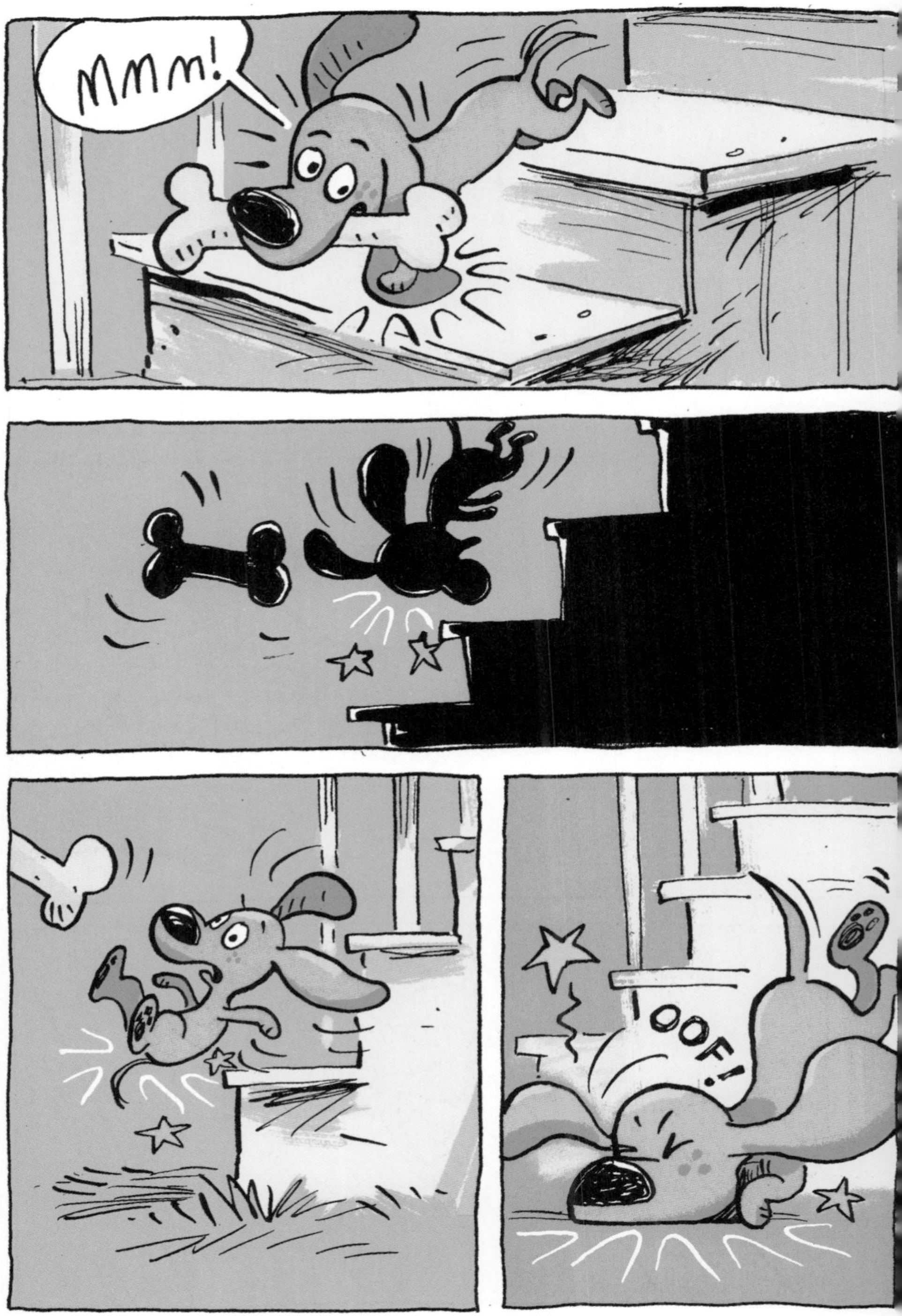
MMM!
OOF!

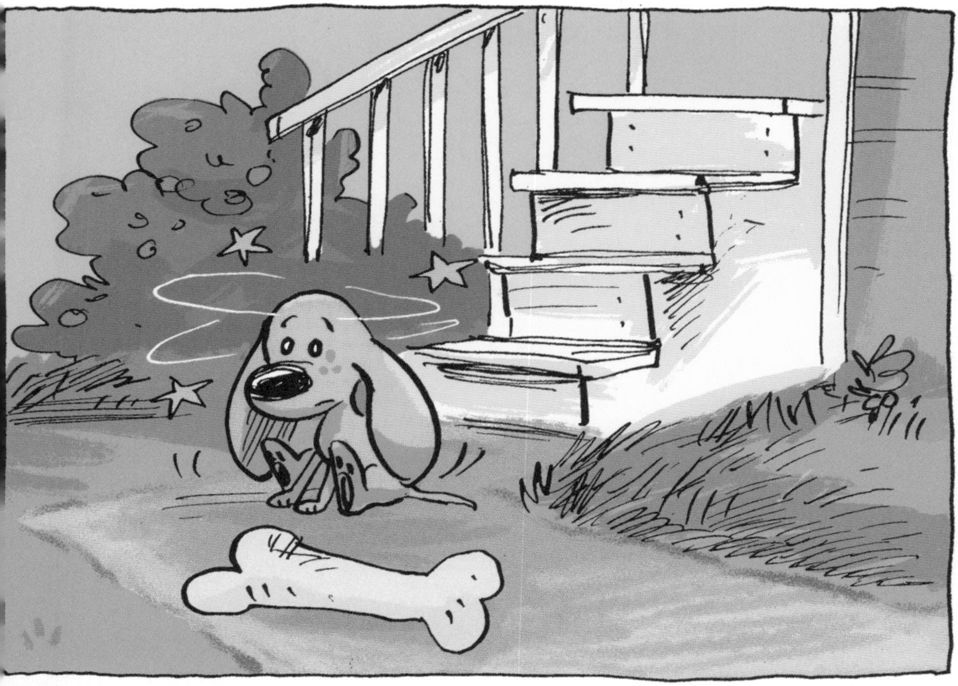

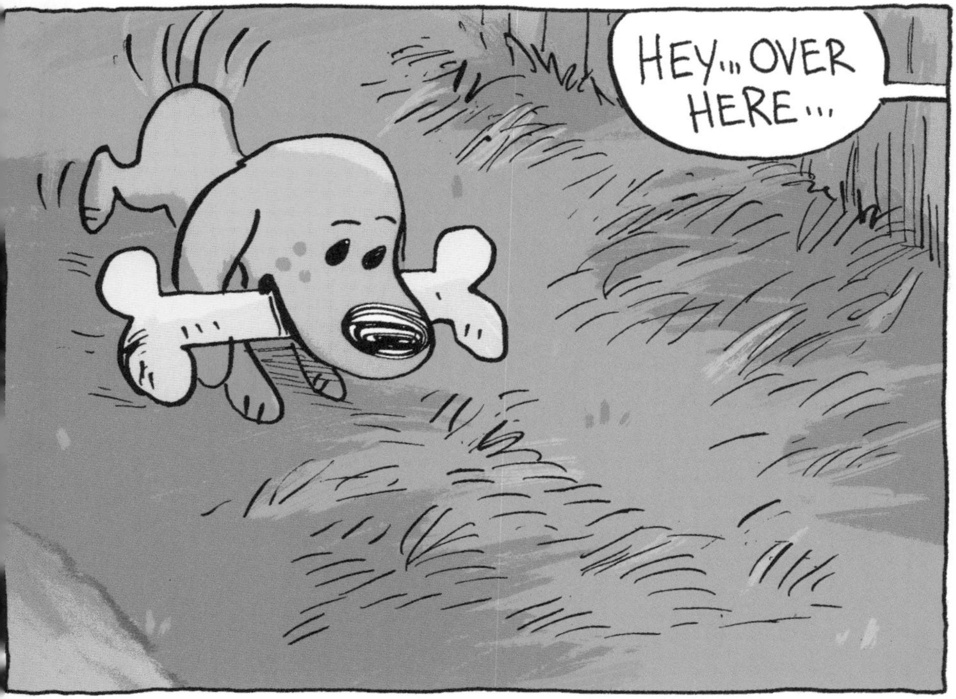
HEY... OVER HERE...

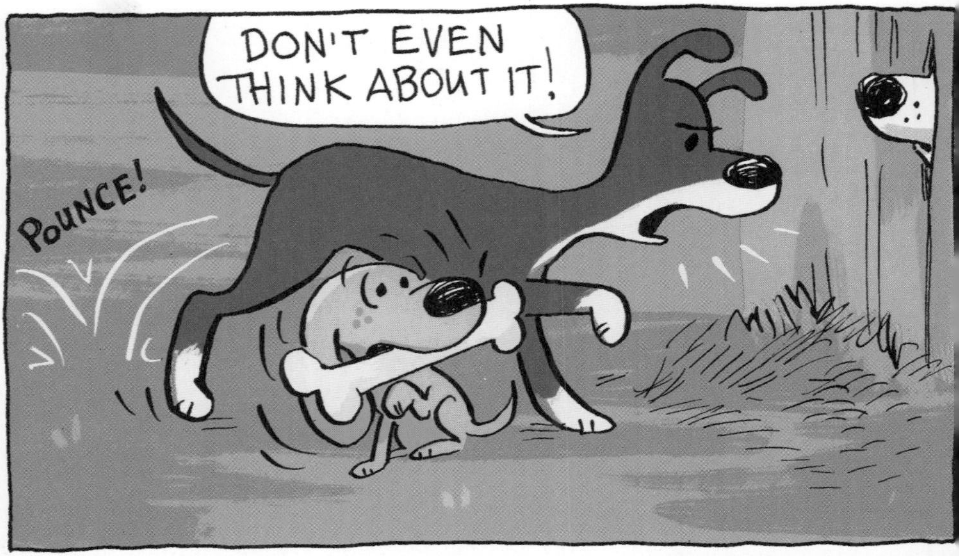
DON'T EVEN THINK ABOUT IT!
POUNCE!

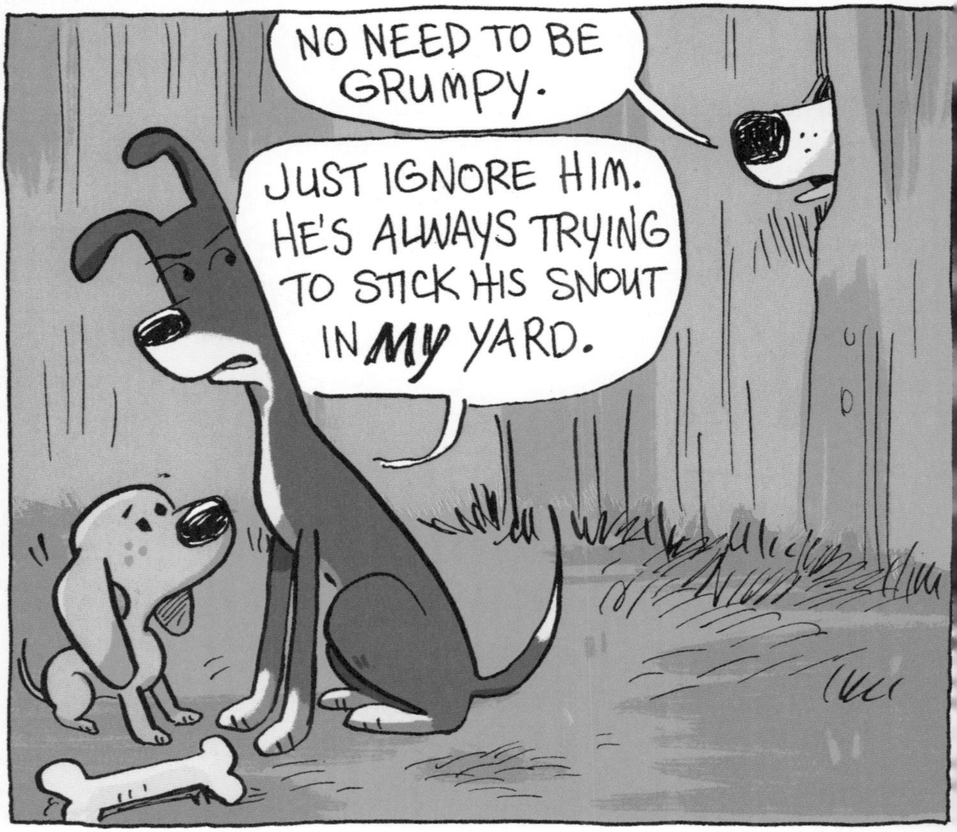
NO NEED TO BE GRUMPY.
JUST IGNORE HIM. HE'S ALWAYS TRYING TO STICK HIS SNOUT IN MY YARD.

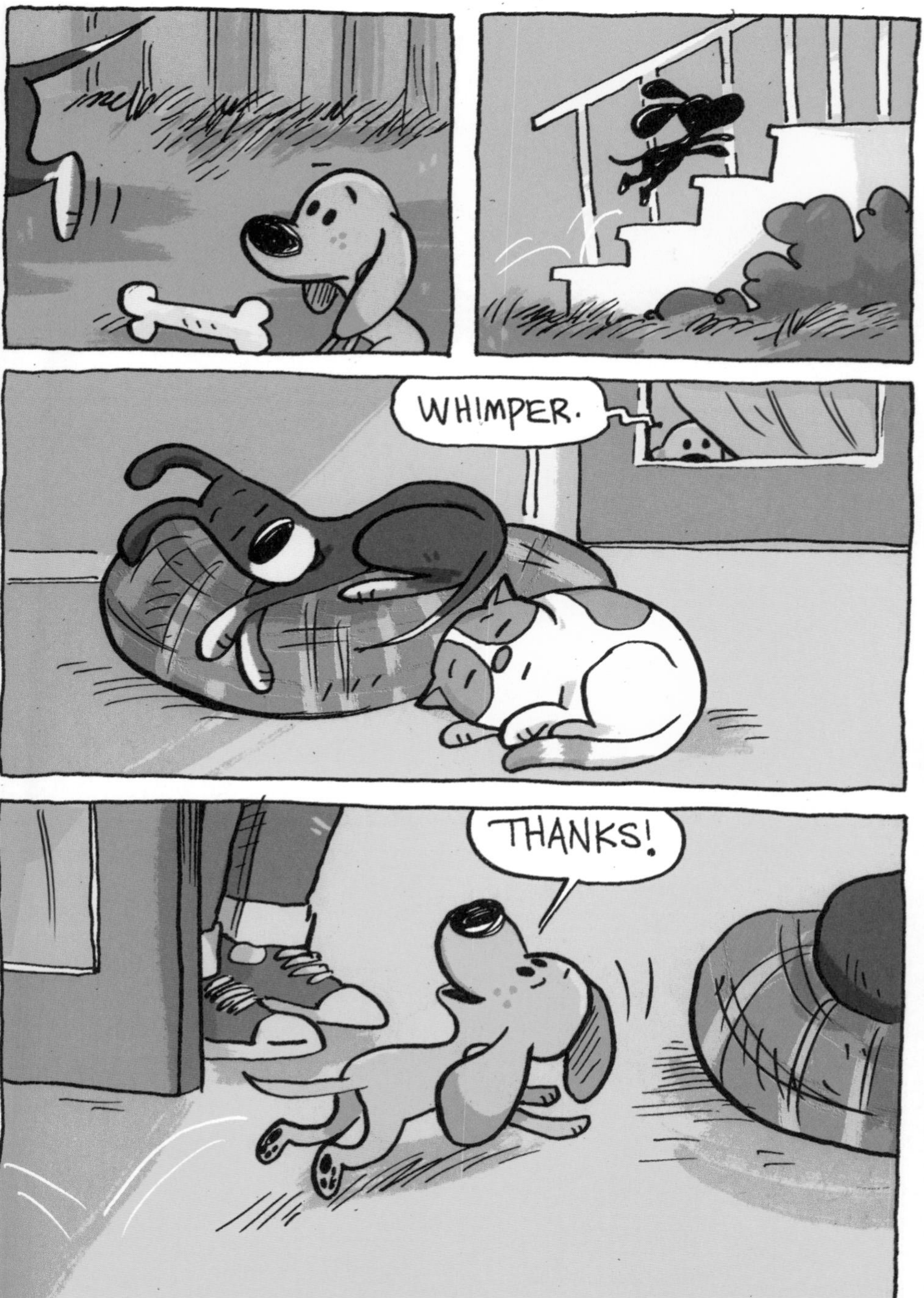
WHIMPER.
THANKS!

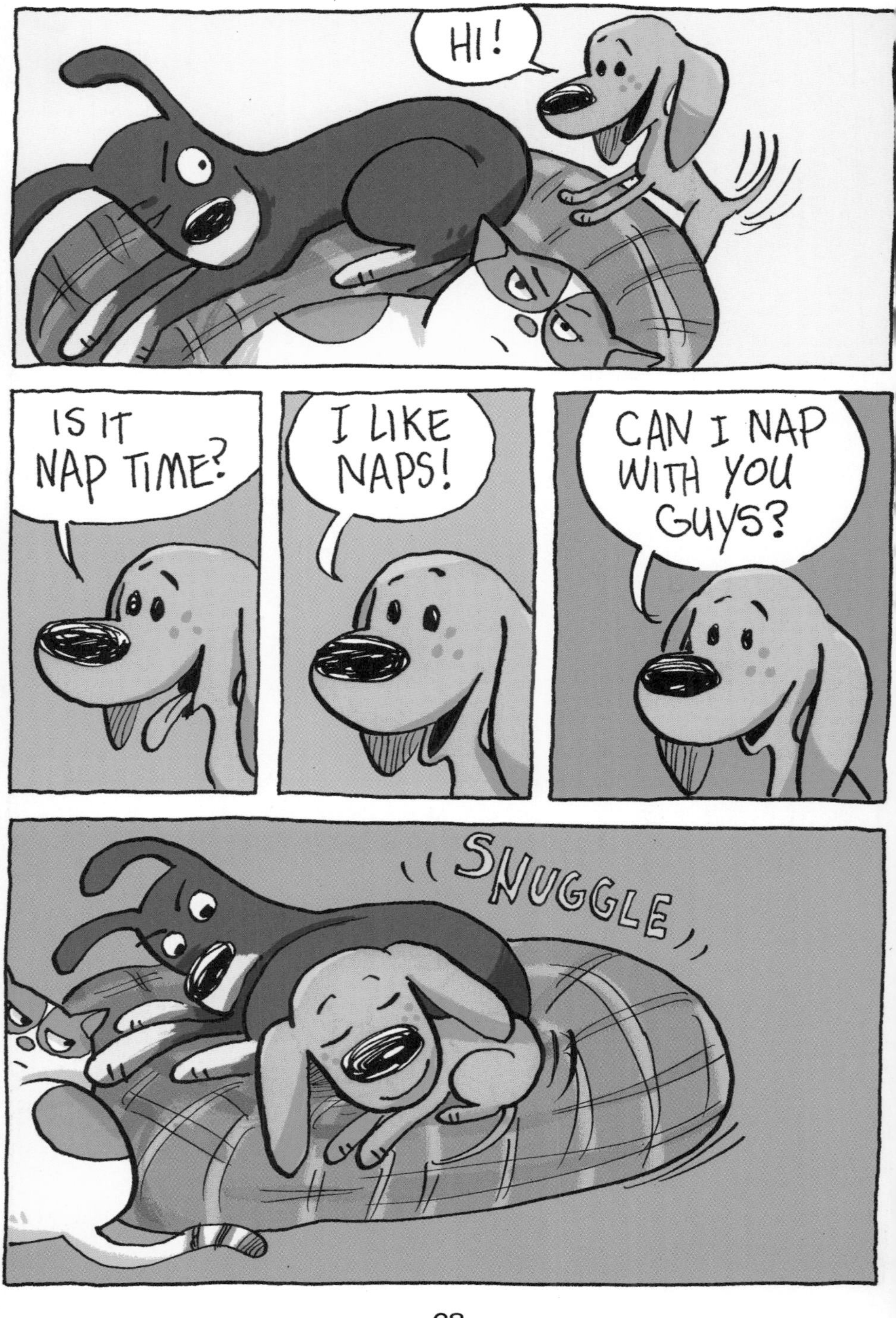
HI!
IS IT NAP TIME?
I LIKE NAPS!
CAN I NAP WITH YOU GUYS?
SNUGGLE

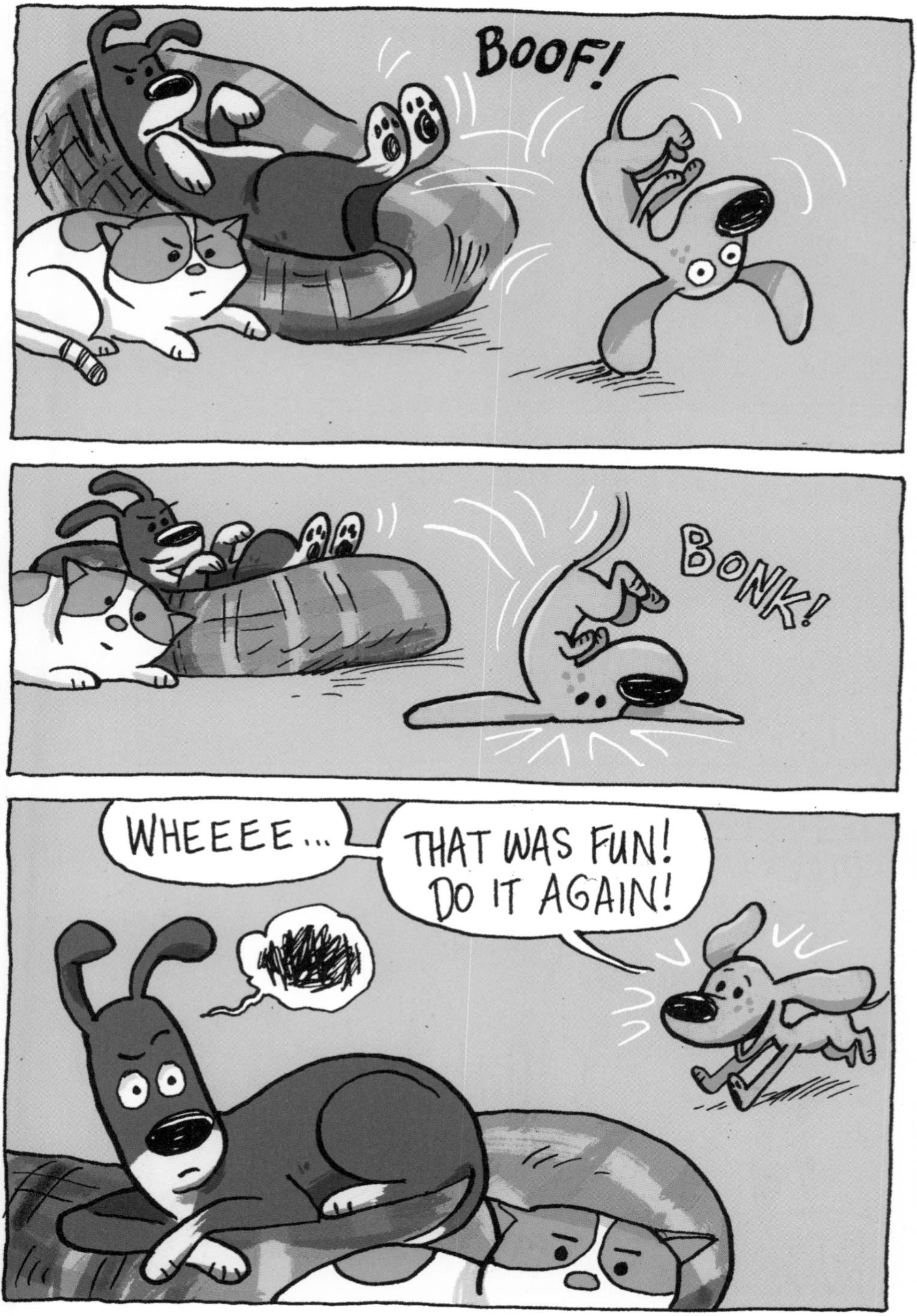
BOOF!
BONK!
WHEEEE...
THAT WAS FUN! DO IT AGAIN!

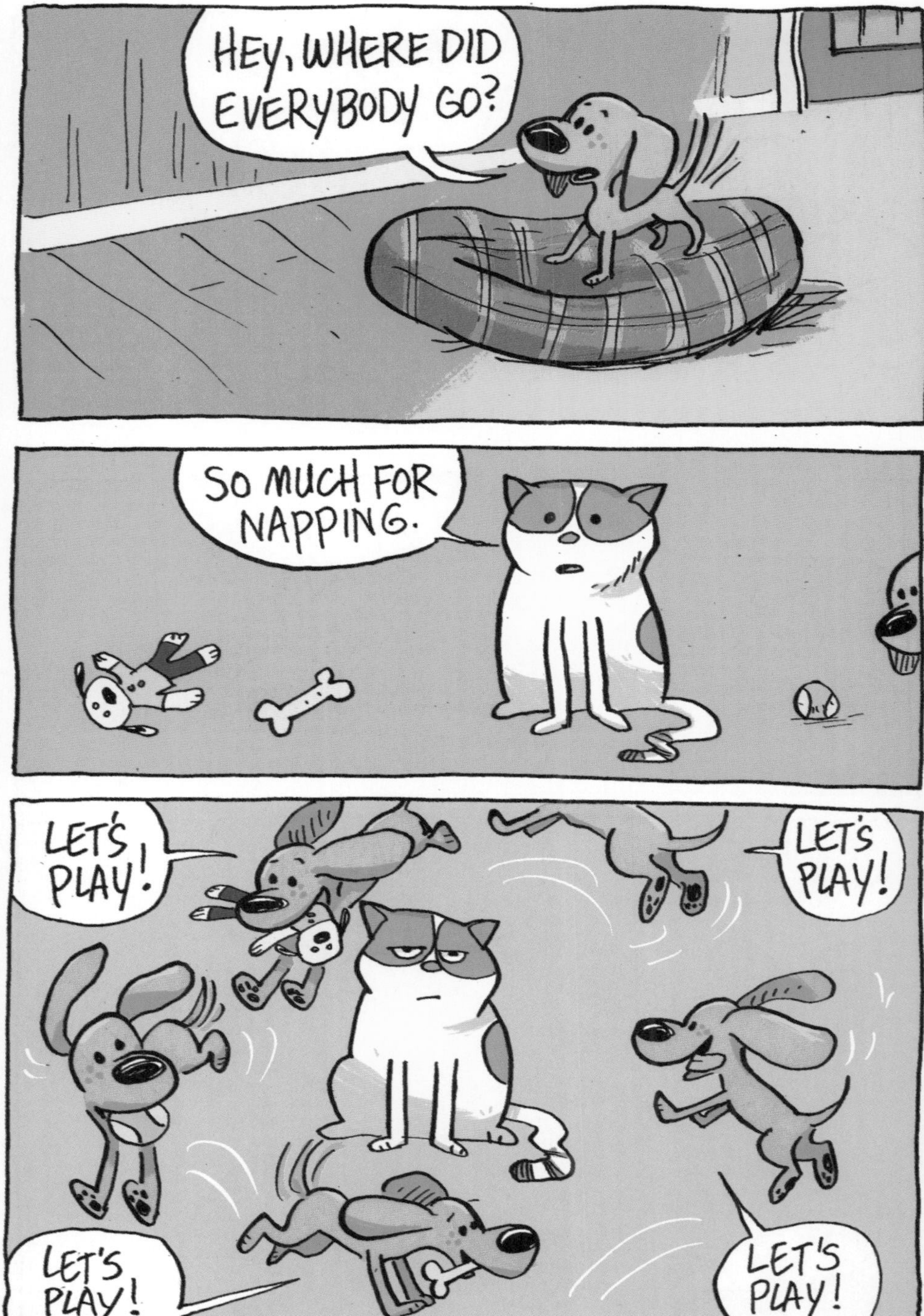
HEY, WHERE DID EVERYBODY GO?
SO MUCH FOR NAPPING.
LET'S PLAY!
LET'S PLAY!
LET'S PLAY!
LET'S PLAY!

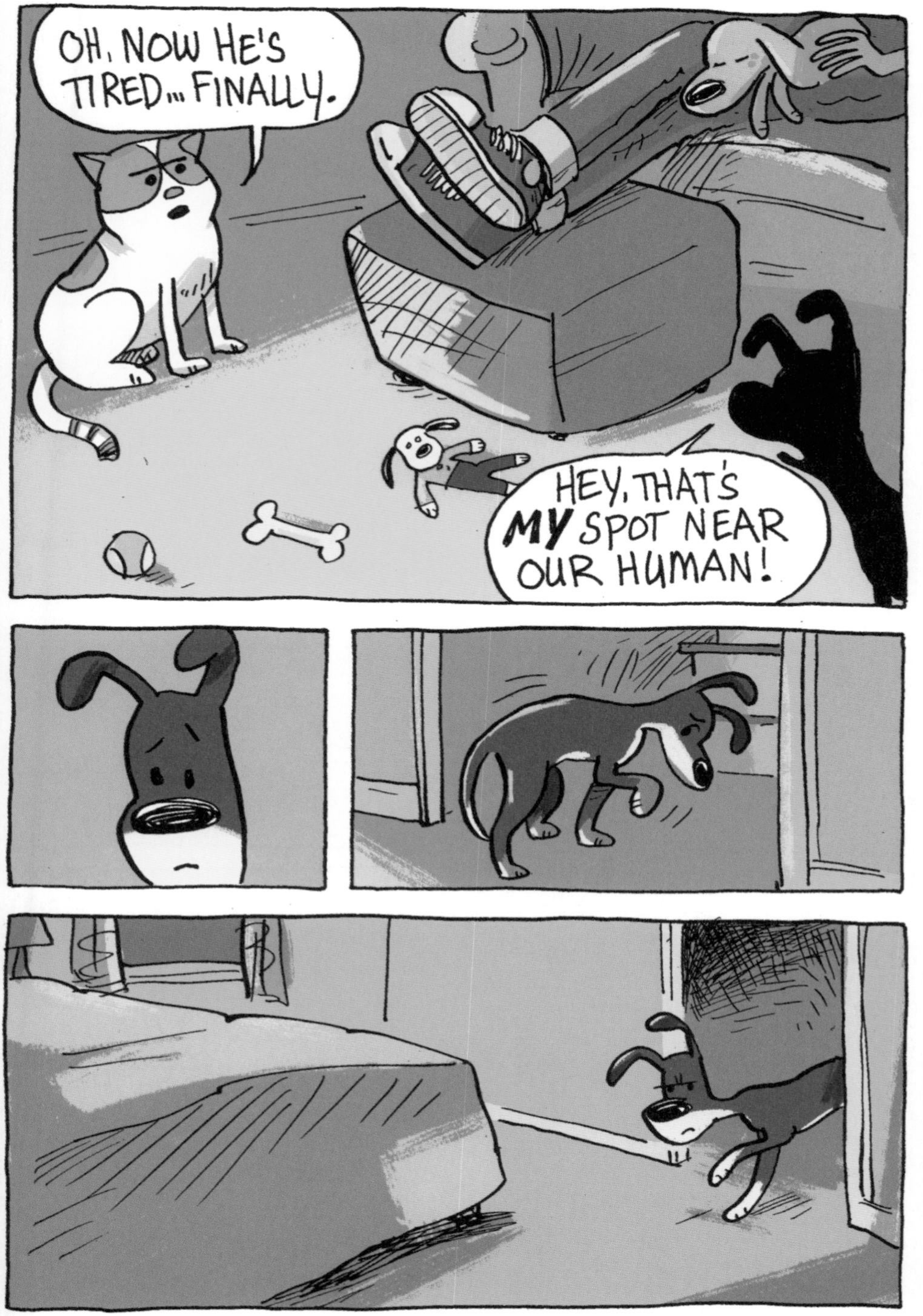
OH, NOW HE'S TIRED... FINALLY.
HEY, THAT'S **MY** SPOT NEAR OUR HUMAN!

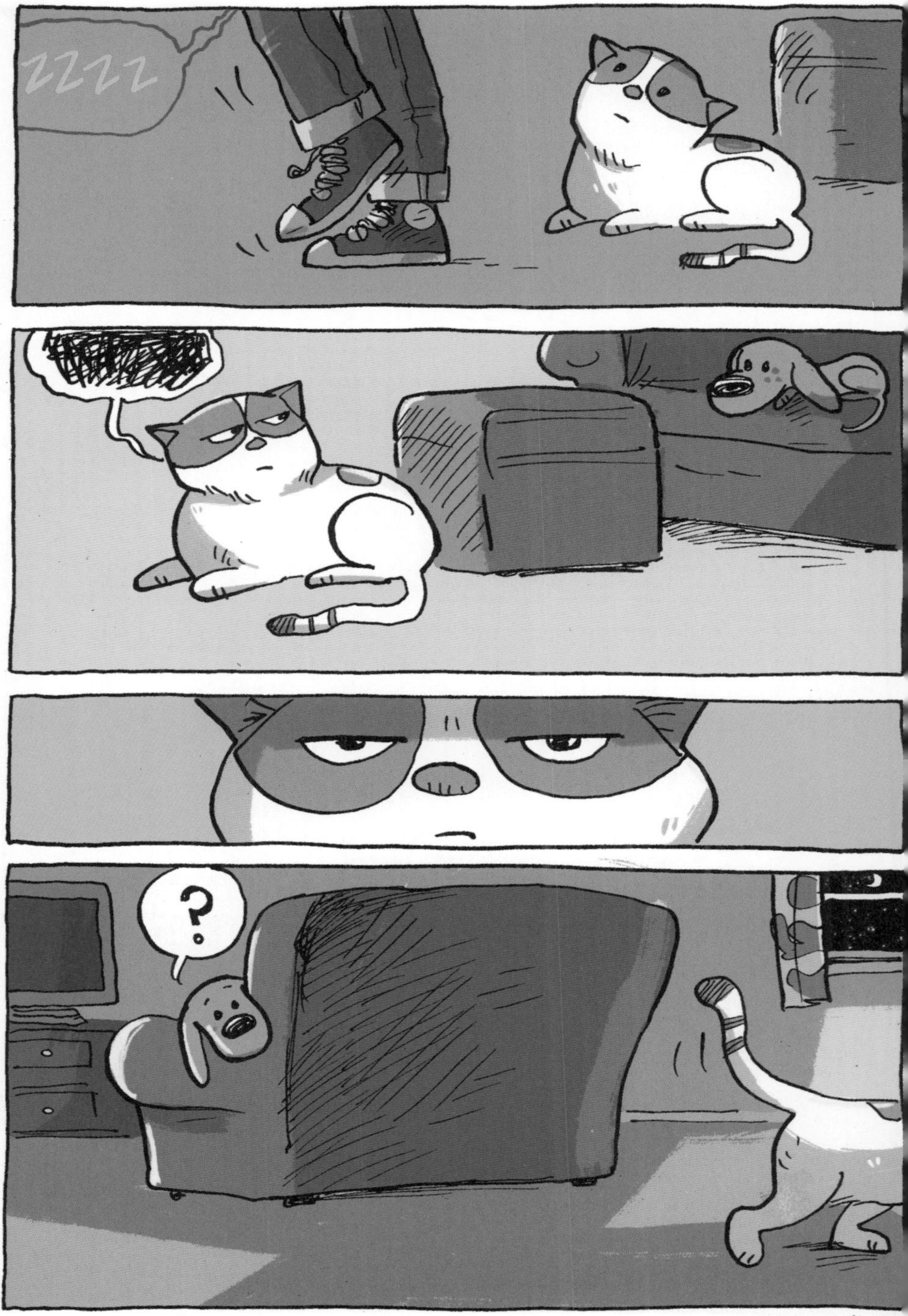
ZZZZ
?

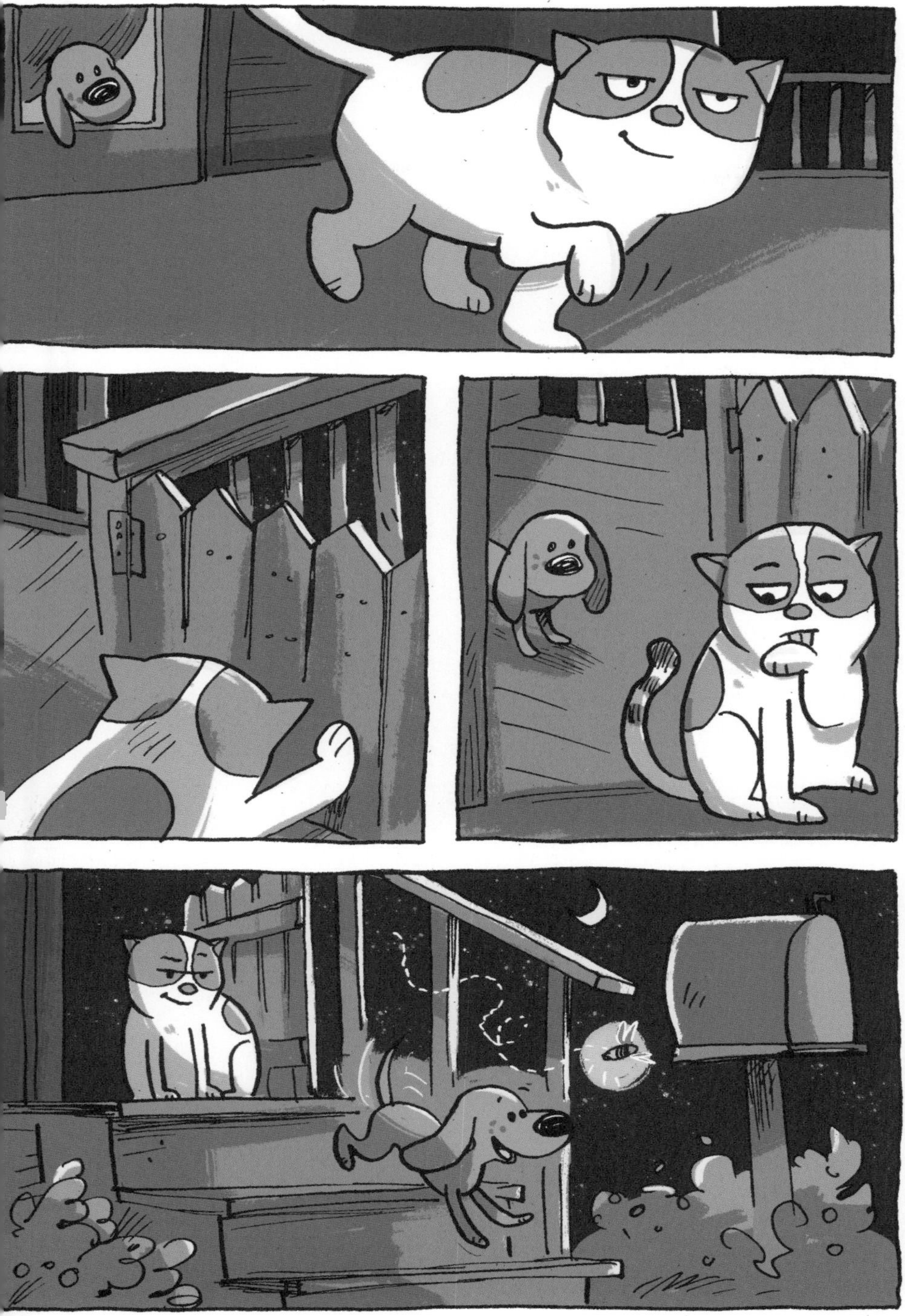

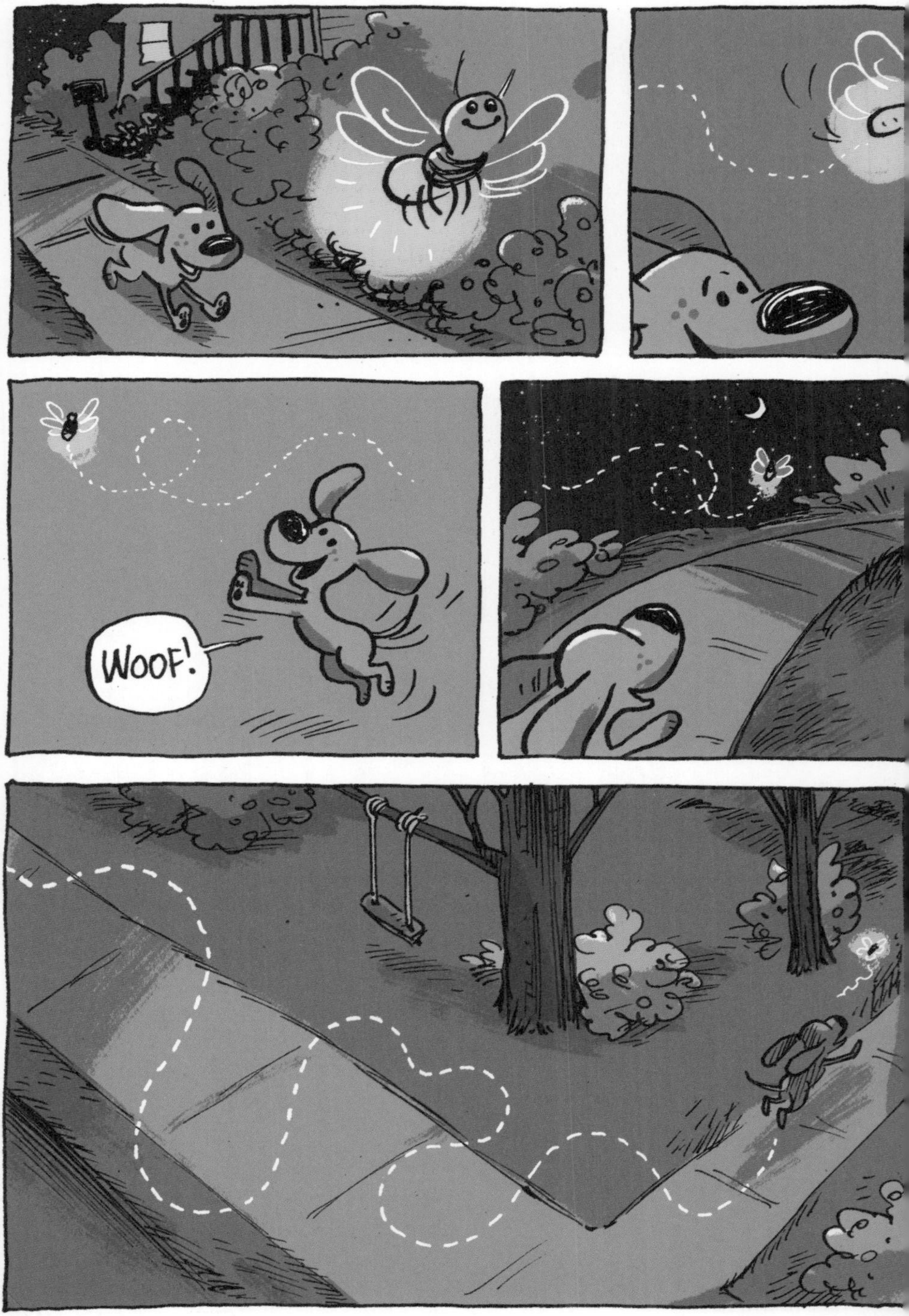
WOOF!

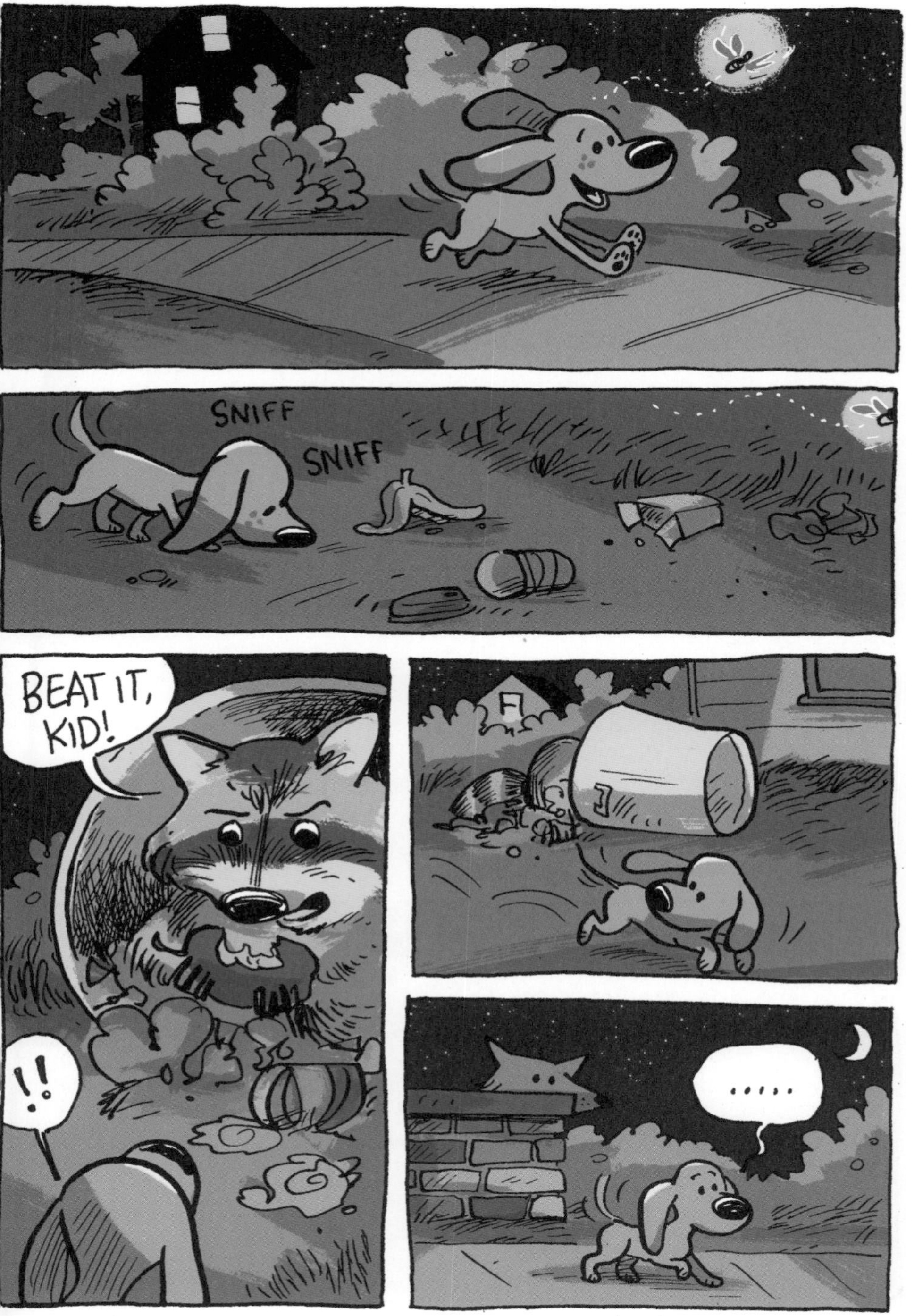

SNIFF
SNIFF
BEAT IT, KID!
!!
.....

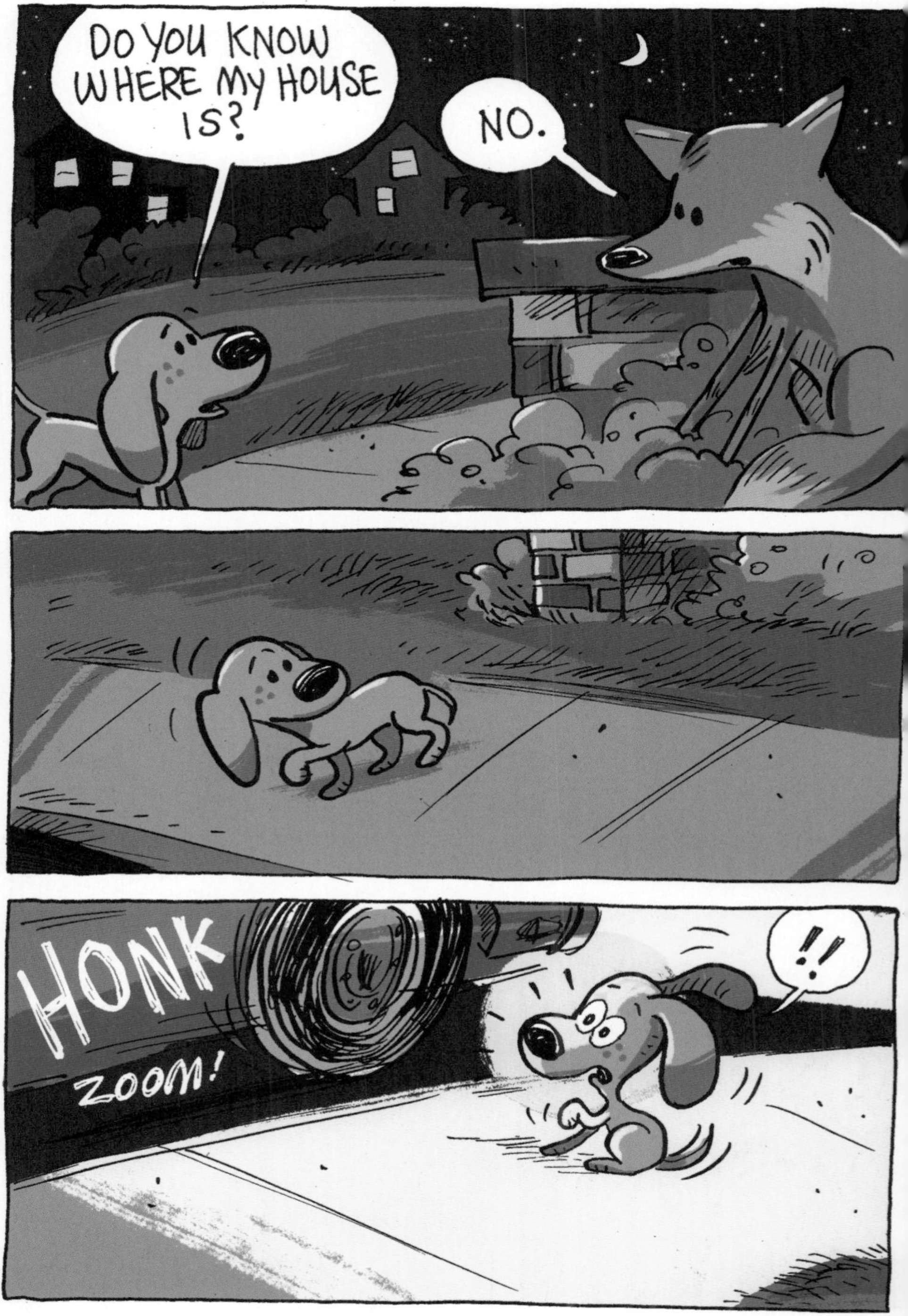
DO YOU KNOW WHERE MY HOUSE IS?
NO.
HONK
ZOOM!
!!

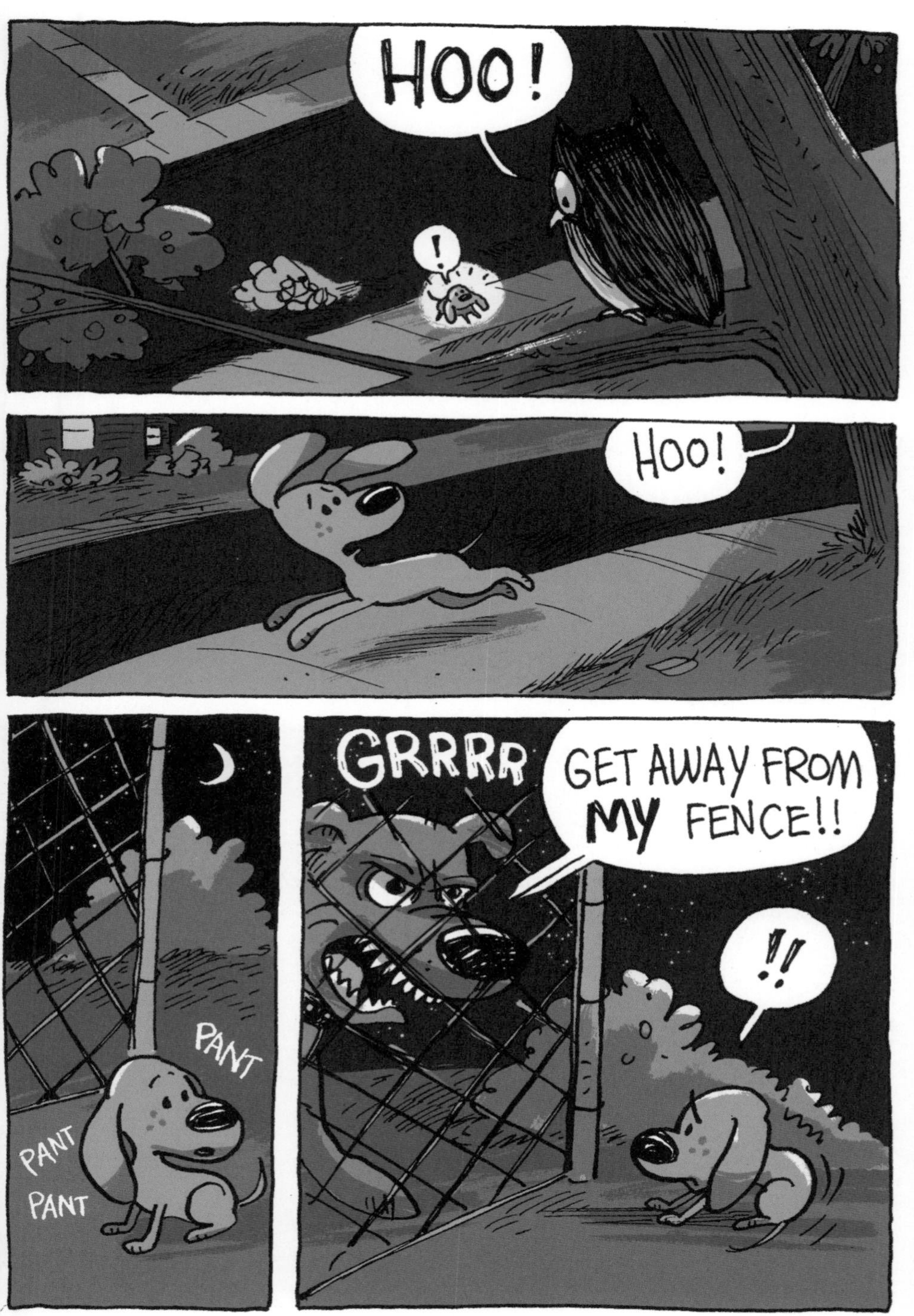
HOO!
!
HOO!
PANT
PANT
PANT
GRRRR
GET AWAY FROM MY FENCE!!
!!

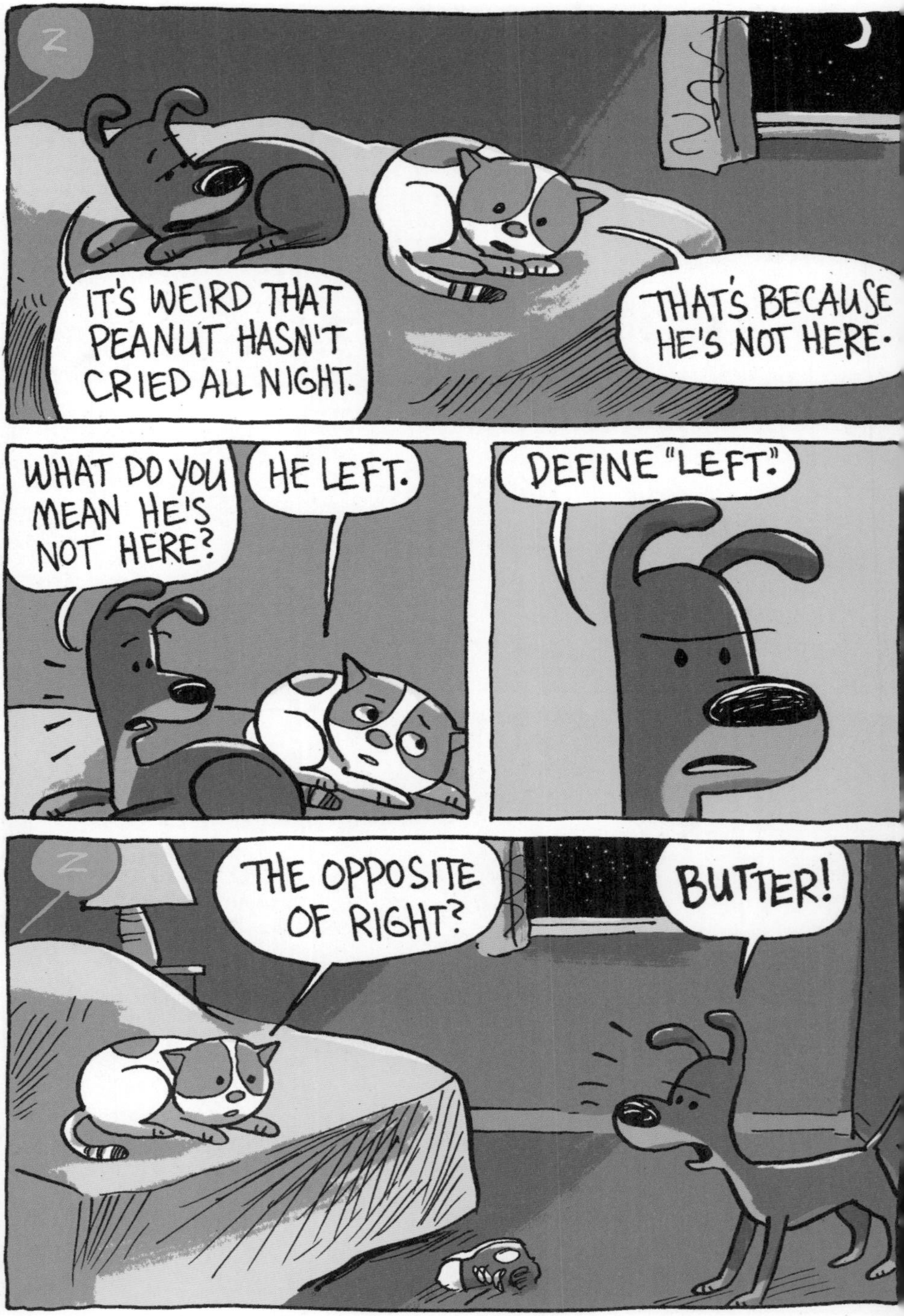
Z
IT'S WEIRD THAT PEANUT HASN'T CRIED ALL NIGHT.
THAT'S BECAUSE HE'S NOT HERE.
WHAT DO YOU MEAN HE'S NOT HERE?
HE LEFT.
DEFINE "LEFT."
Z
THE OPPOSITE OF RIGHT?
BUTTER!

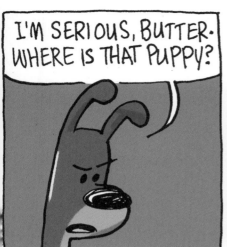

I'M SERIOUS, BUTTER. WHERE IS THAT PUPPY?

UH...I MIGHT HAVE OPENED THE FRONT GATE.

WHAT?!

ACCIDENTALLY, OF COURSE...

IT'S THE MIDDLE OF THE NIGHT!

SO?

I LOVE BEING OUTSIDE AT NIGHT.

CATS ARE NOCTURNAL!! BUT DOGS AREN'T!

KEEP YOUR VOICE DOWN. YOU'RE GOING TO WAKE OUR HUMAN.

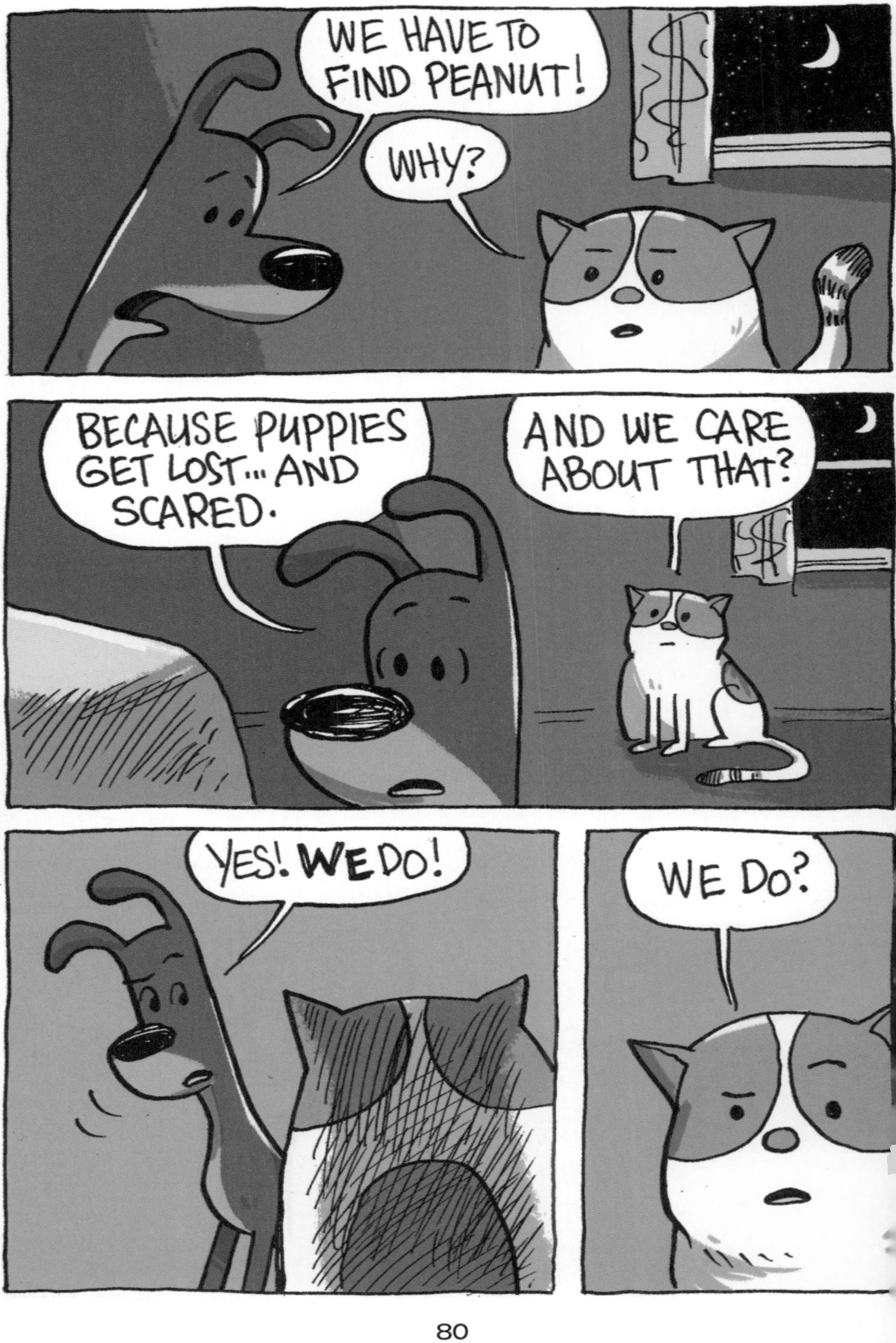

WE HAVE TO FIND PEANUT!
WHY?
BECAUSE PUPPIES GET LOST... AND SCARED.
AND WE CARE ABOUT THAT?
YES! **WE** DO!
WE DO?

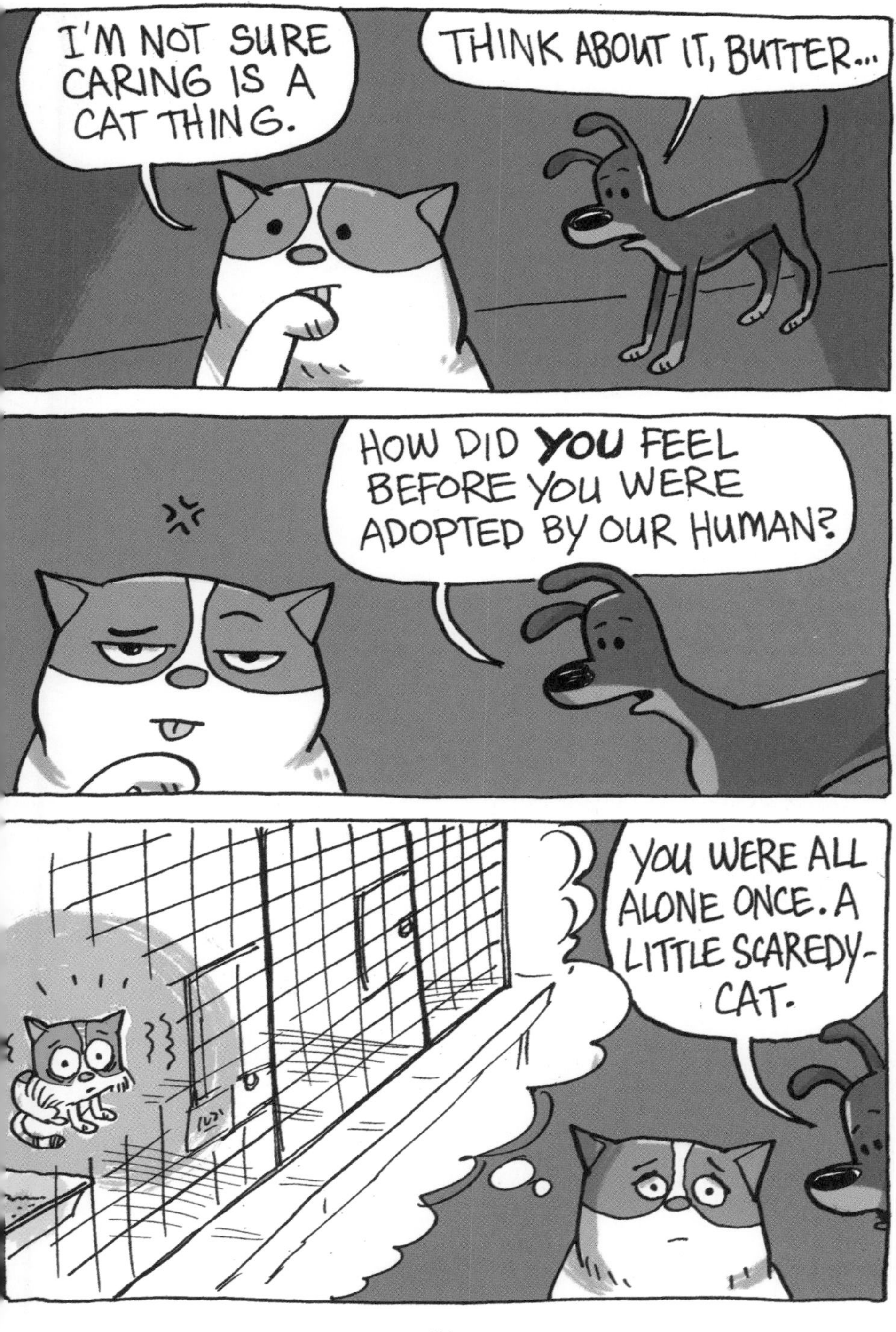

I'M NOT SURE CARING IS A CAT THING.
THINK ABOUT IT, BUTTER...
HOW DID **YOU** FEEL BEFORE YOU WERE ADOPTED BY OUR HUMAN?
YOU WERE ALL ALONE ONCE. A LITTLE SCAREDY-CAT.

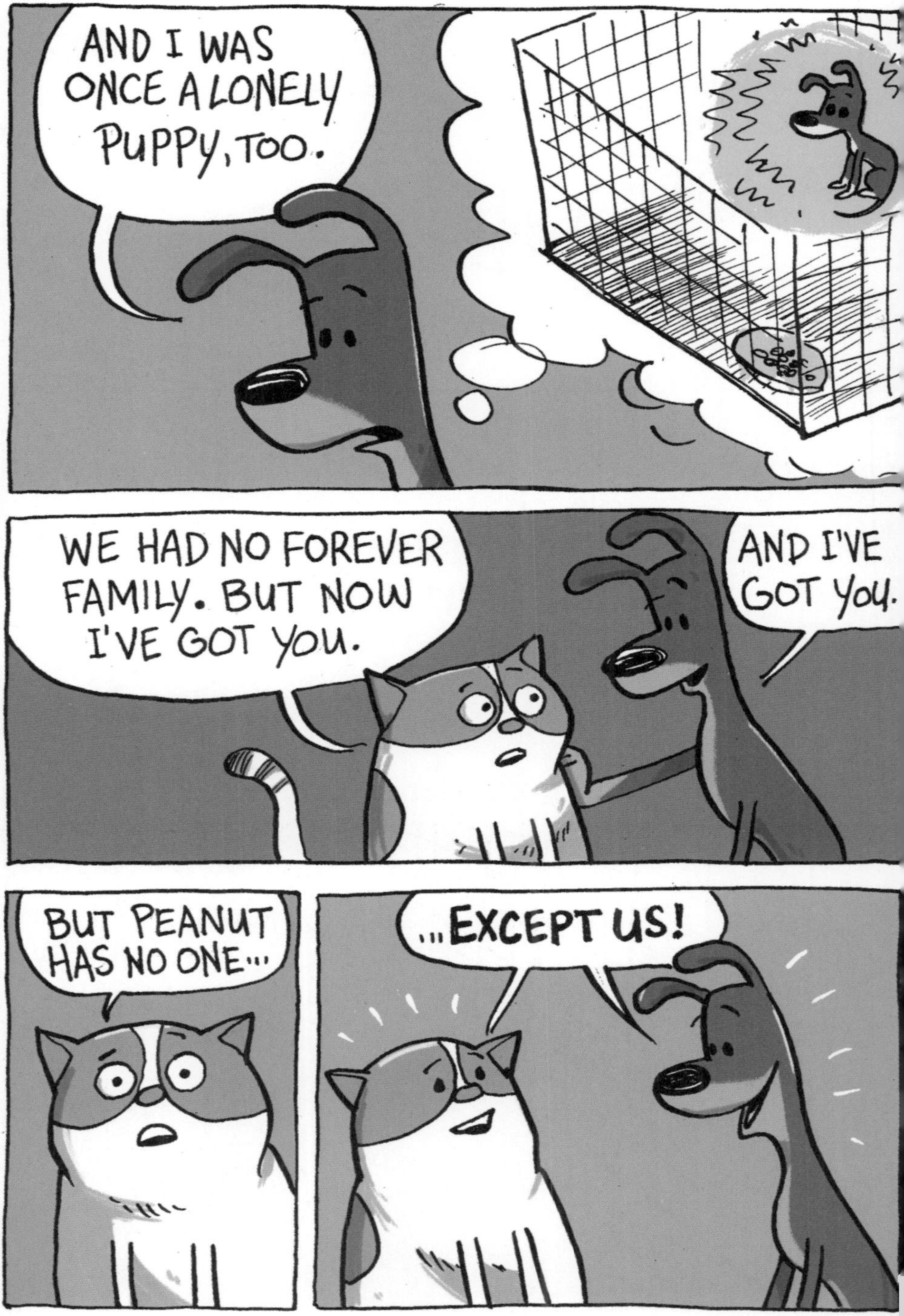
AND I WAS ONCE A LONELY PUPPY, TOO.
WE HAD NO FOREVER FAMILY. BUT NOW I'VE GOT YOU.
AND I'VE GOT YOU.
BUT PEANUT HAS NO ONE...
...EXCEPT US!

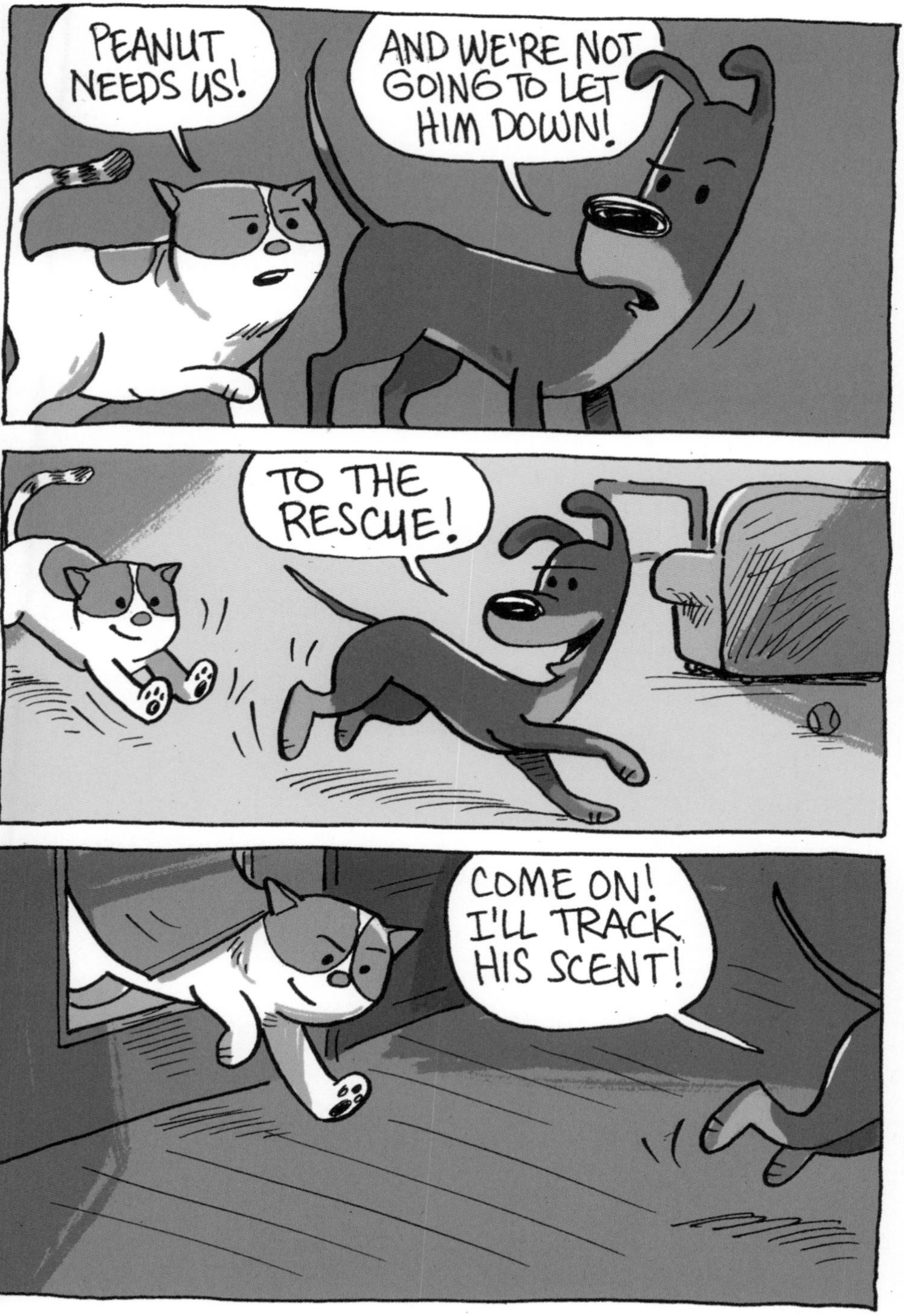
PEANUT NEEDS US!
AND WE'RE NOT GOING TO LET HIM DOWN!
TO THE RESCUE!
COME ON! I'LL TRACK HIS SCENT!

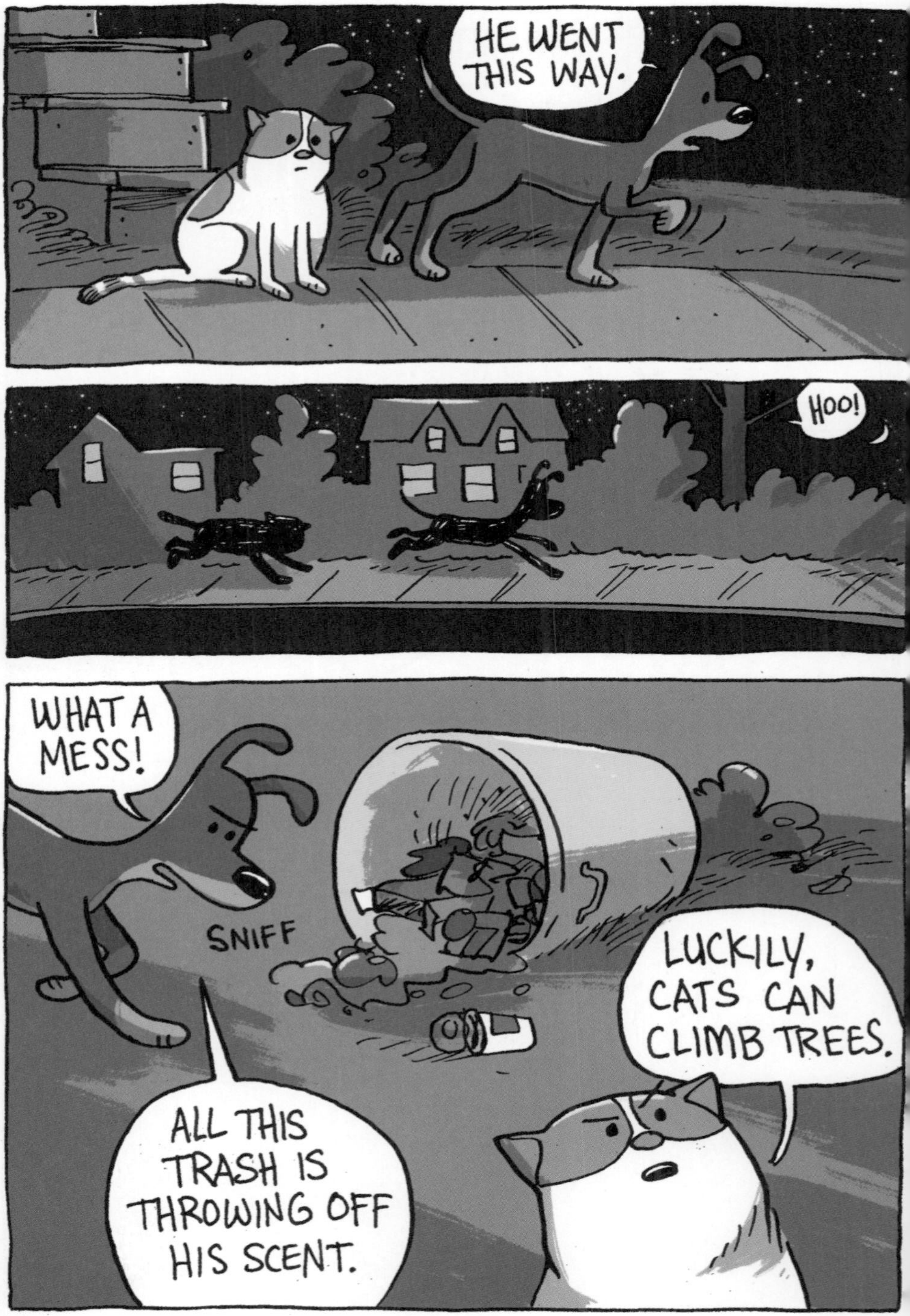
HE WENT THIS WAY.
HOO!
WHAT A MESS!
SNIFF
ALL THIS TRASH IS THROWING OFF HIS SCENT.
LUCKILY, CATS CAN CLIMB TREES.

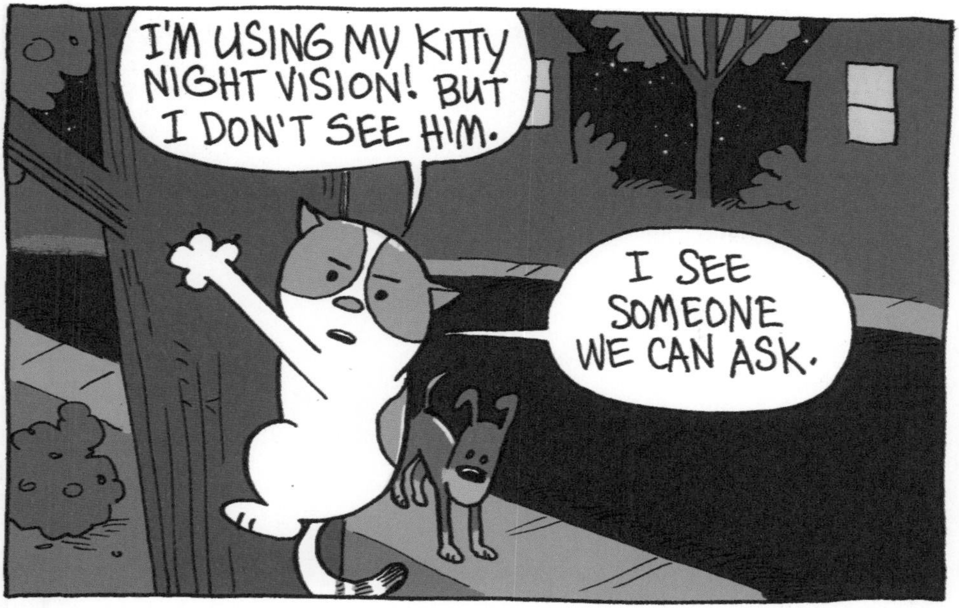
I'M USING MY KITTY NIGHT VISION! BUT I DON'T SEE HIM.
I SEE SOMEONE WE CAN ASK.

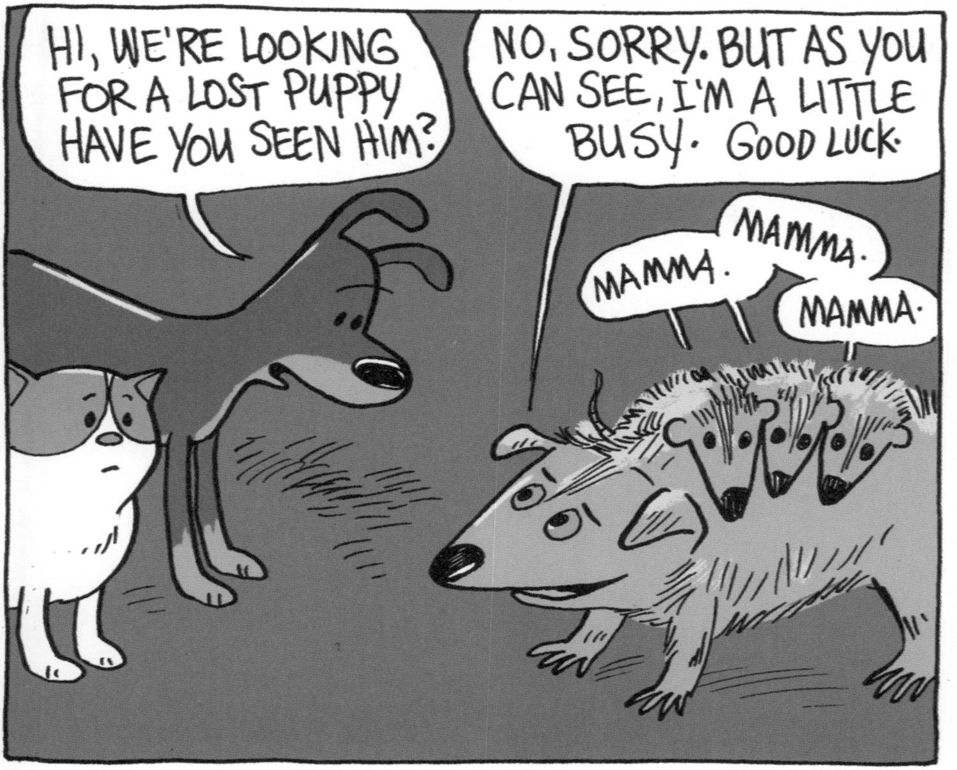
HI, WE'RE LOOKING FOR A LOST PUPPY HAVE YOU SEEN HIM?
NO, SORRY. BUT AS YOU CAN SEE, I'M A LITTLE BUSY. GOOD LUCK.
MAMMA.
MAMMA.
MAMMA.

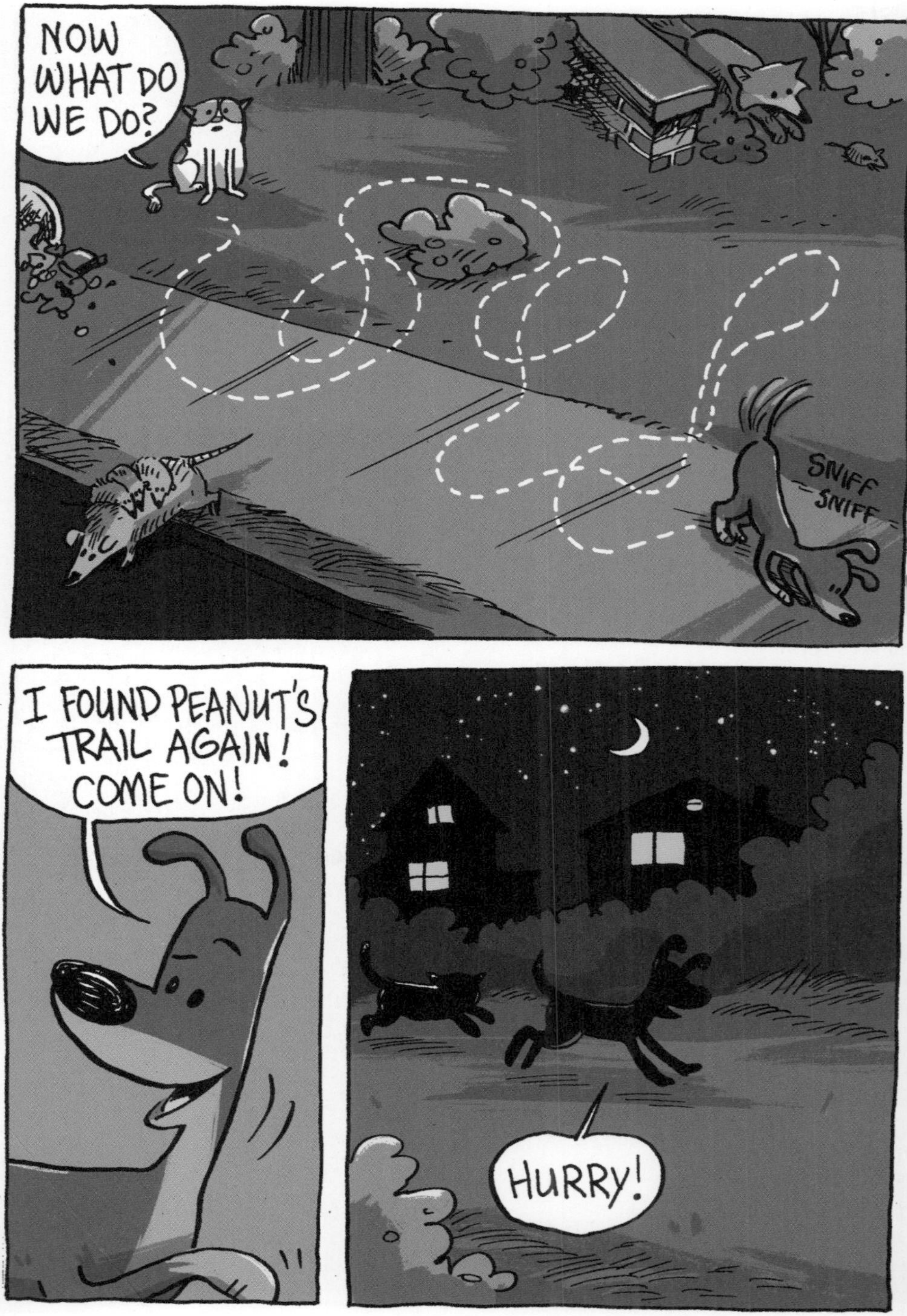
NOW WHAT DO WE DO?
SNIFF SNIFF
I FOUND PEANUT'S TRAIL AGAIN! COME ON!
HURRY!

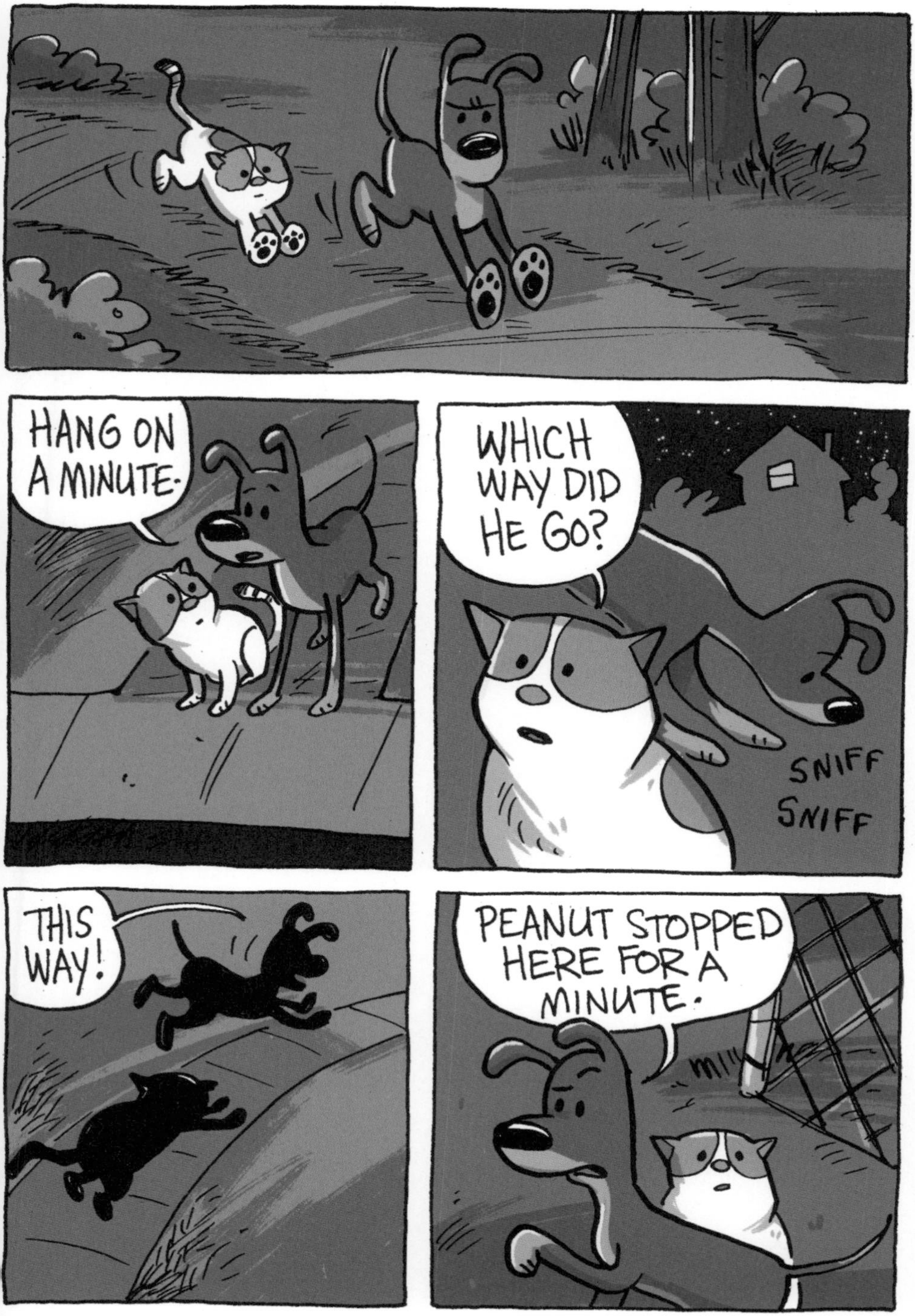
HANG ON A MINUTE.
WHICH WAY DID HE GO?
SNIFF SNIFF
THIS WAY!
PEANUT STOPPED HERE FOR A MINUTE.

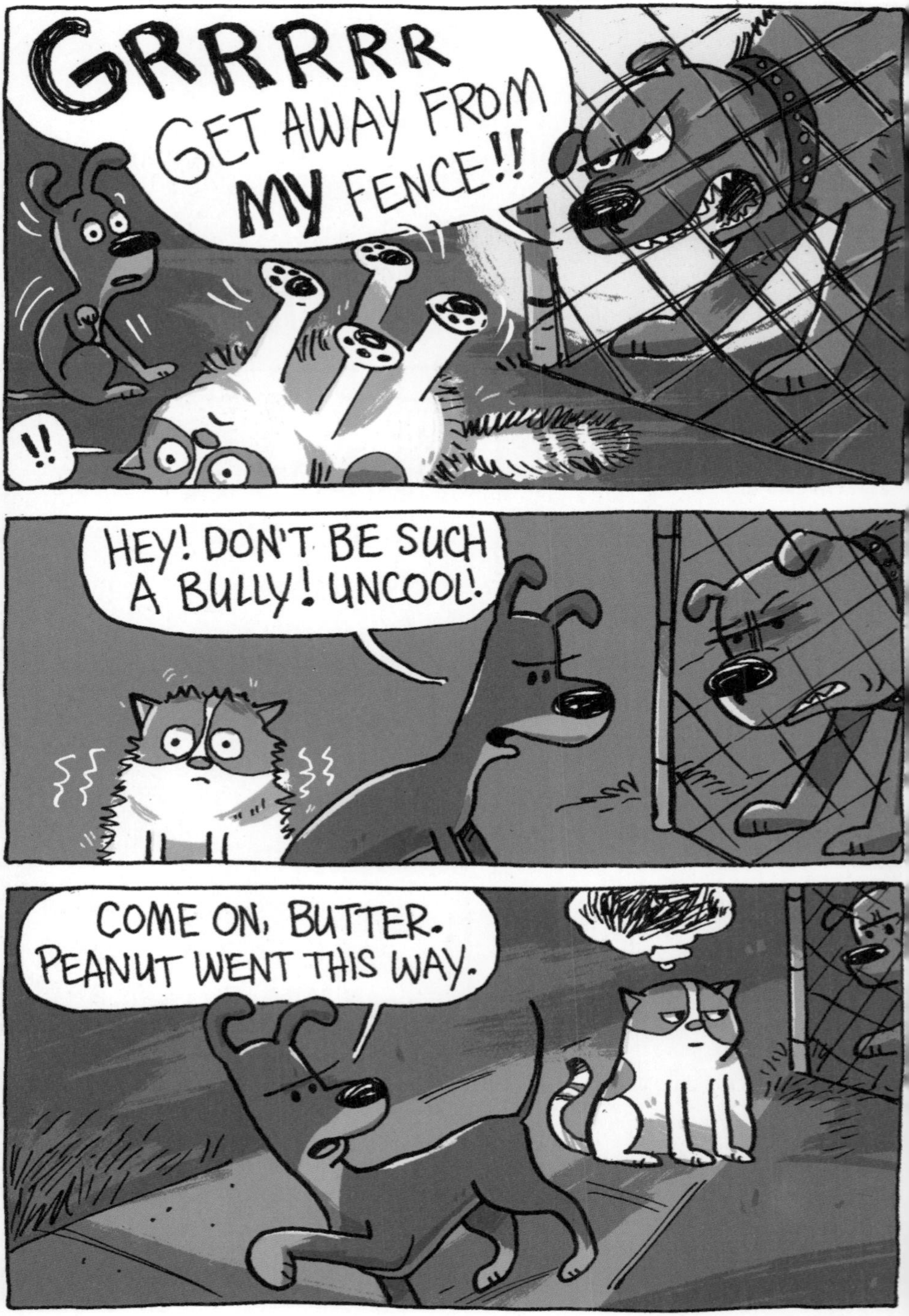
GRRRRR
GET AWAY FROM MY FENCE!!
!!
HEY! DON'T BE SUCH A BULLY! UNCOOL!
COME ON, BUTTER. PEANUT WENT THIS WAY.

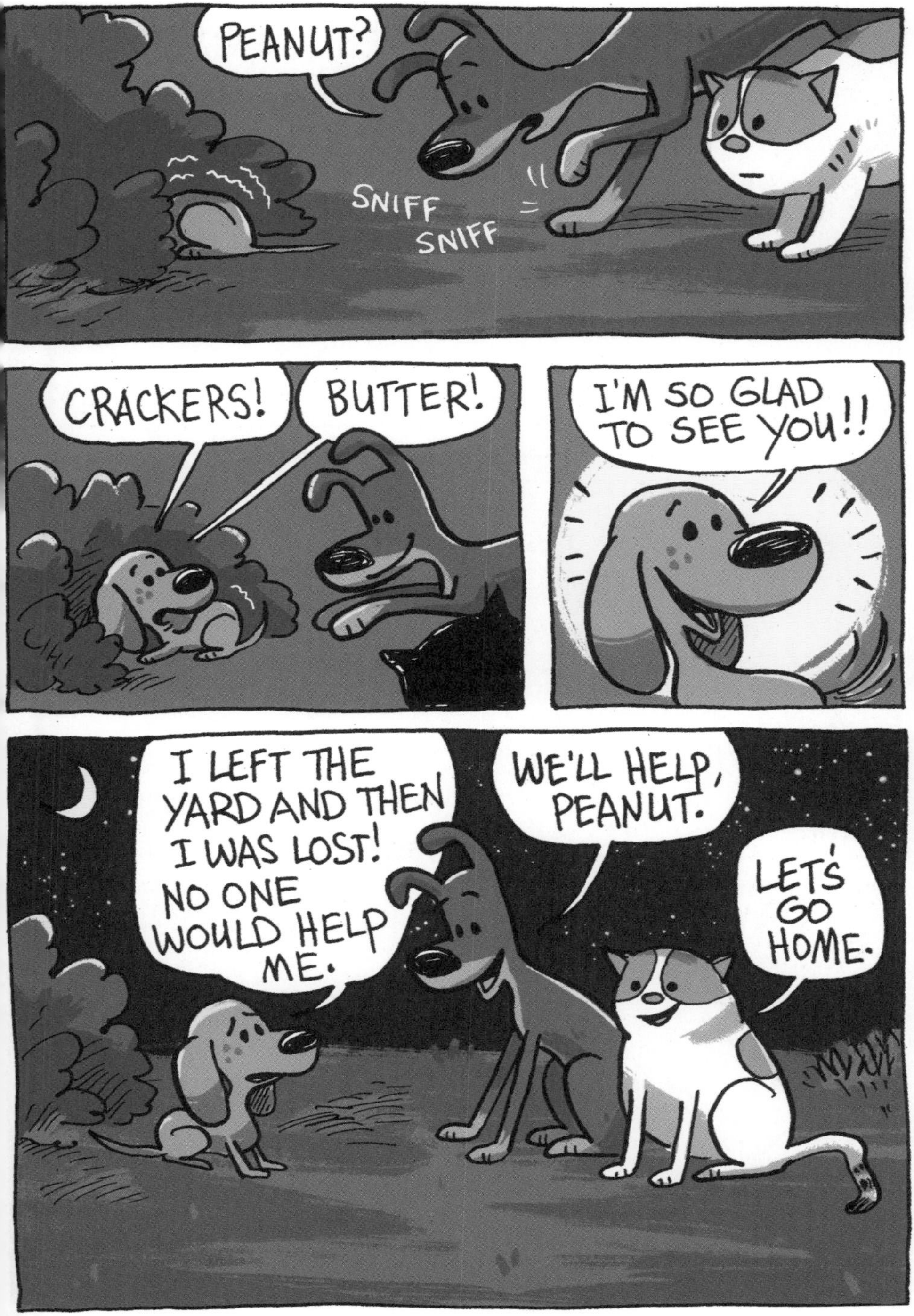
PEANUT?
SNIFF
SNIFF
CRACKERS!
BUTTER!
I'M SO GLAD TO SEE YOU!!
I LEFT THE YARD AND THEN I WAS LOST! NO ONE WOULD HELP ME.
WE'LL HELP, PEANUT.
LET'S GO HOME.

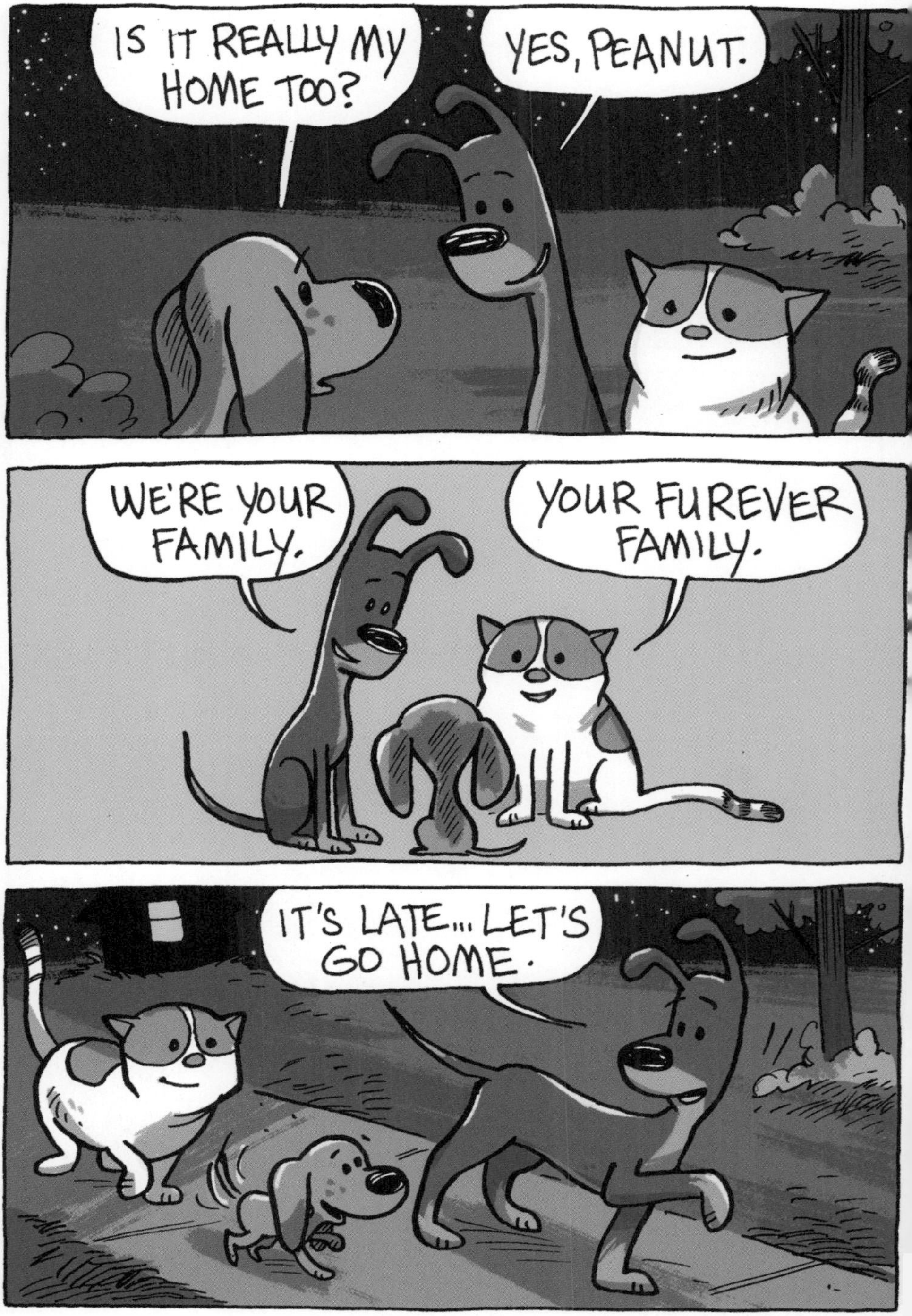
IS IT REALLY MY HOME TOO?
YES, PEANUT.
WE'RE YOUR FAMILY.
YOUR FUREVER FAMILY.
IT'S LATE... LET'S GO HOME.

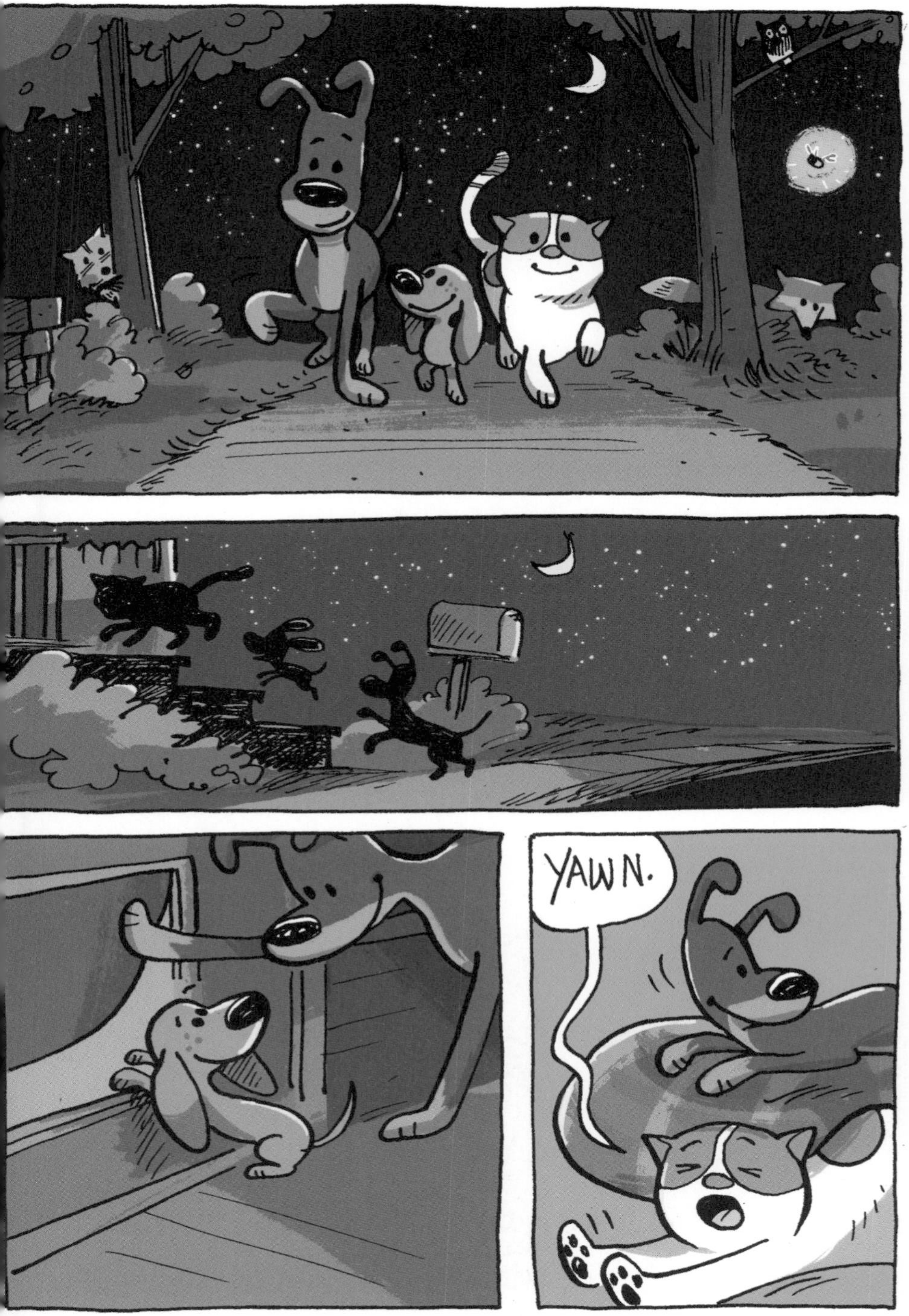
YAWN.

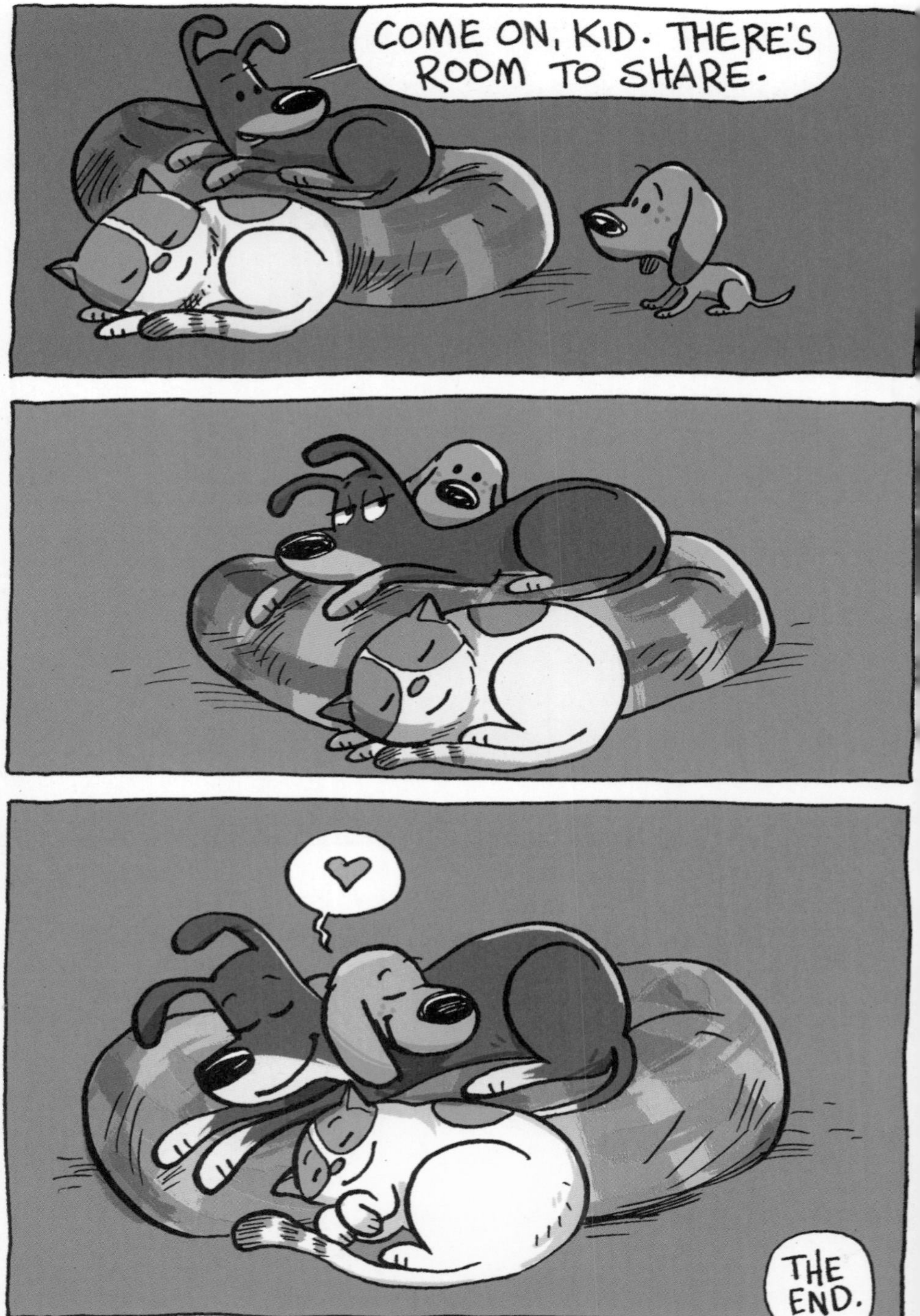
COME ON, KID. THERE'S ROOM TO SHARE.
THE END.

MEET **PAIGE BRADDOCK**

I started drawing comics when I was seven years old. Wiggins, Mississippi, the town I grew up in, was very small. Wiggins didn't have a comic shop or a bookstore. Mostly, I learned about comics by reading the Sunday funnies in the newspaper. My favorite characters to draw were Snoopy, Popeye, and Beetle Bailey. It wasn't long before I started creating my own characters. *Captain Lightning* was the first comics story I wrote and drew. It starred a very clumsy superhero whose cape was always getting snagged on fences and bushes.

Comics have always been one of my favorite things. I majored in illustration in college at the University of Tennessee and later worked as an illustrator for several newspapers. Then I got my dream job: working with Charles M. Schulz at his studio in California. He was the creator of Charlie Brown, Snoopy, and the whole *Peanuts* gang. It's funny how things work out sometimes. Snoopy was one of my all-time favorite characters and now I get to work with him every day.

I've always loved to draw dogs, but when our pet Buddy Barker came to live with us, I started drawing dogs even more often. Buddy was one of the main inspirations for the Peanut, Butter, & Crackers series. Of course, I can't leave out our cat, Otis—who once ate a *whole stick* of butter—and when we added our little dachshund, Charlie, to the mix, we really did have puppy problems!

It's important as artists and writers to figure out what inspires us and to make that part of our story—and *everybody* has a story to tell!

ACKNOWLEDGMENTS

I'd like to offer special thanks to the colorist for this book, Kat Efird. Her colors really brought this story to life in such a vibrant way. Also, big thanks to my editor, Sheila Keenan. I greatly appreciate your sense of humor and your ability to nurture stories. Thank you to my wife, Evelyn, for always suggesting ways to make drawings cuter and funnier.